"Once again, Benedict shines a literary spotlight on a historical figure whose talents and achievements have been overlooked, with sparkling results. *The Only Woman in the Room* is a page-turning tapestry of intrigue and glamour about a woman who refuses to be taken for granted. Spellbinding and timely."

—Fiona Davis, national bestselling author of *The Masterpiece*

"Deftly portrays the fascinating life of a Hollywood icon whose scientific accomplishments have long been eclipsed by her sensuous beauty…follows a remarkable path of survival through the dangers of world war—and those at home, behind closed doors. A read as intriguing and captivating as Ms. Lamarr herself."

—Kristina McMorris, *New York Times* bestselling author of *The Edge of Lost* and *Sold on a Monday*

"An amazing story that once begun must be finished! Benedict is a master of historical fiction."

—Stephanie Crowe, Page & Palette (Fairhope, AL)

"A novelist that makes a career out of writing about 'The Only Women in the Room'… In Benedict's telling, that story is a ready-made thriller as well as a feminist parable."

—*New York Times*

"In writing her narratively connected, fictionalized biographies, Benedict is not unlike an archaeologist digging up clues to moments of epiphany."

—*Newsweek*

"Benedict paints a shining portrait of a complicated woman who knows the astonishing power of her beauty but longs to be recognized for her sharp intellect. Readers will be enthralled."

—*Publishers Weekly*

"Benedict's compelling fictionalized biography pays tribute to the overlooked scientific contributions and the hidden depths of a stunning beauty and beloved movie star of superior intelligence and verve through an irresistible combination of Hollywood glamour and international intrigue."

—*Booklist*

"A captivating story of a complicated woman blazing new trails."

—*Kirkus Reviews*

"This. Book. Is. Amazing. The Only Woman in the Room tells the fascinating true story of actress Hedy Lamarr, whose little-known journey involves escaping the Nazis and her secret life as a scientist and inventor. Jaw dropped? Same."

—*Woman's Day*

"One of the best women's fiction of 2019."

—*Marie Claire*

"The next book you won't be able to put down."

—*Pop Sugar*

"One of the best new fiction books of 2019."

—*Bustle*

"A spotlight on how often women are omitted from historical records, despite the influence and innovations they may have been responsible for…'The Only Woman in the Room' not only succeeds as a novel about a woman's search for peace with herself but also as an imagined glimpse of a decade in the life of a movie star whose contributions to the world are still felt today."

—*Pittsburgh Post-Gazette*

"I was absolutely fascinated… I devoured this book and would have been happy if it had been twice as long. Whether you are interested in Old Hollywood or World War II, there is much to learn and enjoy here."

—Carrie Deming, The Dog Eared Book (Palmyra, NY)

"Relevant today, especially women's worth in a man's world… A worthy read about this gorgeous and talented woman."

—*New York Journal of Books*

PRAISE FOR *CARNEGIE'S MAID*

"[An] excellent historical novel."

—*Publishers Weekly*

"In *Carnegie's Maid*, Marie Benedict skillfully introduces us to Clara, a young woman who immigrates to America in the 1860s and unexpectedly becomes the maid to Andrew Carnegie's mother. Clara becomes close to Andrew Carnegie and helps to make him America's first philanthropist. *Downton Abbey* fans should flock to this charming tale of fateful turns and unexpected romance, and the often unsung role of women in history."

—Pam Jenoff, *New York Times* bestselling author
of *The Orphan's Tale* and *The Lost Girls of Paris*

"With its well-drawn characters, good pacing, and excellent sense of time and place, this volume should charm lovers of historicals, romance, and the Civil War period. Neither saccharine nor overly dramatized."

—*Library Journal*

"Feels like *Downton Abbey* in the United States… Benedict demonstrates the relevance of history to the present day in this impeccably researched novel of the early immigrant experience. Deeply human, and brimming with complex, vulnerable characters, *Carnegie's Maid* shows the power of ambition tempered by altruism, and the true realization of the American Dream."

—Erika Robuck, national bestselling
author of *Hemingway's Girl*

"*Carnegie's Maid* brings to life a particular moment in the ascendancy of Andrew Carnegie while enriching that moment with a sympathetic understanding of what it meant to be an immigrant living in poverty at that time. This would be an accomplishment for any book, but for one that cleverly disguises itself as a historical romance, it's an absolute treasure. The Carnegie legacy may be debatable, but Ms. Benedict's talent for bringing history to life is not."

—*Pittsburgh Post-Gazette*

"Marie Benedict has penned a sensational novel that turns the conventional Cinderella story into an all-American triumph. Young Clara Kelley steps off the boat from Ireland into Andrew Carnegie's affluent world, where invention can transform men and women into whatever they dare to dream."

—Sarah McCoy, *New York Times* and international bestselling author of *The Mapmaker's Children* and *The Baker's Daughter*

"As she showed in *The Other Einstein*, Benedict again proves that behind every great man is a great woman…readers will be highly satisfied."

—*RT Book Reviews*

"They say behind every great man is a great woman supporting him, and that may have been the case with famed American philanthropist Andrew Carnegie. Or at least, that is the fascinating story *Carnegie's Maid* tells about Clara, a young American immigrant working in Carnegie's house."

—*Bustle*

"A special addition to the *Downton Abbey* canon…an absorbing exploration of the influence one plucky young woman might have had on this pioneering philanthropist."

—*Toronto Star*

PRAISE FOR
THE OTHER EINSTEIN

"Superb…haunting story of Einstein's brilliant first wife who was lost in his shadow."

—Sue Monk Kidd, *New York Times* bestselling author of *The Invention of Wings*

"Beautifully written and filled with fascinating historical detail, *The Other Einstein* is a finely drawn portrait of not only what it was like to be a woman in love with physics at that time, but also what it was like to be a woman in love with the wrong man."

—Jillian Cantor, author of *Margot* and *The Hours Count*

"Marie Benedict brings us into the life and times of Mileva Marić Einstein, Albert's first wife. A brilliant mathematician in her own right, Mileva and Albert plan a life together of equal scholarship, but Albert's ambitions and Mileva's role as a wife and mother at the turn of the twentieth century make this an impossibility. Could the theory of relativity actually have been conceived by 'the other Einstein'? In this fascinating and thoughtful novel, we learn that this is more than possible."

—B. A. Shapiro, *New York Times* bestselling author of *The Art Forger* and *The Muralist*

"In her compelling novel, Benedict makes a strong case that the brilliant woman behind [Albert Einstein] was integral to his success, and creates a rich historical portrait in the process."
—*Publishers Weekly*

"A compelling read...[putting] Marić at the forefront of the narrative, letting her tell her own story."
—*Pittsburgh Post-Gazette*

ALSO BY MARIE BENEDICT

The Other Einstein
Carnegie's Maid
Lady Clementine

THE
ONLY
WOMAN
IN THE
ROOM

MARIE BENEDICT

Published by Sourcebooks Landmark, an imprint of Sourcebooks
P.O. Box 4410, Naperville, Illinois 60567-4410
(630) 961-3900
sourcebooks.com

The Library of Congress has cataloged the hardcover edition as follows:

Names: Benedict, Marie, author.
Title: The only woman in the room / Marie Benedict.
Description: Naperville, Illinois : Sourcebooks Landmark, [2019]
Identifiers: LCCN 2018009020 | (hardcover : acid-free paper)
Subjects: LCSH: World War, 1939-1945--Fiction. | Women scientists-
-Fiction. |
   Jewish women--Fiction. | GSAFD: Historical fiction.
Classification: LCC PS3620.E75 O55 2019 | DDC 813/.6--dc23
LC record available at https://lccn.loc.gov/2018009020

Printed and bound in the United States of America.
VP 11

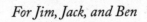

For Jim, Jack, and Ben

PART I

CHAPTER ONE

May 17, 1933
Vienna, Austria

M Y LIDS FLUTTERED OPEN, BUT THE FLOODLIGHTS blinded me for a moment. Placing a discreet, steadying hand on my costar's arm, I willed a confident smile upon my lips while I waited for my vision to clear. The applause thundered, and I swayed in the cacophony of sound and light. The mask I'd firmly affixed to myself for the performance slipped away for a moment, and I was no longer nineteenth-century Bavarian empress Elizabeth, but simply young Hedy Kiesler.

I couldn't allow the theatergoers of the famed Theater an der Wien to see me falter in my portrayal of the city's beloved empress. Not even in the curtain call. She was the emblem of the once-glorious Habsburg Austria, an empire that ruled for nearly four hundred years, and the people clung to her image in these humiliating days after the Great War.

Closing my eyes for a split second, I reached deep within myself, putting aside Hedy Kiesler with all her small worries and comparatively petty aspirations. I summoned my power and assumed the mantle of the empress once again, her necessary

steeliness and her heavy responsibilities. Then I opened my
eyes and stared out at my subjects.

The audience materialized before me. I realized that they
weren't clapping from the comfort of their plush, red-velvet
theater seats. They had leaped to their feet in a standing ovation, an honor my fellow Viennese doled out sparingly. As the
empress, this was my due, but as Hedy, I wondered whether
this applause could truly be for me and not one of the other
actors of *Sissy*. The actor who played Emperor Franz Josef to
my Empress Elizabeth, Hans Jaray, was, after all, a legendary
Theater an der Wien fixture. I waited for my costars to take
their bows. While they awarded solid applause for the other
actors, the theatergoers became wild when I took center stage
for my bow. This was indeed *my* moment.

How I wished Papa could have watched my performance
tonight. If Mama hadn't feigned illness in an obvious ploy to
take attention away from my important evening, Papa could
have seen my Theater an der Wien debut. I know he would
have reveled in this reaction, and if he had witnessed this adulation firsthand, it might have washed away the stain of my
risqué performance in the film *Ecstasy*—a portrayal I desperately wished I could forget.

The sound of clapping started to grow fainter, and a chord
of disquiet descended upon the audience as a procession of
theater ushers paraded down the center aisle, arms laden with
flowers. This grandiose gesture, with its inappropriate, very
public timing, unsettled the otherwise reserved Viennese. I
could almost hear them wonder who would have dared disrupt
opening night at the Theater an der Wien with this audacious

display. Only the overzealousness of a parent could have excused it, but I knew my cautious parents would have never dared the gesture. Was it one of my fellow actors' families who'd made this misstep?

As the ushers proceeded closer to the stage, I saw that their arms brimmed not with ordinary flowers but with exquisite hothouse roses. Perhaps a dozen bouquets. How much would this abundance of rare red blooms cost? I wondered who could afford the decadence at a time like this.

The ushers mounted the stairs, and I understood that they'd been instructed to deliver these bouquets to their intended recipient in full view of the audience. Uncertain how to manage this breach of decorum, I glanced at the other actors, who looked equally perplexed. The stage manager gesticulated to the ushers to halt this display, but they must have been well paid because they ignored him and lined up in front of *me*.

One by one, they handed me the bouquets until my arms could no longer hold them all, at which time the ushers laid them at my feet. Up and down my spine, I felt the disapproving glances of my castmates. My stage career could rise or fall upon the whims of these venerable actors; they could dislodge me from this pinnacle with a few well-placed words and replace me with any one of the number of young actresses clamoring for this role. I felt compelled to refuse the bouquets, until a thought struck me.

The giver could be anyone. He could be a prominent member of one of the feuding government parties—either a conservative Christian Social Party member or a socialist Social Democrat. Or worse, my benefactor could sympathize with the

National Socialist Party and long for the unification of Austria with Germany and its newly named chancellor, Adolf Hitler. The pendulum of power seemed to sway with each passing day, and no one could afford to take chances. Least of all me.

The audience had stopped clapping. In the uncomfortable silence, they settled back into their seats. All except one man. There, in the center of the third row, the most prized seat in the theater, stood a barrel-chested and square-jawed gentleman. Alone among all the patrons of the Theater an der Wien, he remained standing.

Staring at me.

CHAPTER TWO

May 17, 1933
Vienna, Austria

THE CURTAIN FELL. MY FELLOW ACTORS SHOT ME QUIZZI-cal looks, and I gave them a shrug and a shake of my head that I hoped conveyed my confusion and disapproval of the gesture. As quickly as seemed appropriate amid the congratulations, I returned to my dressing room, shutting the door. Anger and worry surged through me at how these flowers distracted from my triumph, this role that would help me firmly put *Ecstasy* behind me. I needed to find out who'd done this to me—and whether it was meant as a compliment, however misguided, or something else.

Pulling out the envelope hidden amid the flowers of the largest bouquet, I reached for my nail scissors and slit it open. I pulled out a heavy cream card rimmed in gold. Holding it close to the lamp on my dressing table, I read:

> *To an unforgettable Sissy. Yours, Mr. Friedrich Mandl*

Who was this Friedrich Mandl? The name sounded familiar, but I couldn't place it.

My dressing room door shuddered with an authoritative knock. "Miss Kiesler?" It was Mrs. Else Lubbig, veteran dresser to the star of every Theater an der Wien production for the past twenty years. Even during the Great War and the despondent years following the Austrian loss, the gray-haired matron had assisted actors onto the stage for the performances that buoyed the Viennese spirits, like the character of Empress Elizabeth, who reminded the people of Austria's historical prowess and prompted them to imagine a promising future. The play, of course, didn't touch upon the later years of the empress, when the golden tether of the emperor's displeasure became a yoke around her neck, constricting her every movement. The Viennese people didn't want to think about that, and they were expert at denial.

"Please come in," I called out.

Without a single glance at the profusion of roses, Mrs. Lubbig began unlacing me from my sun-yellow gown. As I rubbed cream into my face to wipe away the heavy stage makeup and the last vestiges of my character, she brushed out my hair from the complicated chignon the director thought befitted Empress Elizabeth. Although Mrs. Lubbig was silent, I sensed that she was biding her time until she asked the question undoubtedly buzzing around the theater.

"Beautiful flowers, miss," Mrs. Lubbig commented finally, after she complimented my performance.

"Yes," I answered, waiting for her true question.

"May I ask who they are from?" she asked, turning her attention from my hair to my corset.

I paused, weighing my response. I could lie and attribute the flowery gaffe to my parents, but this bit of gossip was currency with which she could trade, and if I shared the answer with her, she would owe me a favor. A favor from Mrs. Lubbig could be quite useful.

I smiled up at her, handing her the card. "A Mr. Friedrich Mandl."

She said nothing, but I heard a sharp intake of breath that spoke volumes. "Have you heard of him?" I asked.

"Yes, miss."

"Was he in the theater tonight?" I knew Mrs. Lubbig watched every performance from the wings, always scanning her assigned actress so she could readily assist with a torn hem or a lopsided wig.

"Yes."

"Was he the man who remained standing after the final applause?"

She sighed. "Yes, miss."

"What do you know of him?"

"I wouldn't like to say, miss. It isn't my place."

I hid my smile at Mrs. Lubbig's false modesty. In many ways, with her treasure trove of secrets, she wielded more power than anyone else at the theater.

"You would be doing me a great service."

She paused, patting her immaculately upswept hair, as if considering my supplication. "I've only heard gossip and rumor. Not all of it flattering."

"Please, Mrs. Lubbig."

I watched her in the mirror, seeing her finely lined face

work as if she was sifting through the carefully kept dossier in her mind to decide upon the appropriate morsel of information.

"Well, Mr. Mandl has quite a reputation with women."

"Along with every other man in Vienna," I said with a chuckle. If that was all, I needn't worry. Men, I could handle. Most anyway.

"It's a bit more than the usual chicanery, miss. One particular romance led to the suicide of a young German actress, Eva May."

"Oh my," I whispered, although, given my own past history of breaking hearts and an attempted suicide on the part of a suitor when I rejected him, I could not judge too harshly. While terrible, this tidbit was not everything she knew. I sensed from her tone that she was still withholding something, that she had more to report. But Mrs. Lubbig was going to make me work for it. "If there's more, I would be in your debt."

She hesitated. "It's the sort of information one feels cautious about sharing these days, miss." In these uncertain times, knowledge was currency.

I took her by the hand and stared into her eyes. "This information is for me only, for my safety. I promise you that it will not be shared with anyone else."

After a long pause, she said, "Mr. Mandl owns the Hirtenberger Patronenfabrik. His company manufactures munitions and other military weaponry, miss."

"An unsavory business, I suppose. But someone must do that work," I said. I couldn't see why the industry must be the man.

"It isn't so much the armaments he manufactures, but the people to whom he sells them."

"Oh?"

"Yes, miss. They call him the Merchant of Death."

CHAPTER THREE

May 26, 1933
Vienna, Austria

NINE DAYS AFTER MY STAGE DEBUT IN *SISSY*, A GIBBOUS moon loomed over the Viennese sky, leaving dark-violet shadows in its wake. It emitted enough light to illuminate the city streets, so I decided to walk the remainder of the way home from the theater in the fashionable nineteenth district and hopped out of the cab, even though the hour was late. I longed for the quiet interlude, a pause between the post-performance theater madness and the parental inundation I had been getting at home after each performance.

The sidewalks contained only a few passersby, a gray-haired couple ambling home after a late dinner, a whistling young man, and I felt safe enough. The route home grew increasingly affluent and well-heeled the closer I got to my parents' home in the neighborhood of Döbling, so I knew the streets would be safe. But none of this would have appeased my parents' concerns if they had known I was walking alone. They were very protective of their only child.

Pushing aside thoughts of Mama and Papa, I allowed myself

to smile over the review published in *Die Presse* this week. The glowing words about my portrayal of Empress Elizabeth had led to a run on ticket sales, and the theater had been standing room only the past three evenings. My status in the theater ranks had grown, with audible compliments from our usually critical director. The accolades felt good after the scandal of my nudity in *Ecstasy*—a decision that had seemed acceptable and in keeping with the artistic sensibility of the film until the public, my parents among them, reacted with shock—and I knew that the return to the theater after my foray into film had been the right decision. It was like coming home.

Acting had been a ward against childhood loneliness, a way to fill my quiet existence with people beyond the ever-present nanny and tutor but the ever-absent Mama and Papa. It started as the simple creation of characters and stories for my many dolls on an impromptu stage created under the huge desk in Papa's study, but then, unexpectedly, role-playing became much, much more. When I went to school—and suddenly became introduced to a wide, dizzying array of people—acting became my way of moving through the world, a sort of currency upon which I could draw whenever I needed. I could become whatever those around me secretly longed for, and I, in turn, got whatever I wanted from them. It wasn't until I stepped on my first stage, however, that I comprehended the breadth of my gift. I could bury myself and assume the mask of an entirely different person, one crafted by a director or a writer. I could turn my gaze on the audience and wield my capacity to influence them.

The only darkness cast over all this light from *Sissy* was the nightly delivery of roses. The color had changed, but the volume did not. I had received fuchsia, pale pink, ivory, bloodred, even a rare, delicate violet, but always exactly twelve dozen. It was obscene. But at least the method of delivery had changed. No longer did the ushers bestow my roses onstage with a grand flourish; now, they discreetly placed them in my dressing room during the show's final act.

The mysterious Mr. Mandl. I thought I had seen him amid the theatergoers in the coveted third-row seat on several occasions, but I wasn't certain. He had made no effort to communicate with me after the letter accompanying the first roses—until tonight. A gold-rimmed card tucked between vibrant yellow blooms—precisely like the color of my gown—contained the handwritten words:

> *Dear Miss Kiesler, I would very much like the honor of taking you to dinner at the restaurant at the Hotel Imperial after the performance. If this is amenable to you, please send word to my chauffeur, who will be waiting at the stage door until midnight. Yours, Mr. Friedrich Mandl*

While my parents would despair if I even considered meeting a strange man unaccompanied—particularly at a hotel restaurant, even if it was the landmark establishment created by architect Josef Hoffmann—the knowledge I'd gathered about Mr. Mandl ensured that I would not cross that breach. Cautious inquiries had yielded more information about my mysterious benefactor. The few friends I had in the insular theater world had heard he was driven by profit, not the morality of those to whom he sold his weaponry. But the most salient nugget came unprompted from the purveyor of secrets, Mrs. Lubbig, who whispered that Mr. Mandl was favored by the crop of right-wing autocrats that were springing up all over Europe. This report troubled me most of all, as Austria was struggling to maintain its independence while geographically surrounded by land-hungry dictatorships.

But while I didn't dare dine with him at the Hotel Imperial, I couldn't continue my practice of ignoring him entirely. By all accounts, Mr. Mandl was a politically connected man, and the current situation required that all Viennese act cautiously. Still, I didn't know how to properly manage his attention, as all my past dalliances had been with malleable young men close to my own age. Until I could formulate a plan, I enlisted Mrs. Lubbig's help to distract Mr. Mandl's chauffeur so I could side-step the stage door and exit out the front.

My heels tapped in a staccato rhythm as I continued my progress to Peter-Jordan-Strasse. I ticked off the familiar homes of our neighbors as I neared what my parents referred to as our "cottage," a misnomer that all Döbling residents used to describe their houses. The name was meant as an homage to the English architectural style of the neighborhood's large airy homes, built around enclosed family gardens, but it belied their substantial size.

A few houses away from my parents' home, the light seemed to diminish. I glanced up to see if clouds were obscuring the moon, but it continued to shine brightly. I had never noticed the phenomenon before, but then I almost never walked alone into our neighborhood at night. I wondered if the darkness could be explained by the proximity of Peter-Jordan-Strasse to the dense Vienna Woods, the Wienerwald, where Papa and I liked to take our Sunday walks.

There was not a twinkle of electric light on the block save for my parents' home. Pitch-black windows with the occasional hint of dwindling candlelight stared back at me from the houses bordering that of my parents, and I suddenly remembered the reason for the increased darkness. Many of the inhabitants of our Döbling enclave honored the tradition of refraining from electrical use beginning at sundown on Friday until sundown on Saturday, even though their religious habits didn't incline toward the orthodoxy that mandated such a practice. I'd forgotten because it was a practice my parents had never observed.

It was the Sabbath in Döbling, a Jewish neighborhood in a Catholic land.

CHAPTER FOUR

May 26, 1933
Vienna, Austria

T HE MOMENT I CROSSED THE THRESHOLD, I WAS
assaulted with the scent. I didn't need to see the roses to
know that the entire house was bursting with them. Why on
earth had Mr. Mandl sent them here as well?

The desultory chords of Bach sounded out from the
Bechstein grand piano in the parlor. As the door clicked shut
behind me, the music stopped, and my mother called out,
"Hedy? Is that you?"

As I handed my coat to Inge, our housemaid, I called back,
"Who else would it be at this hour, Mama?"

Papa came out of the parlor to greet me. With an intricately
carved wooden pipe dangling from the corner of his mouth, he
asked, "How is our Empress Elizabeth? Did you 'own the stage'
as *Die Presse* proclaimed?"

I smiled up at my tall Papa, handsome even with gray at
his temples and wrinkles around his blue eyes. Even at this
late hour, after eleven o'clock, he was immaculately dressed in a
pressed charcoal suit with a striped burgundy tie. He was ever

the reliable, successful manager of one of Vienna's most prominent banks, the Creditanstalt-Bankverein.

He took me by the hand, and for a moment, I was reminded of my childhood weekend afternoons when he would patiently answer all my questions about the world and its workings. No query was off-limits, whether historical or scientific, about literature or politics, and I gobbled up my time with him, the only with his undivided attention. On one favorite sunlit afternoon, he'd spent a full hour describing the nature of photosynthesis in response to my childlike ruminations on what plants ate; his patience in answering my relentless questions about the natural world and the physical sciences never faltered. But those hours were few, as Mama and work and social obligations demanded nearly every other piece of him. And without him, I faced long hours of rote schoolwork with teachers or homework and routines with my nanny and, to a lesser extent, Mama, who paid attention to me only when I sat before a piano and she berated my skills. Even though I adored music, I now only played the piano when Mama wasn't at home.

Leading me into the parlor, he settled me into one of the four brocade chairs that surrounded the fireplace, which was lit for the cool spring evening. As we waited for Mama to join us, Papa asked, "Are you hungry, my little princess? We could have Inge prepare a plate for you. You still look too skinny after that bout of pneumonia."

"No, but thank you, Papa. I ate before the performance."

I glanced around the room, family portraits crowding the walls already busy with their striped wallpaper, and saw that someone—my mother, most likely—had arranged the dozen bouquets of pale-pink roses artfully around the room. But for a single raised eyebrow, Papa remained silent on the subject of the flowers. We both knew that Mama would dole out the questions.

Mama entered the room and busied herself with pouring a glass of schnapps. Without speaking a word or meeting my eye, she conveyed her disappointment in me.

The room grew quiet while we waited for Mama to speak.

"It seems you have an admirer, Hedy," Mama said after a long draw on her schnapps.

"Yes, Mama."

"What could you have possibly done to encourage such a display?" Her tone held its usual judgment. The finishing school she'd insisted upon had failed to polish me into the marriageable, young hausfrau-in-training for which she'd hoped. When I'd pursued a profession she deemed "crass," even though the theater was held in high esteem among the Viennese, she had decided that, very likely, all my behavior followed suit. And sometimes, I admit, I obliged her with whatever young man I was currently allowing to court me. I'd occasionally let certain suitors—whether the aristocratic Ritter Franz von Hochstetten or the upstart actor and *Ecstasy* costar Aribert Mog—touch me in all the ways that Mama imagined, in my own private rebellion against her. *Why not?* I asked myself. She thought I was engaging in the salacious behavior anyway. And I liked learning that the power I had over men mirrored the power I had over the audience—to keep them in my thrall.

"Nothing, Mama. I have never even met the man."

"Why would a man give you all these roses if you've given him nothing in return? If you don't even know him? Has this man seen your reprehensible *Ecstasy* perhaps and figured you for a loose woman?"

Papa interjected rather sharply, "Enough. Perhaps it was the gift of her performance, Trude." Mama's given name was Gertrude, and Papa only called Mama by her nickname when he was trying to soften her.

After smoothing an errant black hair back into her perfect coif, Mama rose. Looking much taller than her tiny five feet, she strode over to her desk, where the bouquet bearing the card sat. She reached for her silver letter opener and sliced open the familiar cream envelope.

Holding the gilt-edged card close to the lamplight, she read aloud:

> *To Mr. and Mrs. Kiesler, I have been fortunate enough to watch your daughter play Empress Elizabeth four times in the past week, and I congratulate you on her talent. I wish to introduce myself to you in person in order to request your permission to call upon your daughter. If that is acceptable to you, I will come to your home this Sunday evening at six o'clock, the only evening when the theater is dark. Yours truly, Friedrich Mandl.*

Mr. Mandl was forcing my hand.

To my great surprise, my parents fell silent. I thought my mother would scoff at the invitation as bold and inappropriate or chide me for some invented offense surrounding Mr. Mandl's attention. And I assumed my father—mild-mannered in all matters excepting me—would rail against the supplication by a man unconnected to us by family or friends. Yet the favorite mantelpiece clock, a gift from Mama's parents on their wedding, ticked loudly for nearly a minute, and still they said nothing.

"What's wrong?" I asked.

Papa sighed, something he'd done with more frequency in recent months. "We must tread carefully, Hedy."

"Why?"

Mama drained her glass and asked me, "Do you know anything about this Mr. Mandl?"

"A little. When he started sending roses to my dressing room, I asked around the theater. It seems that he owns a munitions business."

"He sent you flowers before?" Papa sounded alarmed.

"Yes," I answered quietly. "Every night since *Sissy* opened."

They shot each other an inscrutable glance. Papa answered for them both. "I will respond to Mr. Mandl. We will have him here for a cocktail on Sunday at six o'clock, and, Hedy, you will dine with him afterward."

I was shocked. While my mother was eager for me to conform and marry a nice Döbling boy, and I guessed my father felt the same though he never said so, they had never overtly meddled in my personal life before. Not even when I refused to give up my career to accept the marriage proposal of the son of one of Germany's most distinguished families, the Hochstetten fellow. And they'd certainly never insisted that I go on a date with a particular boy. Why now? "Do I have any choice in this matter?"

"I am sorry, Hedy, but you must. This is not a man we can risk offending," Papa said with a sad expression.

Even though I'd guessed that I'd eventually have to meet Mr. Mandl, I wanted to resist. But the pained look on my father's face stopped me. Something, someone was forcing his hand. "Why, Papa?"

"You were born after the Great War, Hedy. You don't understand how politics can be a force of destruction." He shook his head and sighed again.

But he did not elaborate. When did Papa start withholding information from me and thinking that I was unable to understand complicated matters? He had always told me that I was capable of anything, and I had believed him. His assurances had prompted my confidence to pursue acting.

I tried to keep the anger and disappointment from my voice. "Just because I've chosen acting doesn't mean that I can't comprehend issues unrelated to the theater, Papa. You of all people should know that."

I was irritated at Papa's patronizing tone, unusual after years of treating me as an intellectual equal. How many Sunday nights had we spent discussing the newspaper by the fire after a family supper? Since I'd been a relatively young girl, he'd reviewed with me every detail of the headlines until he felt certain that I understood the nuances of the national and international political scene, not to mention the economic developments. All the while, Mama would sip her schnapps and shake her head in disapproval, muttering "a waste of good time" under her breath. Why would Papa think I'd changed simply because the theater now occupied my nights instead of fireside conversations?

He gave me a weak smile and said, "I suppose that's true, my little princess. So you must know that, only two months ago in March, Chancellor Dollfuss took advantage of an irregularity in parliamentary voting procedures to seize the Austrian government and dissolve Parliament."

"Of course, Papa. It was all over the newspapers. I don't just read the theater section. And I saw the barbed wire around the Parliament building."

"Then you must understand that this move turned Austria, like Germany, Italy, and Spain, into a dictatorship. Theoretically, we are still a country with a democratic constitution and two parties—Dollfuss's conservative Christian Social Party, which appeals to rural and upper-class folk for different reasons, and the opposing Social Democrat Party. But the reality is different; Chancellor Dollfuss is in charge and working to consolidate total power. Rumors abound that he's going to ban the Schutzbund, the military arm of the Social Democratic Party."

My stomach churned at Papa categorizing Austria with its fascist neighbors and lumping its leaders in the same category as Adolf Hitler, Benito Mussolini, and Francisco Franco. "I don't know if I ever saw it written quite so plainly, Papa." I knew Austria was surrounded by fascist dictators, but I'd thought our country had remained largely free of such rulers. For now, anyway.

"You might not read the word 'dictator' in the newspapers, but indeed, that is what Chancellor Dollfuss has become, with the Heimwehr, which, as you know, is a paramilitary organization, effectively serving as his personal army, since the treaty ending the Great War limits Austria's ability to amass troops.

The ostensible head of the Heimwehr is Ernst Rüdiger von Starhemberg, but behind Starhemberg is his close friend and business colleague Mr. Friedrich Mandl. Mr. Mandl supplies all the military needs for the Heimwehr and, by all accounts, is involved in strategy as well."

I had thought Papa was meandering in this political lecture, but now I comprehended. He was leading me to Mr. Mandl, and the power this mysterious man exerted was becoming clear. "I understand, Papa."

"I'm not certain that you do. There is more, Hedy. I'm sure that you read in the newspapers that this Adolf Hitler became chancellor of Germany in January."

"Yes," I said as my mother rose for a second schnapps. Typically, she only drank one, sipping it slowly throughout the evening.

"Are you also familiar with the anti-Semitic policies Hitler has been adopting in Germany?"

I hadn't really paid much attention to the articles on this topic, as I didn't really think it applied to us. But I didn't want to admit ignorance to Papa, so I said, "Yes."

"Then you know that as soon as the Nazis came to power, they began a formal boycott of Jewish businesses and banned all non-Aryans from the legal profession and civil service. Jewish German citizens have not only been subject to violent attacks, but they've been stripped of their citizenship rights—rights that Austrian Jews have counted upon since the 1840s."

"I've read about that," I said, although in truth, I skimmed those stories.

"Well, then maybe you've also read the articles about the

Austrian Nazis who long for a unification of our country with Germany, and whatever people's political views about Dollfuss, everyone's primary fear is that this Chancellor Hitler will stage a coup to take over Austria. Nothing has been said publicly, but I've heard rumors that Chancellor Dollfuss met with Italian leader Mussolini last month and that Mussolini has agreed to aid Austria in protecting our country should there be a German invasion."

"I suppose that's good news, although I'm not sure Austria should be beholden to Italy," I offered. "I mean, Mussolini is a dictator too, and we might just end up with Mussolini instead of Hitler."

Papa interrupted me. "That's true, Hedy, but Mussolini doesn't advocate the same strident anti-Semitic policies as Hitler."

"I see," I said, although I couldn't see why Papa was so concerned. Such policies wouldn't really affect us. "But what does that have to do with Mr. Mandl?"

"Mr. Mandl has a long-standing relationship with Mussolini; he supplied him with weaponry for years. The rumor is that *he* arranged the meeting between Dollfuss and Mussolini."

My head spun as I began to see the thread stitching Mandl into this nefarious tapestry. This was the man pursuing me?

"This Mr. Mandl is the man behind Chancellor Dollfuss's throne. *But* he may also be the man behind Austria's continued independence."

CHAPTER FIVE

May 28, 1933
Vienna, Austria

ICE CLINKED ON CRYSTAL, AND LIQUID POURED ON ICE. Forced laughter and the hum of small talk drifted up the steep mahogany staircase. A conversational lull transpired, rectified by the dulcet tones of Beethoven played by my mother's expert hands. My parents were attempting to manage Friedrich Mandl.

We had decided that I would wait upstairs until Papa summoned me. That way, my parents could engage in the charade of assessing Mr. Mandl to see if he was worthy of calling upon their only child, even though we all knew that this was a ruse, that Papa's permission had been granted the moment Mr. Mandl signed his name on the letter to my parents.

My palms were sweaty, an unfamiliar experience for me. My nerves had never been an issue in the past, not with men anyway. I might feel a flutter in the second before the curtains lifted onstage or in the long minutes before the director called out "take one," but never in the context of dating. Boys did not intimidate me; I'd always had the upper hand in past relationships, committing and severing ties with ease. I treated them as subjects upon whom I could practice my chameleon skills, the building blocks of my acting career.

I rose from my perch on the chaise longue and stood before my full-length mirror for the hundredth time. Mama and I had debated the appropriate attire to navigate this encounter— nothing too suggestive, or he might receive the wrong impression of me; nothing too childlike, or he might take offense that we weren't taking him seriously. We had settled on an emerald-green crepe dress with squared shoulders and a high neckline, with a skirt that hit well below my knee.

Pacing my room, I strained to hear the conversation downstairs. Snippets became audible periodically, but nothing I could place in context. A loud burst of laughter sounded out, and then Papa called upstairs, "Hedy, please come downstairs if you are ready."

After a final glance in the mirror, I headed down the staircase, my heels making an unseemly clatter. Papa waited in the doorway to the parlor for me, his face carefully assembled in a mask of pleasantness. It belied the worry I knew lurked beneath.

Taking Papa by the elbow, I crossed the threshold into the parlor. Mama sat on the sofa facing Mr. Mandl, a cautious expression on her face. Of my caller, I could see only the back of his carefully combed head.

"Mr. Mandl, may I introduce my daughter, Miss Hedwig Kiesler. I believe you're familiar with her, although you have never formally met." Papa gently propelled me forward.

Together, Mama and Mr. Mandl rose, and he turned toward me. From the ugly rumors about politics and women, I expected to find him repulsive. In fact, I'd braced myself for it. After he made a formal bow to me, our eyes met, and I found him unexpectedly attractive. Not in the physical sense exactly, although he was handsome in a polished way with his impeccable navy Savile Row suit and gleaming cuff links, but in the power and confidence that exuded from him. Unlike all my past suitors, he was a man, not a boy.

He took the lead. "It is a true honor, Miss Kiesler. I am an admirer of your work, as I think you know."

Heat spread across my cheeks, another rarity for me. "Thank you for the flowers. They were beautiful and"—I searched for the right word—"generous."

"A paltry reflection of my enjoyment of your work." Smooth words slid out of his mouth like liquid.

An uneasy silence settled upon the room. Usually Mama, ever socially astute, had the right response at the ready, but Mr. Mandl seemed to have unsettled everyone. Papa came to the rescue. "Mr. Mandl has been sharing his love of the arts with us."

"Yes." He turned to me and said, "I learned that your mother was a concert pianist before she married. I confess that I implored her to play, even when she protested that she no longer performed outside the family. Her rendering of Beethoven was masterful."

It was Mama's turn to blush. "Thank you, Mr. Mandl."

The fact that Mama played for Mr. Mandl told me more about my parents' fear than Papa's earlier monologue about Mr. Mandl's political and military maneuverings ever could. When she gave up her career twenty years ago to marry Papa, she had sworn that she would never play for anyone again, save family. And my stubborn mother had adhered to that vow until tonight.

"I'm guessing you taught your daughter to play beautifully as well," he said.

"Well..." Mama hesitated.

I knew Mama couldn't bear to compliment my playing. She demanded perfection, and all my efforts displeased her, as much as my looks—as if she believed that I chose my beauty on purpose, exclusively to defy her.

"Have you seen any of the other new plays that opened this month, Mr. Mandl?" I turned the attention away from my visibly apprehensive mother to the broader conversational topic. I didn't want Mama to fill the silence with nervous chatter unflattering to me.

He fixed his brown eyes on mine. "In truth, Miss Kiesler, your performance in *Sissy* spoiled me for any other actor or actress. I keep returning to the Theater an der Wien."

His intensity made me uncomfortable, and I longed to avert my eyes. But I sensed that he didn't want demureness from me but strength. So I met his gaze while I said the words etiquette demanded. "You flatter me unduly, Mr. Mandl."

"I mean every compliment, and you deserve every rose."

Mama returned to herself and blurted out a phrase she had repeated over and over since my childhood. I'd heard it every time someone called me pretty or complimented my piano or acting skills and every extra moment Papa spent explaining to me the inner workings of a car engine or a porcelain factory. "You'll spoil the girl, Mr. Mandl."

The phrase was not the affectionate admonition it seemed

on the surface. It reflected her feelings that I didn't deserve spoiling, that I had already been given too much, that I was—at my core—unworthy.

Could this stranger decode the criticism hidden behind my mother's words?

If Mr. Mandl sensed her true meaning, he didn't react. Instead, without averting his eyes from mine, he said, "It would be my pleasure to spoil her, Mrs. Kiesler." Turning back to Papa, he asked, "Do I have your permission to take your daughter for dinner?"

After a discreet, apologetic glance at me, he said, "Yes, Mr. Mandl, you do."

CHAPTER SIX

May 28, 1933
Vienna, Austria

T HE MOMENT WE STEPPED OUT OF MR. MANDL'S CHAUF-
feured limousine into the lobby of Hotel Imperial,
the staff flocked to his side. Even the notoriously persnick-
ety maître d' of the hotel's legendary restaurant raced to Mr.
Mandl, offering his services. On the few special occasions I'd
dined at the restaurant with my parents—for birthdays and a
school graduation—we'd practically begged for attention and
waited nearly an hour to place our orders. The establishment,
known for its fine cuisine and the haughtiness of its staff, felt
like it was a different place on Mr. Mandl's arm. But I tried to
hide my amazement, to play the part of the worldly actress.

Whispers trailed behind us, and we were led to a table placed
in the enviable center of the wood-paneled room. I'd always
thought of Papa as a successful man, and he was, but only now
did I understand true power. Funny how it could be conveyed by
the service at a restaurant and the stares of other diners.

Roses of every imaginable color decorated the table, bright-
ening the otherwise luxurious but monochromatic room. None

of the other tables had flowers, only bronze candlesticks topped with gleaming white candles, and Mr. Mandl must have specially ordered them for this occasion. Clearly, he'd had no real concern that my parents would withhold permission for our date.

As I settled into the striped upholstered chair pulled out for me by Mr. Mandl, who eschewed the attempts by the maître d' to seat me, I felt dowdy in the dress Mama and I had selected. In the mirror, it had appeared simple but appropriately modest. But here, wives and girlfriends alike wore the latest couture, which mostly consisted of flimsy slips of expensive fabric stitched together by crystal strings. I looked positively nunlike in comparison.

He asked me a few pointed questions about the types of food I enjoyed and the wine I preferred and then asked, "Do you mind if I order for you? I eat here frequently and have a reasonable sense of their best dishes. I would hate for you to be disappointed."

Many men would have taken charge of the ordering without even asking permission, and I appreciated the courtesy. Still, I knew I shouldn't just dutifully acquiesce; his strength demanded strength in return. "I usually like to order for myself, but in this instance, that would be fine."

My caveat surprised and pleased him, as I'd sensed it would. He laughed, a rich, melodic sound, as he signaled for the waiter to return to the table. After he ordered oysters and champagne for us to begin, followed by chateaubriand, he initiated a conversation about the theater world. He was quite familiar with Vienna's established directors, writers, and actors and solicitous of my opinions about the staging and casting of recently opened plays. The knowledgeable exchange was rare for me—most men knew little, or cared little, about the theater world—as was his active encouragement of my own thoughts. I found him refreshing and unexpected.

We grew quiet over the oysters, until he asked, "I suppose you have heard a lot about me?"

The blunt question startled me. I'd been enjoying his company and had momentarily forgotten about the unpleasantness of his reputation. Unsure about the safest response, I settled on honesty; his own bluntness seemed to deserve its match. "Yes, I have."

"I'm guessing you've heard nothing good."

A knot formed in my stomach. My parents and I had hoped the evening would pass without any foray into his character. "Not *all* of it bad," I answered with a smile. I hoped to inject a note of levity into this unsettling exchange and perhaps divert it back to our former topic.

He placed his fork down on his plate and carefully wiped the corners of his mouth with his linen napkin before speaking. "Miss Kiesler, I will not insult your obvious intellect by claiming that the rumors you've heard are *all* lies. It's true that I've dated several women and that I've been married once before. It's also true that, in my line of work, I must occasionally deal with political figures and movements that others find unsavory. All I ask is that you allow me the opportunity to demonstrate that I am different from the men with whom I do business and that I am more respectful than the number of women to whom I've been linked would suggest. I am not my reputation."

Although I knew I should feel otherwise, that I should guard myself against this man, his words moved me. I understood him. I too had been trying to restore the harm to my honor wreaked by *Ecstasy*. Immediately after its release, the movie's nudity and depiction of sexual intercourse—in which the director poked me with a pin to achieve an orgasmic expression on my face—led to the movie's banning in several countries and censorship in others, which cast a shadow upon my name. Although, of course, the scandal only increased people's desire to actually see the elusive movie. Didn't this man deserve the same chance at redemption that I myself sought?

Before I could answer, he spoke again. "You seem hesitant, Miss Kiesler, and I would be surprised—maybe even a little disappointed—if you weren't. I have no interest in playing games, so I ask that you please allow me to make my feelings and my intentions plain."

I nodded my assent, even though his request made the knot in my stomach tighten.

"I am not a particularly religious man, Miss Kiesler. Nor am I especially romantic."

Without thinking, I raised my eyebrow and glanced at the roses.

"Well, not usually," he said with a smile. His face quickly became serious again. "But when I saw you on the stage, there was a moment when I felt a surge of recognition, as if I knew you. Not as if we had met in the normal manner—at a social occasion or through acquaintances—but as though I'd always known you. It happened just before your curtain call; for a few seconds, you were no longer Empress Elizabeth but yourself. And I felt that I knew you."

He continued to speak, but I didn't hear him. I was too astounded by his statement and deep in my own thoughts.

"It has been a singular experience for me, and I feel strangely connected to you—" He stopped talking suddenly and shook his head. "If my business colleagues could hear me talking to you in this way, they'd consider my words the ravings of a demented fan. As you must."

I could have allowed him to flounder. I could have stayed silent and watched this man who was reported to hold the fate of Austria in his hand falter. His behavior could have provided the excuse for me to refuse future encounters. But I felt a peculiar link to him. "No, I could not possibly think of you in that way."

"If you mean that, would you consider seeing me again?"

I had been pursued by boys before, and even though I was only nineteen, I was no innocent. There had been many admirers: Wolf Albach-Retty, Count Blücher von Wahlstatt, even a young Russian academic whose long, unpronounceable last name had faded from memory, among others. Some had held my attention briefly, and others I had entertained for slightly longer periods. A few I'd allowed access to my body, while most I'd held at bay. But none of them had afforded me the respect of this frankness. Instead, they'd engaged in the intricate courting dance so typical of most men but so insulting to my intelligence, so predictable. Notwithstanding their titles or money or degrees, none had seemed my equal, so I stayed with them only briefly. But Friedrich Mandl was different.

I paused, allowing him to think I was mulling over his request. He didn't bother to hide his anticipation, and I delayed my response as long as possible, enjoying his apprehension and the sway I held over this very powerful man.

I took a long sip of my champagne, carefully licking my lips before I spoke. Then, finally, I said, "Yes, Mr. Mandl. I would consider seeing you again."

CHAPTER SEVEN

July 16, 1933
Vienna, Austria

I ALMOST GIGGLED. PLACING MY HAND OVER MY MOUTH, I stifled the girlish peals about to pour from my lips. Such silliness wouldn't be in accord with the sophisticate I purported to be. Not that Fritz would mind terribly. He seemed to delight in me, even in the aspects of myself that I didn't find delightful.

Once I composed myself, I ran a finger along the rim of the plate. The surface gleamed as if hewn from gold, but surely it was merely gilded porcelain. As if he read my thoughts—an increasingly common occurrence—Fritz answered, "Yes, *Liebling*, the plates are crafted from solid gold."

The laughter I'd suppressed came spilling out. "Solid gold plates? Truly?"

He laughed along with me and then explained, "Nearly solid. Pure gold is too soft on its own, of course, and must be mixed with an alloy. Here, it's been hardened by an addition of silver, which only makes it tougher but no less beautiful... like you."

I smiled at the compliment, enjoying the thought of being appreciated for my strength. Most men found my confidence intimidating, but Fritz solicited my opinions and welcomed my views, even those different from his own. "Did you commission them? I cannot imagine you'd find gold plates at a typical *Geschäft das Porzellan verkauft.*"

"Let's just say they became available after the recent unrest at the universities. And at a reasonable price."

His words confused me. Was he speaking about the riots that broke out last winter and spring when Jewish students were barred by socialists from the University of Vienna? Why would such turmoil lead to the fire-sale selling of gold plates? The two events seemed unrelated, but a connection teased at the edges of my consciousness.

Fritz interrupted my thoughts, holding his finely etched crystal goblet high. "A toast to the past seven weeks. The happiest of my life."

As we clinked crystal until the glasses sang and sipped on the crisp, bubbly Veuve Clicquot, I thought about the past weeks. Seven lavish dinners, one for every night the theater was dark. Twenty lavish lunches, for those afternoons I did not have a matinee and he did not have a business meeting. Forty-nine deliveries of fresh flowers, never repeating the color two days in a row. Seven weeks forcing myself to not glance at the third-row seat that he'd purchased as his own for the show's run and that he inhabited many of the nights I was onstage. Seven weeks with the Theater an der Wien aflutter at my affair, all except Mrs. Lubbig, whose lips sealed upon learning of my fledgling relationship and had not opened since. Seven weeks with my parents' nerves on edge until I returned home from my evenings on the arm of the richest man in Austria, who said I made him feel young again. Even hopeful.

I surrendered my world to him. Except for the hours that I performed on the stage, I became his. As he'd requested, I allowed him to prove himself to me.

We'd dined in every fine establishment in Vienna and its environs, but we'd never visited even one of his three homes—an enormous Viennese apartment; a castle called Schloss Schwarzenau near a town of the same name, approximately 120 kilometers northwest of Vienna; and a lavish, twenty-five-room hunting lodge dubbed Villa Fegenberg, over 80 kilometers south of Vienna—before tonight. Dining alone in a grown man's house without an appropriate escort went against every protocol my parents held dear. So I didn't tell them.

Earlier that evening, he'd led me through the columned and gated entryway to his white stone building at 15 Schwarzenbergplatz, in the most affluent section of Vienna and adjacent to the Ringstrasse, past the uniformed concierge and three doormen, and up the gated elevator to the top floor of the building. There, he'd spun me around his twelve-room apartment—a space more aptly described as a mansion, as it took up three floors—which I complimented in a reserved tone, although I felt like gushing. His home was decorated in a style that, at first, seemed the stark antithesis of the cozy, multi-patterned decor with which I had grown up in Döbling. But the longer I studied the luxurious simplicity of the monochromatic furnishings, rugs, and artwork, the more cloying I perceived the excess of decoration found in most Viennese homes. And instead of feeling sterile, his home felt wonderfully modern and fresh.

As we lingered over the five courses of French haute cuisine laden with unfamiliar sauces that Fritz had ordered his chef to prepare in honor of the fine French champagne we were drinking, I ran my finger along the fabric of the dining room table chair and linens. The nubby silk felt wondrously decadent under my fingertips. Although Fritz's face was turned toward the servant refilling his champagne, I caught a glimpse of his expression through the reflection on a hefty mirror on the opposite wall. He was beaming at my pleasure.

Lifting the champagne to his lips, he asked another question about my upbringing. Fritz seemed endlessly curious about me, but he never spoke about his own youth. It seemed impossible that the impeccable, powerful man sitting before me could have ever been a soft, vulnerable child. Had he been born hard-edged and strong? Had he marched out of the womb with that confident stride?

"Enough about me, Fritz. Surely, by now, you see that the life of Hedwig Kiesler of Döbling is not terribly exciting. But you, well, you are a different matter. What is the origin story of Friedrich Mandl?"

Grinning, he launched into the tale of Hirtenberger Patronenfabrik. His narrative of the stolid family munitions business that Fritz had rescued and grown exponentially when it fell bankrupt after the Austrian defeat during the Great War sounded well rehearsed, almost glib. Clearly, he trotted it out whenever the occasion called for it, but I wanted more than a practiced account of a company. I wanted the real Fritz's history.

The private story of the boy who became the country's richest man, not the public narrative he'd carefully crafted about a company's rise.

"How impressive, Fritz. Particularly the bank loan you negotiated to return the factory to family ownership after the bankruptcy. That was a stroke of brilliance."

He smiled. How he loved praise.

I continued. "But what of your family life? Tell me about your mother."

The broad smile disappeared. His jaw clenched, becoming more square in shape. Where was the besotted, eager Fritz I knew? I felt a chill. I leaned back in my seat, and registering my reaction, he forced a grin back onto his face.

"Nothing much to share there. She was a very typical Austrian hausfrau."

I knew better than to probe further. Changing the subject in order to alter the mood, I asked, "Would you mind showing me the drawing room?"

"Excellent suggestion. Why don't we have our digestifs and desserts there?"

He led me by the hand to a sofa that sat before a wide window with a fine view of the imposing architecture around the Ringstrasse. The lights of the ornate buildings sparkled and reflected off the many mirrored surfaces in the drawing room, and as I sipped the festive *Bowle* he poured for me, I felt an irrational sense of happiness. The success in *Sissy*, my burgeoning relationship with Fritz—they felt too perfect to be real. Unearned, Mama would say.

Glancing over at Fritz, I realized he was staring at me,

smiling at my smile. Leaning toward me, he kissed me, gently at first. The tenderness gave way to intensity, and his hands slid from my waist to my back. I felt his lips on my neck, and his fingers began unclasping my dress.

I had been intimate with other boys before. Lingering kisses and embraces on balconies and backstage. Fumbling caresses and gropes in the back seats of cars. Three stolen afternoons in the empty apartment of a boyfriend's professor parents where I let go of all my inhibitions. But I sensed that I should hold back with Fritz, that I should wait and allow him to pursue me. So even though I longed for him, I broke away.

"I should leave," I said, nearly breathless. "My parents will be furious if I'm home later than midnight."

He released his arms and gave me an enigmatic grin. "If you wish, *Hase*."

I pulled him toward me for a final kiss. "I don't wish, but I must. My parents are steadfast in their rules."

Breathing into me, he said, "I think, upon your return home, you might be surprised at the status of those rules. There may be change on the horizon."

CHAPTER EIGHT

July 16, 1933
Vienna, Austria

The chauffeur opened my door, but Fritz's fingers lingered on mine. "I wish you didn't have to say good night," he whispered.

"I wish the same," I whispered back. And it was true. I had started this relationship telling myself that I didn't like him, that all this listening and nodding and talking and laughing and even kissing was a role urged upon me by my parents, by necessity. Another performance. I figured I would find a way out. But the Hedy I truly was underneath all the external play-acting had developed real feelings. And I realized that my heart was now as vulnerable as all the hearts I'd broken in my past romantic games.

Still, in some ways, my actual feelings were of no consequence, just as they held no real weight onstage. I pulled my hand away from his and stepped out of the car without another word. My parents' house was dark. If not for rays of the waning moon, I might have tripped on the stone passageway to the front door. Feeling in the dark for the door handle, I opened

and closed the door quietly behind me, careful not to waken
anyone in the sleeping house, not even Inge, our housemaid.
The hour was well past midnight, and if my luck continued its
hold, Mama and Papa would already be in a deep slumber and
any noises I made wouldn't rouse them. My shoulders relaxed
as I thought about the prospect of retiring to bed without the
usual interrogation.

Unbuckling my silver heels, I slid my feet out of my shoes. I
gingerly placed them down on the floor to avoid a clatter. Treading
with a light step, I avoided the floorboards known to creak as I
made my way to the staircase and started up without a sound.

But when I pushed open my bedroom door, Papa sat upon
the edge of my bed, pipe between his lips.

"Is everything all right, Papa?" He had never waited for me
in my bedroom before. He and Mama either awaited my return
in the parlor, smoking and sipping schnapps after a night at
the theater with friends, or retired to bed. Until I started seeing
Fritz, that was.

"No one is ill, if that's what you mean, Hedy."

Gathering the folds of my long blue gown, I sat down next
to him on the edge of my bed, tucking my bare feet underneath
me. "What's wrong, Papa?"

"Mr. Mandl came to visit me today at the bank," he said
with a long pull on his pipe.

"He did?" Why would Fritz have gone to see my father
today? And more importantly, why hadn't Fritz mentioned it
during our long evening together?

"Yes. He invited me to lunch at his private club, and Mr.
Mandl being who he is, I accepted."

My mind raced with possible reasons, and my voice quivered as I asked, "What did you talk about over lunch?"

He blew a smoke ring toward the ceiling and watched as it ascended, touched the swirling plaster, and dissipated. Only then did he answer. "We exchanged the usual pleasantries, but of course, we primarily discussed you. Mr. Mandl is very taken with you, Hedy."

My cheeks felt hot, and I was thankful for the darkness. Despite all the warnings we'd received and all the sordid tales we'd heard, I was extremely drawn to Fritz. And I liked the way his power coursed through me when we were together. The man was not the reputation, he had proven to me.

"It was certainly kind of him to invite you to lunch." I didn't know what else to say. It felt awkward asking Papa for the details of their conversation.

"I don't think I've made myself very clear, Hedy. There was a purpose to our lunch, beyond the mere extolling of your many virtues."

"Oh?" My voice shook, out of excited anticipation or fear, I didn't know.

"Yes. Mr. Mandl asked for your hand in marriage."

"Marriage?" I was shocked. We'd only known each other seven weeks.

"Yes, Hedy. He is quite determined to have you for his wife."

"Oh," I whispered. Conflicting emotions swirled through me—flattery, fear, power. Fritz was no starstruck boy, as were all my previous entanglements. He was a grown man who had any number of women at his disposal, and he wanted me.

Papa set his pipe down. His hands now free, he wrapped

his arms around me. "I'm so sorry, Hedy. My insistence that you not offend this powerful man has yielded this terrible result."

"Do *you* think it's terrible, Papa?"

"I don't know what to think, *Liebling*. You've just met this man, whom we otherwise know only by a rather awful reputation. Even though you've accepted many dates with him, I have no sense of how you really feel. And I'm scared. I really fear—even if you did care for him—what life as Friedrich Mandl's wife would entail." He paused, weighing his next words. "But I may be more scared about the repercussions to you—to us—if you refuse."

I whispered, "I don't think his proposal is terrible."

"Are you telling me that you care for him?" He sounded shocked. And wishful. For what, I wasn't yet certain.

"Well…" I paused, unsure about the proper language to use for this conversation. It felt strange to speak with Papa about my emotions for a man. In my past relationships, euphemisms had ruled the day. "I'm certainly flattered, Papa. And I do have feelings for him."

He pulled back and stared into my eyes. In the low light of my nightstand lamp, I saw tears well in my stoic father's eyes. "You're not saying this because you think it will please me, are you?"

"No, I mean it."

"There is a wide gulf—a vast ocean, if you like—between caring for someone and wishing to marry them, Hedy."

I wondered if he was thinking about his tense relationship with Mama when he said those words. But instead of answering Papa's implicit question—or asking him about my supposition—I deflected. "What do you think, Papa?"

"Normally, no matter your feelings, I'd object on any number of grounds. He's too old for you. You hardly know each other. We don't know his family. His sullied reputation in business and with women. I could go on and on. And I'm certain your mother would agree, but I've waited to discuss this with her. I wanted to know what your feelings were first."

Was Papa telling me to refuse his proposal? His opinions mattered quite a lot to me. Mama's thoughts on the matter of Fritz hardly impacted me. Her disdain for me colored her views, rendering them self-serving for her and useless for me. Unless I trod the precise path she deemed appropriate, I was a fallen woman in her eyes.

Papa wasn't finished. "But in truth, I'm torn. If you care for him, this match could protect you in the days to come. He's powerful. Whether you share his political views and his alignment with Chancellor Dollfuss, he's committed to keeping Austria independent from Germany and that vile anti-Semite Chancellor Hitler. And if the rumors are true, the situation is going to get more dangerous for us Jews."

What was Papa talking about? We weren't really Jewish, not like the émigrés who'd flooded into Austria during the Great War and again in the bleak, impoverished days that followed our defeat. Those Eastern Jews, the *Ostjuden,* lived apart from the rest of Austrian society, holding fast to their orthodox beliefs and practices. I didn't even know any like that, who dressed in the traditional garb. The few religious Jews I knew in our neighborhood, those who kept Sabbath or displayed menorahs or mezuzahs in their homes, did so quietly, not with the bold insouciance of the *Ostjuden,* and they looked like everyone else. And my family, well, we really didn't consider ourselves Jewish, except in a vague, cultural sense. We were fully assimilated into the vibrant cultural life of the capital city. We were Viennese above all else.

"But we're not like those Eastern European Jews who've immigrated here in the past few years."

His voice was brittle. "Just because I don't wear a yarmulke and we don't celebrate the High Holidays doesn't mean we aren't Jewish, particularly in the eyes of others. We live in Döbling, for God's sake, a town with its own synagogue, where nearly all four thousand of the inhabitants are Jewish. And both your mother and I were raised in Jewish homes. If the *Hakenkreuzler*, those thugs who strut about with their damn swastikas, broaden their reach, Döbling could certainly be targeted. And its people."

"No, Papa. Not Döbling." It seemed almost laughable that picturesque, secure Döbling could be anyone's idea of a target.

Papa's brittle tone softened to allow for sadness. "The attacks on Jews are increasing, Hedy, even if it's not reported in newspapers. Only violent public attacks, like the one that happened in the Café Sperlhof prayer room last year, cannot be kept quiet by the government. In Jewish areas populated by the orthodox community, like *Leopoldstadt*, anti-Semitic flyers are distributed on a regular basis, and there are frequent skirmishes. Tensions are mounting, and if Hitler gets his hands on Austria, then God help us."

I was speechless. Papa and I had discussed our Jewishness only one time before. A memory of that talk broke free from the past and entered the present moment as fresh and alive as when the event first occurred. I was perhaps eight years old, and for several hours, I'd been sitting under Papa's desk, staging a dance scene for my dolls; I adored using the dark, private area under his ornate escritoire as my theater. It suddenly seemed that Mama—always just around the corner, especially when I didn't want her to be—had been gone all day. Instead of experiencing elation at the unexpected liberation from Mama and her timetable—a freedom that had allowed this long expanse of theatrics—I felt panic. Had something terrible happened to her?

Racing from the study, I found Papa sitting before the fire in the parlor, reading the newspaper and puffing on his pipe quite contently. His composure troubled me. Why wasn't he worried about Mama? "Where is she?" I yelled from the doorway.

He looked up from his newspaper, eyes alarmed. "Whatever is wrong, Hedy? Who is 'she'?"

"Mama, of course. She's missing."

"Oh, not to worry. She is just making a shiva call at Mrs. Stein's family home."

I knew that Mrs. Stein, one of our neighbors four doors down, had recently lost her father, but what on earth was a shiva call? It sounded exotic.

"What's that?" I asked, scrunching my nose up in a way that Mama described as "unseemly." But Mama wasn't here, and Papa would never chastise me for something as silly as my nose.

"When a Jewish person dies, their family mourns for them for a week by receiving into their home callers expressing condolences. This is described as 'shiva.'"

"So the Steins are Jewish?" It was a word I'd heard my parents say occasionally, but I wasn't certain what it meant, other than that people seemed to fall into two groups—Jewish or not. I felt quite grown-up saying the word aloud.

Papa's eyebrows raised at my question, and his eyes widened in an unfamiliar expression. It resembled surprise, but I'd never known my unflappable Papa to be surprised about anything. "Yes, Hedy. They are. And so are we."

I wanted to ask Papa a question—something about what it meant to be Jewish—but the front door slammed. The unmistakable sound of Mama's heels on the entryway floor traveled into the parlor, and Papa and I exchanged a glance. The time for questions had passed, but from that moment forward, I knew what category my family fell into, if not precisely what the religion entailed.

This second conversation was the longest Papa and I had ever spoken about our Jewishness—although, in the intervening years, I'd gleaned a rough sense of the religion and the fact that our family came from Jewish stock—and his words terrified me. Before now, the acts of violence I'd read about in the newspapers seemed to happen to another group of Jews, a people separate and apart from my own remote heritage. Now, I wasn't certain.

"Should we be worried, Papa?"

My fear must have been apparent, because Papa clasped my hands in his and tried to reassure me. "I've said too much, Hedy, about my private worries. No one knows what will transpire in this tumult. But if anyone can protect you, he can. Friedrich Mandl may be able to keep you safe in unsafe times."

CHAPTER NINE

July 18, 1933
Vienna, Austria

THE EVENING FELT AS THOUGH IT HAD BEEN BURNISHED bright. Our table was perfectly positioned at the dining room's center, where all eyes could linger upon us. Our faces gleamed in the flickering light from two silver candelabra, which bore candles on arms shaped like tree branches. The warm glow cast by this silvery confection made the crystal glasses sparkle brighter and the silverware glint from their many reflective surfaces. On the table's center stood a porcelain vase full of roses in every one of the hues that had been delivered to my dressing room, a bouquet trimmed by expert hands such that the blooms sat at the perfect height and would not interfere with our views of each other. The restaurant hummed with the low chatter of other late-night diners and the gentle playing of a piano. I felt as if all the elegant dinners and lunches we'd experienced together were a dress rehearsal for this moment and the curtain had lifted on our own opening night. Or was I just reading theatrics and momentousness into inconsequential details because I thought Fritz would propose tonight?

I knew Papa had spoken to Fritz yesterday. They'd arranged another lunch at Fritz's club, and in the morning before he left, Papa and I had rehearsed what he would say. Tendrils of Papa's pipe smoke had lingered in the front hall when I had returned home from the theater last night, and I'd raced to where he waited in the parlor to tell me the details of their conversation. According to Papa, it had transpired precisely as we'd planned, with one exception. Fritz had made clear to Papa that he wanted me to give up acting if we married, the same condition I'd rejected from another young suitor. But this proposal—from this man—was different, even though my dislike of the condition was no less. With the heightened fear over the political threats, the stakes were much higher now, and anyway, my feelings about Fritz were far more intense. After much tearful discussion with Papa—watched over by Mama, who offered turns of phrase as we practiced my response—I began to see Fritz's caveat through an altered lens and had come to accept it, if not embrace it.

But Fritz had said nothing about this second lunch, just as he'd said nothing about the first. The pressure to keep the mood playful and my tone light and teasing—as I sensed Fritz wanted—was immense. I leaned heavily on my training as an actress to mask the anxiety making my stomach flutter and my palms clammy. I willed myself to suppress the nervous, young Hedy Kiesler from Döbling, and I became stage darling Hedwig Kiesler, accustomed to and deserving of the attentions of Austria's richest man.

I was regaling Fritz with a backstage tale of my costar and the increasingly ridiculous demands from our stage director when a man appeared beside our table. During our restaurant dates, many men paid their respect to Fritz with a quick bow and a quiet word, but he never rose, never introduced the men to me. But this time, Fritz leaped to his feet and gave a hearty handshake to the tall gentleman.

"Ah, Ernst. May I introduce Miss Hedwig Kiesler? Hedy, this is Prince Ernst Rüdiger von Starhemberg."

Prince von Starhemberg. Even if Papa hadn't recently described him as a leader in right-wing—and sometime fascist—Austrian politics and the head of the Heimwehr, I would have known that surname. The Starhemberg family, a long, ancient line of Austrian nobles, owned thousands of acres and multiple castles all over the country.

The gentleman turned his close-set eyes, long aristocratic nose, and stern expression in my direction. "I've heard of your triumph in *Sissy*, Miss Kiesler. It is an honor to meet you," he said with a low bow.

Prince von Starhemberg had heard of me? My head swam with the notion of a man of his nobility and importance familiar with *me*, and for a moment, I forgot myself. A sharp stare from Fritz mobilized me, and I nodded my head. "It is a pleasure, Prince von Starhemberg. Thank you for your kind words about my performance."

The prince's eyes lingered on me uncomfortably, and I wondered how Fritz would react as he took note of Starhemberg's attention. To my surprise, I watched as approval—not jealousy—passed across his face.

The two men faced one another again. "The plans are proceeding well with our Italian friend?" Starhemberg asked.

"Oh yes, very well. Do we have a date set for our next meeting?" Fritz said.

As their voices dropped to a hush, I tried not to listen, not to make guesses about the machinations concerning their "Italian friend," who had to be Mussolini. I busied myself studying the restaurant's famed decor. A nod to the future and an homage to the past with its sleek French furniture and luxurious Belgian linens balanced out by hints of Tyrolean style, the restaurateurs had created the quintessential Austrian establishment.

The men broke apart, and Starhemberg took my hand in his. "I will have to come and watch your performance as our legendary Empress Elizabeth. Our people are in dire need of heroines these days," he said and then kissed the top of my hand. With a final bow, he strode toward the wide front doors of the restaurant, the waitstaff scurrying to open the doors before he could reach them.

Fritz and I settled back into our seats, each taking a healthy drink from our champagne.

"My apologies for the interruption, Hedy," Fritz said.

"No need for apologies, Fritz. It was my pleasure to meet Prince von Starhemberg."

"I'm glad to hear that. Ernst is more than just a good friend. The alignment in our political and economic views has led to a strong alliance between us, and I imagine you will see much of him in the future."

With the word *future*, I swallowed hard. Was this it? Was this the moment when my life changed?

I tried to downplay my mounting anxiety and excitement.

"It was very kind of him to compliment my acting. A man such as Prince von Starhemberg must have many more pressing matters than my performance in *Sissy*."

Fritz grew quiet, and I worried that I'd made a misstep. Had I insulted him by suggesting that an important man wouldn't have time for the theater or an actress? And that he, by inference, was not as important as the prince?

"*Hase*, do you love the limelight so much?" he blurted.

With this question, I sensed we were coming to the crux of it. My response required that I tread carefully, or the chance could be lost. Papa and I, with Mama in the wings, had hashed out this thorny issue and my even thornier answer last night until dawn. Even though I'd lamented the sacrifice of acting, I'd begun to see the exchange of my career for the security and safety Fritz could offer as a necessary trade. But now that the moment had arrived, could I say the words?

I took a deep breath. "The limelight, the applause, was never the focus for me, Fritz. I relish the art of inhabiting another role, leading another life." These were the lines that Papa and I had practiced.

"What if you were offered another life? A role you could inhabit every minute of every day, not only when you were on the stage? Would you need the theater?"

I knew what he wanted me to say, what was necessary to secure this opportunity. Assuming an expression of demureness, I lowered my eyes and said, "It would depend on the role I was offered. And the person making the offer."

He cleared his throat and announced, "The role is wife. And I am asking you to be mine."

Glancing up at Fritz through the fringe of my lashes, I asked, "Truly?"

He slid a black velvet box across the table, opening it as it reached my side. A wide gold band, imbedded with a blaze of diamonds, sat inside. The piece of jewelry was the most extravagant I'd ever seen; I couldn't even guess at the number of carats contained in its setting. I nearly laughed thinking of me, a nineteen-year-old girl who'd been in a Swiss finishing school not even two years ago, adorned by a ring better suited to the mature hand of a born princess.

"What do you say, *Hase?*"

"Yes, Fritz. I will be your wife."

He slipped the ring on my finger and signaled the waiter for more champagne. As we toasted the future Mrs. Mandl, I felt an expected loss over Hedy Kiesler the actress. Who might she have become if Fritz Mandl had never come to see *Sissy?* Because, I knew, this new role of wife that Fritz offered me was permanent. It wasn't one I could push aside when a rehearsal was over or a curtain had fallen.

And this toast and this marriage were a farewell.

CHAPTER TEN

August 10, 1933
Vienna, Austria

*T*HE AISLE IS SIMPLY ANOTHER STAGE, I TOLD MYSELF. *Nothing to be nervous about.*

I smoothed my gown again and tucked a wispy hair back into my low chignon through which delicate white orchids had been woven. Pacing back and forth in the small space reserved for us in the chapel sanctuary, I nearly bumped into Papa. He noticed my fidgeting and drew me close, careful of the elegant swath of orchids I carried and the intricate folds of my dress, which, despite its Mainbocher label, seemed too simple against the baroque interior of the Karlskirche. "You look beautiful, *Liebling*. You have nothing to fear."

Papa had always told me that the beauty I was born with must have a purpose. At first, I thought he must have meant the Viennese theater, the highly valued cultural world for which attractiveness was a prerequisite. But now I wondered. Had he really meant that my appearance was destined to help me make an important marriage? One that could help me and my family?

"Only the eyes of hundreds of strangers," I answered him.

Papa almost snorted with laughter. "That should have no impact on you, my little actress. Every night, you face hundreds of strangers."

"Former actress," I corrected him, then regretted my words when I saw the look of sadness on his face.

"You will see many familiar faces from Döbling in the crowd too," he said, trying to change my focus.

"Undoubtedly cringing at this church wedding. No *chuppah* here," I retorted. Now that Papa had opened the door to discussions of Jewishness, I could not resist the barb.

"Now, now, *Liebling*. Most of the Döbling folk have lived in Vienna for generations and are hardly strangers to a Christian ceremony."

"Maybe they've witnessed a Christian wedding as guests, Papa. I doubt many have seen one of their own participate in the Christian ceremony."

"I think you'd be surprised."

The weeks since Fritz's proposal had passed in a blur. As we'd agreed, I gave my final performance of *Sissy*, releasing a statement saying, "I am so happy about my engagement that I am unable to be sad about my departure from the stage. My excitement over my impending marriage has made it easy to give up my lifelong ambition to be successful in the theater." While drafting the public remarks, I felt anything but happy at giving up acting, and though I never confessed my distress to Fritz, he must have sensed it, because he tried to soften the sting with a surprise trip to Paris for my wedding gown the following day.

With Mama as escort, we spent three days in Paris. I longed for the theater and museums I'd experienced with my parents in past trips. During those visits, Mama, Papa, and I had splurged and stayed at the luxurious Hôtel Le Meurice, chosen for its proximity to the Louvre Museum, where we'd spend mornings strolling past its incomparable painting and sculpture collections—Mama preferred the pink-hued color schemes of Fragonard while Papa lingered over the muted portraits by Rembrandt—before lunching at the exquisite hotel restaurant. Afterward, while Mama rested, Papa and I spent the afternoon strolling through the nearby Tuileries Garden, where we examined the ancient mulberry trees first planted by Henry IV, the elegant sculptures, and occasionally indulged in the more plebeian delights of which Mama would disprove, such as the roving acrobats, puppet theaters, and miniature boats sailing across the small lake. Then together, we'd step out for an evening of opera at the *Palais Garnier* or symphonic music at one of several theaters, depending on which orchestra Mama and Papa selected. Some of my fondest familial memories stemmed from these Parisian jaunts.

But this visit to Paris contained none of the culture and exploration of my prior trips. Fritz had mapped out a series of appointments with the finest dressmakers in the city, located on the high-fashion boulevards of rue Cambon, avenue Montaigne, Place Vendôme, and avenue George V. During these hours with the designers at Chanel, Vionnet, Schiaparelli, and finally Mainbocher, Mama sat by, uncharacteristically mute, as Fritz watched me model gown after gown for him.

In the privacy of my dressing room at Mainbocher Couture,

I watched as an assistant dressmaker pinned me into a pale-blue gown with formfitting swaths of fabric draped like a Grecian goddess. She stepped back to allow me to study the design in the three-way mirror before I showed it to Fritz and Mama, and I couldn't repress a cry of delight. It suited me as no other dress had before, highlighting my figure in a way that was both flattering and appropriate for the wedding, all the while drawing attention to my face, almost like a soft beam of light. A singular dress for a singular occasion. It was perfect.

I couldn't wait to see Fritz's reaction. Strutting out into the private parlor outside the dressing room, where Mama and Fritz sat ensconced in hand-embroidered silk chairs with glasses of champagne in their hands, I slowed and presented myself to them. To him.

A slow smile spread on Fritz's face as he inspected me. His eyes lingered on the curve of my bosom, and his gaze began to feel indecent in Mama's presence.

"So what do you think?" I asked with a twirl to draw his eyes away from my chest.

"Very flattering, *Hase*."

"It's the one," I announced with a glance at Mama. Even she couldn't hold back a smile.

Fritz rose and drew so close that I could feel the heat of his breath. "It is quite pretty, Hedy, but it is not the one."

"How can you say that, Fritz?" I asked with a coquettish look. Pulling away from him and spinning around again, I said, "Doesn't it suit me perfectly?"

He reached for me, and for a moment, I thought he was going to draw me in for a kiss. Instead, his fingers wrapped around my upper arm tightly, and in a low, angry voice only I could hear, he said, "It is *not* the one. You will try on the others."

I stepped back from him, almost stumbling, and retreated to the dressing room. Had Fritz just threatened me?

Shaking, I allowed the assistant dressmaker to unpin me from the Grecian gown. She selected a striking black-and-white-print dress from the rack and slid it on me. Staring into the mirror, I could see that it drew attention to my raven hair and pale skin, but the sharp edges and geometric design of the gown seemed better suited for a formal ball than for a bride at her wedding. But would I even be allowed to voice these concerns to Fritz? Did I dare? I felt conflicted. I didn't want to hear that tone in Fritz's voice again or feel his fingers dig into my arm, but I didn't want to sacrifice everything—including the selection of my own wedding gown—to keep the peace.

Without a twirl or a saunter, I walked into the parlor, ready for Fritz's judgment. He jumped to his feet when he first caught sight of me and pulled Mama up alongside him.

"*That* is the one," he said without asking my mother or me what we thought.

When Mama saw color rise in my cheeks, she shook her head at me. Disagreement with Fritz, it seemed, was not acceptable. Not after the scene she'd just witnessed.

"It's lovely," I said, trying to bury the anger I felt at him for his earlier harshness and instead focus on his delight observing me in this dress. I asked myself whether a particular dress was really that important anyway. Wasn't the most critical thing securing my marriage to Fritz with all its attendant security and protection?

Swiveling back to the mirror, I tried to see myself as Fritz saw me, as he wanted me to be. I did look arresting in the dress. Catching his eye in the mirror, I nodded my accord with his decision.

After the fitting for the Mainbocher gown, we dropped Mama at the hotel and strolled briefly through the familiar Tuileries Garden, then north to the Place Vendôme. With their arched ground-floor windows framed by pilasters and ornamental pillars, the grandeur of the buildings lining the octagonal square awed me, and Fritz delighted in telling the story behind the Vendôme Column at the Place Vendôme's center. Over forty meters high and modeled after Trajan's Column, the famous triumphal tower in Rome, it was originally commissioned by Napoleon in the early 1800s to commemorate his victories. The bronze column, with its climbing bas-reliefs, became the subject of controversy, and, as Napoleon's status rose and fell, it was taken down until the late 1800s when it was restored for good.

"Rulers and movements may rise and fall, but the power of money always prevails," Fritz said. While ostensibly a summary of some facet of Napoleonic history, it seemed a fitting statement of Fritz's own political beliefs. Power, it seemed, was an end unto itself for Fritz.

We sauntered past the luxurious stores that occupied the prime space around the square, lingering in front of Cartier's arched bronze windows. The golden afternoon sunshine made the jewels on display glitter, and I marveled at a set of earrings, necklace, and bracelet inlaid with a geometric pattern of diamonds, rubies, sapphires, and emeralds. It was a picture-perfect moment, and I tried to let my earlier distress slip away.

"The jewelry isn't nearly as beautiful as you, *Hase*. Nothing is," Fritz said, wrapping his arm around my shoulders.

Turning the conversation back to our wedding day as we walked away from Cartier, he began to review the plans for the celebratory meal following the ceremony. Fritz had taken charge of the wedding, dictating nearly every element—the flowers, gown, music, restaurant venue, meal, guest list—with as much detail as a set designer or stage director. The only item left as yet untended by Fritz was the ceremony itself, and I assumed he'd address that next. At first, in the privacy of our home, Mama muttered her displeasure over this "inappropriate" arrangement of the groom organizing the wedding instead of the bride. But as she spent more time with Fritz and witnessed his almost frenetic focus on the event, even these complaints fell away. Instead, not only did she not dare intervene, but she cautioned me against interference.

The sole aspect of the wedding planning in which I involved myself was the guest list. Fritz insisted on inviting not only high society, such as Prince Gustav of Denmark, Prince Albrecht of Bavaria, and Prince Nicholas of Greece, but also key political leaders, including Chancellors Engelbert Dollfuss and Kurt von Schuschnigg. My requests were few; I wanted only to include five or six theater friends of my own and some of Papa's and Mama's families, but Fritz had balked. He was worried about the numbers. Fritz had decided upon the Grand Hotel of Vienna, on Kärntner Ring, for the wedding luncheon, and it could only accommodate two hundred people in its largest salon. With Fritz's guests alone, we were nearing that number.

As we walked, I asked about an invitation for my theater mentor Max Reinhardt, an important director and producer in his own right, when Fritz interrupted me with a non sequitur. "What do you think of the Karlskirche? Are you very familiar with it?"

Why was he asking me about one of the most famous buildings in Vienna, the fantastical baroque church with a vast copper cupola flanked by two columns? What on earth did it have to do with my request to add Max to the guest list? Was it larger than some of the other venues he was considering and able to accommodate more guests? No, that couldn't be. It was a Christian church.

"Of course, Fritz." I worked hard to keep the annoyance out of my voice in the hopes that he'd expand our guest list. "No one could live in Vienna and be unfamiliar with the Karlskirche. It dominates our skyline." I shook my head a little and then, after a brief pause, continued discussing the guest list. "Are you certain we don't have the space for Max? What of my aunt and uncle? Papa would be disappointed not to have his brother's family there."

"Hedy, I didn't ask you about the Karlskirche as a way of making general conversation or discussing the guest list. I wondered whether you would like to get married there," he snapped.

Me, married at the Karlskirche? Was it possible that Fritz didn't know that my family heritage was Jewish? We had never discussed religion, not his or mine. Not once. I just assumed that, as Papa had pointed out, because I hailed from Döbling, he would know.

"I'm not a Christian, Fritz," I said carefully. "And even though I'm not religious, my family background is Jewish."

His expression didn't change. "I surmised as much, Hedy. But that shouldn't stop us from marrying in the Karlskirche. My own father converted from Judaism to Catholicism simply so he could marry my mother. I can arrange for a quick conversion for you so we can be married there." He made the suggestion lightly, as if switching from Jewish to Christian was a matter as easy and uncontroversial as changing a dinner order from fish to beef. I had never heard him speak about his own family's religious history, and I was surprised to hear that he had a Jewish ancestry as well.

Conversion? My family wasn't religious, but a conversion was a drastic step. What would Papa say? I knew how scared he was for me and our family in the anti-Semitic political climate and how badly he wanted this marriage to proceed as a means of protection. But would he condone this extreme measure?

Perhaps we could reach an accord without the necessity for conversion. I chose my words with care. "Is there no other place that you'd like us to marry? One of your other homes? What about Schloss Schwarzenau? Or your apartment in Vienna, which is close to the luncheon at the Grand Hotel?"

His eyes narrowed, and his jaw clenched in a way I'd only ever seen when he spoke to those nameless business acquaintances who paid their respects at restaurants or when I mentioned his upbringing. "The Karlskirche is the place where society folk marry, and I intend to have our wedding celebrated properly. Besides, it won't do for me to have a Jewish wife. Not with the sort of business I'll be conducting in the months to come." He nodded as if reaching a conclusion. "Yes, the more I think about it, the more certain I am that we should have a Christian ceremony at the Karlskirche."

I slowed my gait. Papa wanted the security that this marriage could provide, and now the marriage required conversion. What other path could I take without putting my family or myself at risk? Besides, I told myself, my tie to my religious heritage was tenuous at best. My Jewishness had always been the vaguest of shadows, and a conversion wouldn't preclude acknowledgment of that. I was too far down this road to veer off it now.

Giving Fritz's arm a squeeze, I quickened my step to match his stride. Trying to keep my voice light and merry, I said, "Of course. The Karlskirche it is."

That evening, after dinner at the Michelin-starred restaurant Lapérouse, I arrived back to my hotel room to find a large box wrapped in rich red paper and tied with white, silken ribbon sitting on my bed. A white envelope sat under the ribbon. Sliding it out, I opened the envelope and read the unsigned letter that lay within.

For my bride to wear on our wedding day.

Tugging a velvet box out from the heavy wrapping paper, I saw the word *Cartier* emblazoned on the top. Slowly, I lifted the lid of the velvet box. Staring out at me was the jewelry set I'd admired in the Cartier window. The earrings, necklace, and bracelet twinkled in the low chandelier light of my hotel suite, and I couldn't believe that this king's ransom of diamonds, rubies, sapphires, and emeralds belonged to me. Yet the longer I stared, the more I wondered if Fritz hadn't gotten off cheaply.

Weren't these jewels a puny price to pay for my sacrifices? First, my acting career, and now, my family's heritage? Never mind that my own connection to my family's religion was tenuous; it was a momentous surrender.

The music began. Fritz had arranged for the first chairs of the Vienna Symphony to play orchestral versions of some of my favorite pieces before I made my appearance. I smiled at the sound of Cole Porter's "Night and Day" before panic took hold and my palms began to sweat.

Taking a deep, shaky breath, I locked arms with Papa and readied myself to walk down the aisle. But before we stepped out of the chapel sanctuary and onto the red carpet of the Karlskirche, he whispered, "You cannot treat this man as you've treated all those boys that came before, Hedy. When you tire of him, when he angers you, you cannot treat him as one of your past fripperies. The stakes are too high. Do you understand, Hedy?"

Papa had never spoken to me in such a way before. Was I making a horrible mistake?

"I understand," I said, because what else could I say? I could hardly leave Friedrich Mandl, richest man in Austria and the Merchant of Death, at the altar.

"Good, because this is for life, Hedy. For all our lives."

CHAPTER ELEVEN

August 14, 1933
Venice, Italy

L IGHT STREAMED THROUGH THE SLATS OF THE SHUTTERS. Row by row, chunky beams of sunlight illuminated Fritz as he lay sleeping in our bed in the honeymoon suite at the Hotel Excelsior. My new husband.

His eyes opened, and he smiled a slow, lopsided grin. It was a vulnerable expression that my imposing husband would never show the outside world. Only me. "*Hase,*" he whispered.

I wrapped my legs around his but otherwise drew no closer to him. He adored the chase, even if it was only across a single mattress. His fingers wrapped around the silk strings that hung over each of my shoulders and kept my nightgown up. As he began sliding the strings off my shoulders, I pulled away very slightly.

"We've already missed breakfast. If you keep me in this bed any longer, we'll miss lunch too," I said, demurring, but my words belied the coquettish expression on my face. And while I deliberately painted the come-hither look upon my features, I didn't need to feign the desire. Fritz, a man who'd had dozens of women, was a skilled lover with an understanding of women's bodies, unlike the boys I'd known before.

"I think you know by now that I need only you for sustenance, *Hase*," he said softly in my ear as he pulled me atop him.

"Then I will feed you," I said, sitting astride him.

Afterward, when we did indeed miss luncheon at the Pajama Café and instead ordered room service, he sipped an espresso and bit into a dense slice of bread laden with jam while watching me dress.

"Wear the green swimsuit instead. The one by Jean Patou," he commanded. "I like the way it shows off your legs."

I peeled off the striped bathing suit I'd planned on wearing to the Lido beach that stretched in front of the Hotel Excelsior. The green one was skimpier, with a triangular piece cut from the fabric in the midriff area. Oddly, I felt more naked wearing it to the beach than I did filming the scandalous scenes in *Ecstasy*. Perhaps the leering expression in the eyes of the other vacationers—as opposed to the businesslike scrutiny I received on the *Ecstasy* set—made the difference.

As I pulled the designated swimsuit over my hips, he gave another order. "Use the dark lipstick." He'd become increasingly particular—and insistent—about my appearance since the wedding.

I rarely objected to his desires—physical or otherwise—because, in truth, it was far easier to please someone who made their wishes well-known. It was almost a relief not to have to constantly read him and adjust my performance accordingly, as

I did with most others. But this request seemed silly; I'd grown up experiencing the outdoors without layers of artifice. "For the beach? Is heavy makeup really necessary?"

His brow furrowed at my mild objection, and his voice grew angry. "Yes, Hedy. The lipstick emphasizes the curve of your mouth."

His insistence surprised me. I hadn't seen this behavior from him since he demanded I wear the Mainbocher gown for our wedding. What happened to the man who liked my opinions and strength?

Still, I did as he asked. Afterward, we walked down the stairs and through the Venetian-styled lobby tinged with Byzantine and Moorish influences. The Hotel Excelsior was vast, with over seven hundred bedrooms, three restaurants, multiple terraces, two nightclubs, ten tennis courts, a private boat dock, and, of course, its very own beach. Even the walk from our suite to the beach took nearly thirty minutes.

We stepped outside into the blinding Italian sunshine. Pulling the wide brim of my hat down over my eyes and adjusting my sunglasses, I wrapped my silk kimono around me more tightly and linked arms with Fritz. When the promenade to the beach narrowed and we could not saunter arm in arm, he prowled behind me, ever vigilant, until we reached the sea.

Spread before us was the wide beach of Lido, the barrier island separating Venice from the Adriatic Sea. Even though the sand was crowded with cabanas and lounge chairs populated by elegant sunbathers wearing outfits torn from the European fashion pages, it was the sound of the waves and the seagulls that made me feel strangely elated. I breathed in the salty sea air, and for a brief moment, I inhabited my old self instead of the role of Mrs. Fritz Mandl.

The mood broke when Fritz lifted his hand casually, signaling the cabana boy to tend us. A young fellow in a striped shirt scampered over, towels draped over his arm. "May I help you, sir?" he said in German heavy with an Italian accent. How had he known we were German speakers? I supposed the staff, well used to the international crowd that stayed at the hotel, had their ways of discerning the nationality of their visitors.

"We would like two loungers and two umbrellas."

"Yes, sir," the boy said, leading us to the only available two chairs on the beach. The loungers, cushioned with a red striped fabric that matched the boy's shirt, sat in the back row, and dense rows of other hotel guests blocked the view of the sea.

In the few days we'd been staying at the Hotel Excelsior, the hierarchy of the guest beach chairs had become clear. Only the richest and most noble were given chairs in rows nearest the edge of the sea. Guests without any particular notoriety were allotted chairs farther away from the water wherever they were available.

I knew what Fritz would say to the boy before he uttered the words. "Why would you think these chairs would be acceptable?"

"I'm sorry, sir, but all the other chairs are taken."

"Tell your manager that one of his guests would like to speak with him. I'm Mr. Mandl, and I will wait right here for him."

The poor boy froze. When he finally mustered the courage to speak, his voice was quivering. "Did you say Mr. Mandl, sir?"

"Yes. Are you hard of hearing?" Fritz barked.

"My deepest apologies, sir. We were told by the hotel owner to take special care of you, that you are a special friend of—" The boy broke off before he could say who, but I knew of whom he spoke. "I had our two best chairs reserved for you, but when the hours passed and you didn't come, I allowed other guests to use the seats."

"For a nice tip, no doubt."

The boy's face flamed red to match his shirt. "I will inform our manager that you would like to speak with him, but in the meantime, please allow me to address your request."

Fritz shot him a skeptical glance but also granted him a slight nod of acquiescence. We watched as the boy scurried about, carrying the two remaining loungers and umbrellas to a front row of his making. Our spot now blocked several irritated guests in the original front row, who'd undoubtedly paid a hefty sum for their premier spots.

But Fritz was satisfied. Before we could settle in our seats, however, a man in an impeccably cut navy suit, far too hot for sunbathing, marched over to us, a waiter in tow. He extended his hand and, in practically unaccented German, said, "Please allow me to introduce myself, Mr. and Mrs. Mandl. My name is Nicolo Montello. I am one of the proprietors of the Hotel Excelsior."

"Ah, a pleasure, Mr. Montello," Fritz answered, reaching out to shake the man's hand.

"When I learned of the slight you suffered at the hands of one of our employees, I was horrified. A representative of Il Duce himself asked us to extend you and your new wife the greatest Italian hospitality on your honeymoon, and we failed you. Please allow me to ensure that, from this moment forward, your stay at the Hotel Excelsior will be magical."

"We would appreciate that, Mr. Montello."

The man bowed deeply and then gestured for the waiter to step forward. He lifted the silver dome off the tray carried by the waiter to reveal a bottle of Château Haut-Brion, which even I knew was very expensive. Without a single word from Mr. Montello, another waiter appeared carrying a table with a linen tablecloth, which he set up between our two loungers. A third waiter then arrived with a tray of green figs and melons, of the sort I'd seen next to other sunbathers, along with an array of fresh seafood. The four men then bowed and took their leave.

We settled in our seats. As he sipped the wine, Fritz cracked open a lobster tail. He smiled over at me, and said, "See, *Hase*, what have I told you? Money and power always prevail."

CHAPTER TWELVE

August 14, 1933
Venice, Italy

T HE STRUM OF THE BASS GREW FASTER, AS DID THE WAIL
of the horns and thump of drums. The lyrics of the pop-
ular jazz tune quickened, and I closed my eyes and let the wild
strains of Duke Ellington's "It Don't Mean a Thing" surge
through me.

A fourteen-piece jazz band from America dominated the
stage of Chez Vous, the Hotel Excelsior's jazz club. The luxurious nightclub, decorated with decadent floral centerpieces and
a thirty-foot fountain, focused around an indoor stage. This
in turn opened to an outdoor stage and garden illuminated by
hundreds of twinkling lights that changed colors frequently.

Hotel guests and a few interlopers crowded the outdoor
dance floor where legendary singers like Cole Porter performed
each summer during the season, and the central table arranged
for us by Mr. Montello afforded an excellent view of the merriment. Outfitted in gossamer-thin evening gowns bedecked
with sparkling designs, the women, along with their partners,
engaged in frantic dances like the Lindy Hop and the shag in

an effort to keep time with the up-tempo song. Gazing out at the carefree dancers, it seemed impossible that Papa's worries might come to fruition. How could Hitler's anti-Semitic brand of fascism take hold and spread amid such revelry?

Fritz and I had joined the club merriment around ten o'clock, after relaxing on the beach until five o'clock, imbibing cocktails until seven on the terrace in our bathing gear and silk kimonos like all the other guests, and then enjoying a long and elegant meal in the exquisite pink dining room after changing into formal attire. I itched to join the dancers, but my two days at the Hotel Excelsior had taught me that Fritz liked to keep us a bit separate from the throngs. Well, me anyway.

Earlier on the beach, after we'd polished off the wine and food provided by Mr. Montello, Fritz had excused himself. The still day had turned gusty, and a strong breeze blew the fashion magazine I'd been flicking through out of my hands and across the sand. Sliding on my shoes, I rose to fetch it, but before I walked too far, a man jumped off his lounger and grabbed it for me.

Crumpled issue of *Modenschau* in hand, the man walked toward me. "*Parlez-vous français?*"

"Yes," I answered in French.

"My apologies that I couldn't catch your magazine before it became mangled," he said and handed it to me. The man was younger than Fritz, perhaps in his late twenties, and significantly taller and blond.

Squinting into the sun to look up at him, I thanked him. We were exchanging a few insignificant pleasantries about the changeable weather when Fritz returned. From the set of his jaw, I knew he was upset to find me speaking with another man, no matter how innocent the exchange.

"Ah, here is my husband," I announced to the man in French, thinking my words would appease Fritz before remembering he didn't speak the language.

Fritz wrapped his arms possessively around my waist and, in German, asked the two of us, "What do we have here?" His tone was undeniably accusatory.

I was about to explain the magazine rescue when the man inquired, in halting German, whether we'd like to join his friends for a game of gin or backgammon.

Fritz pulled me so tight, I could barely breathe. "Thank you, but *my wife* and I prefer to be *alone*."

The fast-paced Duke Ellington song came to an abrupt end, and the horns took center stage. They played the slow, sinuous opening notes of Cole Porter's "Night and Day," and the dance floor cleared. I knew Fritz would be pleased not only with the disbursement of the crowd but also the song's sultry pace, as I knew he found dancing to rapid-fire jazz tunes "undignified."

I rose from my chair and stood before him, swaying my hips a little in a suggestive invitation to dance. He joined me, and we glided across the floor in a smooth two-step. Even though the band was performing an instrumental version of "Night and Day," I whispered the lyrics in Fritz's ear.

He smiled at my words, and I congratulated myself on the small victory of getting him to dance. A few more couples joined us on the floor—although nowhere near the numbers of the previous two fast-moving songs—and Fritz and I spun around happily. Two older gentlemen glanced at me appreciatively, and I observed pride on his face. It seemed that Fritz wanted me to be desirable but only from afar. When oglers came too close, even gained possible access to me, pride morphed into rage.

A young couple, both dark-haired and well-dressed with patrician features, danced close to us, too close. Their movements were jerky, even sloppy, and I saw that the woman was trying to steer her inebriated partner toward a more open section of the dance floor. He resisted her efforts until she grew frustrated and stormed off.

Partnerless now, the man staggered toward us. "Can I cut in?" he slurred in unmistakable German.

"No," Fritz said and spun me away from the man. We continued to dance as if nothing had transpired, but Fritz's fingers dug into my hips.

The man stumbled back toward us, across the floor, weaving in and out of other dancers. "Come on. Pretty young girl like that shouldn't have to dance all night with an old *Kerl* like yourself."

Keeping one arm wrapped around me, Fritz pushed the drunkard to the floor. With his hand gripping mine, he stepped over the man, leading us to the bar, where a waiter handed us two flutes of champagne. Fritz quaffed an entire glass before I could even take a sip and then led me out of the club.

He pulled me across the lobby and up the grand staircase to our suite without a single word. By the time I got a good look at his face as he fumbled for the hotel room key, I saw that anger had flared into fury. As soon as he closed the door behind us, he pressed me up against the wall next to our bed. Sliding his hands under my dress, he pushed my underpants aside and took me there, not exactly against my will but without even the courtesy of a kiss. I walled a part of myself off from him in that moment, recognizing that life with Fritz was going to be a more dangerous tightrope walk than I'd imagined.

CHAPTER THIRTEEN

September 28, 1933
Schwarzau, Austria

H E SLIPPED THE BLINDFOLD OVER MY EYES. I HEARD THE
sound of a key in a lock and then a click. Cupping my
hand in his, Fritz guided me up a stair. A door thudded shut
behind me, and he released my hand. I felt his fingers in the
hair on the back of my head, and the silk of the scarf covering
my eyes slipped away. Why did I feel scared?

My new husband said, "You can open your eyes, *Hase*."

I stood in the cavernous entry hall of Villa Fegenberg.
The structure, described by Fritz with the misnomer "hunting
lodge," resembled the country estate of a baron more than anything else. While the entry hall's decor gave a nod to the hunting motif with its mounted bear heads and gilded weaponry,
the ancient tapestries and old Dutch Masters hanging alongside them belied the rustic nature of the house.

Fritz had wanted his beloved Villa Fegenberg to be our first
stop upon returning to Austria from our honeymoon. A way
of prolonging our celebration, he'd said. And in truth, the rest
of our honeymoon had indeed been a luxurious frolic. As we

traveled through Venice, Lake Como, Capri, Biarritz, Cannes, Nice, and finally Paris, Fritz had indulged my every whim, all the while keeping us apart from our fellow travelers and therefore apart from Fritz's anger. I began to believe that the fury he'd taken out upon me after Chez Vous was a singular incident, something that would never happen again.

As we stepped into the parlor, vistas of pristine mountains stared at me through the large windows that lined the parlor from floor to ceiling. Evergreen-covered hills rolled and crested into sharp peaks, some capped by snow. The verdant expanse was dotted with vivid splashes of blue from rambling streams and small lakes. The view reminded me of the landscape of the Wienerwald, the sprawling, forested woodland that bordered Döbling where I took leisurely Sunday walks with Papa.

Fritz marched to the center window and flung it open. Crisp, fresh mountain air flooded the room, and I breathed deeply of it. He strode back to me and, clasping me in his arms, said, "We will be happy here, Hedy."

"Yes," I said, breaking free of his hold just enough to stare up into his eyes.

"Come," he said, releasing me but for my hand. "You will need to meet the staff. They should be assembled in the front hall."

We reentered the front hall, and a phalanx of servants awaited us in a long, formal line. For the servants to have assembled themselves in this fashion without a single cue from Fritz, he must have carefully orchestrated our return in advance, all the way from our last destination, Paris. I greeted the butler, housekeeper, cook, two manservants, and four maids in turn, and all were perfectly respectful, if a bit cold or removed, save one. The pretty parlor maid named Ada, maybe even a year or two younger than myself, met my gaze straight on, almost as if she were challenging me. Perhaps she didn't like having a mistress near in age to herself. I nearly drew Fritz's attention to her manner, but something held me back. I didn't want him to think me unable to handle the staff.

With all the servants maintaining their positions, Fritz took me by the hand and led me up the grand staircase. There, on the landing, in full view of the staff, he kissed me. He then pulled me into what could only be our bedroom. I tried not to think of the servants standing at attention, listening to the noises we made as we fell onto the bed.

A few hours later, with the sun slipping behind the blackening outline of the mountains, Fritz and I sat down to dinner. We'd dressed as if dining at the Hotel Excelsior, Fritz in his dinner jacket and me in his favorite gold-lamé dress with black velvet trim. The formality had seemed excessive, but Fritz had insisted. "This is a momentous evening, *Hase*. Our first day home in Austria."

We touched crystal flutes of champagne in the golden light of the sunset and then walked into the dining room. An enormous rectangular table dominated the room, and without thinking, I squealed in delight.

Fritz chortled at my reaction. "We can seat forty people here with the table fully extended, and we will. This will be your domain."

Hosting forty people for dinner? I hadn't really thought about my wifely duties as hostess to an important businessman. I'd been too swept up in the excitement of the wedding and the glamour of our long travels. The reality of life as Fritz's wife—what that would entail on a daily basis—hadn't registered. I supposed I could not forestall that reality any longer.

"If you like," I said vaguely, unsure of what else to add.

Fritz walked to the head of the table, where a servant hastened to pull out his chair. Instinctively, I gravitated toward the seat next to Fritz and awaited the servant's ministrations. But the man froze, nervously glancing at Fritz for direction.

"Hedy," Fritz scolded. "You will take your rightful seat at the other end of the table."

I stared down the long table and then back at him. Was this a little jest? There must have been ten chairs between Fritz's seat and the one he indicated, and he and I had always dined intimately—à deux—on our honeymoon. "Surely you're joking, Fritz. The distance is so great, I would have to yell to have a conversation with you."

There was no humor on Fritz's face. His voice grew stern and his eyes cold. "No, I'm not kidding. You must practice for the dinner parties that we will begin hosting here next week."

"Next *week*?"

"Yes, Hedy, we have a full schedule of events beginning next week." His voice contained a firm note. "Most of my business deals take place over dinners. And most of my business relationships are cemented over meals as well. With you as the perfect hostess and me as the host and owner of the Hirtenberger Patronenfabrik, we will make a formidable team."

Me, a perfect hostess? I was a nineteen-year-old girl with two years' experience as an actress, nothing more. I'd had no exposure to this lifestyle growing up; my parents had preferred to do their socializing at restaurants and theaters, not at elaborate dinner parties in our Döbling home, which paled in comparison to even one of Fritz's many abodes. What credentials or training did I have to serve as the "perfect hostess" to the richest man in Austria?

None was the answer. But I knew that Fritz would never tolerate ignorance from me. I'd sold him on a version of myself that included proficiency in all the aspects of his world. I supposed I would just have to act the part. Perhaps I wouldn't have to give up my acting career altogether.

What would a worldly woman say to her husband in this moment? I asked myself. I searched my past roles until I settled upon some lines of dialogue that might work, with modifications of course. Keeping my voice strong and confident, I said, "Then I should meet with the housekeeper and the staff first thing tomorrow morning, so I can review our calendar. I will work with them on the guest lists, seating arrangements, menus, and the like."

Fritz gave me a smile of condescending amusement, much like one would give a child. It wasn't the reaction I'd expected. Had I said the wrong thing? In what way were my words humorous?

"*Hase*," he said, warmth and irritation evident in his voice in equal measures. "Don't worry yourself about such things. I've handled these affairs for many years now, and they aren't a mantle you should bear. The only onus that you should carry on your delicate shoulders is that of your beauty."

CHAPTER FOURTEEN

November 24, 1933
Schwarzenau, Austria

I TOOK A LONG DRAG ON MY CIGARETTE AND STARED OUT from the balcony, watching the smoke mix with my exhalation, made visible in the cold night air. Like a cat, I stretched my neck and back in an unsuccessful attempt to relieve the tension. We were hosting the usual mix of political figures and minor royalty for the weekend at Schloss Schwarzenau, our Renaissance-era castle complete with crenelated towers, a marble and stucco chapel with frescoes of the apostles, twelve bedrooms, a ballroom, and a moat. The day, spent riding and picnicking near the castle's own lake with our guests, had been unseasonably warm, and the night had been a welcome respite. Still, despite the drop in temperature, I'd found the endless dinner service and small talk stifling, possibly due to Fritz's cloying guests, and I'd had to excuse myself.

The honeymoon ended the day after our arrival at Villa Fegenberg. That morning, my life as Mrs. Mandl began. Even if I had spent significant time imagining my daily existence as the wife of Austria's richest man, it would have been time ill-spent. Never would I have guessed that Fritz meant what he said over dinner the night of our arrival. He expected every hour of my long days to be spent in preparation for the evenings, preening and heightening my beauty. I was like an exotic bird, only permitted outside my gilded cage for performances and locked up again afterward.

The household and social calendar management that would typically fall to the wife was off-limits to me. Fritz oversaw every aspect of our homes and our entertaining, from running the staff to selecting the menus to arranging our engagements. He believed that shopping for my wardrobe for our many social occasions and adorning myself should be a full-time occupation, and consequently, I spent my days utterly alone, except for dressmaker and salon appointments accompanied by my driver, Schmidt, who squired me around in the Rolls-Royce Phantom that Fritz had given me as a belated wedding present. Socializing with the few friends I had from my theater or school days was discouraged if not specifically prohibited by Fritz, although visits with my parents were permitted. Until evening arrived, aside from family, I had only my books and the piano for company, and the ivory and black keys that I once avoided because they represented Mama became my friends. The strength and independence Fritz seemed to have admired during our brief dating days had evaporated, replaced by a fierce need for my acquiescence and a fervent desire to exact verbal retribution should I not meet his standards.

From time to time, Fritz and I shared a weekend day alone at Villa Fegenberg, where I saw flashes and glimpses of the man I thought I'd married. Afternoons spent on horseback on mountain trails with picnics in flowering fields, where he relaxed his strictures and I could again be the vigorous, opinionated woman he'd dated. These hours sustained me and gave me hope for a different future.

To his many business and social acquaintances, Fritz described my life as "luxurious and indulgent," and any outsider would probably agree. After all, he and I rotated among three enormous homes, each opulently decorated and with a full staff, and I spent my days in a swirl of decadent spending. But in an ironic turn, my life mirrored the last role I had played, the last role I'd likely ever play—Empress Elizabeth. Not the early, romantic part of her story I'd acted out onstage but her later years, when her older husband, the Emperor Franz Josef I, took control over her life and the lives of her children, locking her in a royal cage deprived of the light and air of freedom. Like Elizabeth, I wanted for nothing except liberty and purpose. But how could I complain?

Footsteps interrupted my thoughts. Glancing behind me, I saw the outline of two men walking out onto the balcony. I recognized them as guests brought by the one of the financiers with whom Fritz occasionally did business, but they were otherwise unremarkable. Before every event, Fritz would run through the guest list, highlighting the important players, and these men had neither been singled out nor introduced to me, another of Fritz's signals of the guest's significance. The men had passed the evening as blank spots on my horizon.

Neither had greeted me, a politesse required for the hostess, which meant they must not have seen me behind the colonnade where I stood. But I had no desire to interrupt my all-too-brief hiatus from the evening's duties to make small talk with men Fritz deemed insignificant.

"Are the plans progressing?" one of the men asked the other in a low, gravelly voice.

"Yes. My contact says that they've been undetected," the other answered after inhaling deeply on his cigarette.

"Well, Linz is a good place to stay unnoticed."

"It was the right choice when the Schutzbund decided to go underground."

The word *Schutzbund* put me on high alert. From the many dinner discussions on politics to which I'd listened these past few months, I knew that the Schutzbund was the military arm of the Social Democratic party, run by the Jewish leader Otto Bauer. Chancellor Dollfuss, leader of the opposing faction and a close cohort of Fritz, had banned the Schutzbund last February, leaving his own military group, the Heimwehr—led by Prince von Starhemberg and supplied by my husband—in sole charge. The Schutzbund was, in some ways, Fritz's enemy.

Were these men actually talking about the machinations of the Schutzbund? If so, Fritz would want to know that the prohibited military group in direct opposition to his own faction had not dispersed as commanded but was in hiding. And on the rise.

The men continued talking about the Schutzbund. "Are they nearly ready?"

"I try to stay out of the details. I'm only a money man."

"True enough, ignorance is a virtue these days. I think I'll—"

I'd been listening so intently that my cigarette burnt to the quick. Before my fingers singed, I dropped the butt to the ground and stomped out the final flame with the toe of my navy satin shoe. Even though I'd attempted silence, my movements must have called attention to my presence. As if suddenly realizing that someone else inhabited their space, the men broke off midsentence.

The clomp of men's shoes echoed as they marched over to my corner of the balcony. I quickly grabbed a cigarette and my silver monogrammed lighter out of my purse and pretended to be engrossed in operating it.

When their footsteps grew louder, I shifted to make myself more visible and called out to them. "Ah, gentlemen, you are my saviors. Do either of you have a match? My lighter seems to be out of flame." I put my cigarette between my lips and leaned toward them in a gesture open to multiple interpretations.

They froze for a moment, until the taller man gained hold of himself and said, "Mrs. Mandl, our apologies. We would never have ignored you if we'd realized we had company on the balcony. Have you been here long?"

He was hedging, trying to understand what, if anything, I'd overheard. I painted a broad, vapid smile upon my lips and answered, "Please, sir, no need for apologies. I've been enjoying the night air for only a few minutes, and in truth, I've been lost in my own thoughts, assessing the evening's success thus far. It's quite a responsibility for a young woman like myself to host men such as yourselves, don't you think?" I batted my eyes.

The men shot each other glances of relief. The man who'd been quiet finally spoke. "I think it's safe to say that tonight has been wildly successful, Mrs. Mandl. Your home is breathtaking, and the hospitality has been extraordinary."

"What a relief, sirs." I sighed. "Now, can I extract a little promise from you both?"

They looked toward each other with wary expressions. The taller man said, "Of course, Mrs. Mandl. Anything."

"Promise you won't tell my husband about our little conversation? He'd be distraught if he thought his new bride was hiding away on our balcony, fretting about her party."

"You have our word."

The quartet Fritz had arranged for the evening began playing a slow, mournful jazz tune. "Gentlemen, I believe that's my cue. Will you excuse me?"

They nodded as I took my leave. Passing through the French doors back inside, I walked down the hallway to the salon where the guests would be dancing to the band and drinking the digestifs Fritz had selected to complement the menu.

I didn't have to progress far into the crowd to find Fritz, because he was waiting for me near the doors. His eyes bore such venom that I felt sick. What had I done this time? What condemning words would I hear whispered in my ear? He held my behavior to unbearably high standards on these evenings and would lash out if I didn't meet them.

"Where have you been? The guests have been asking after you." He extended a hand toward me and smiled for the benefit of his guests, but his tone was furious. I guessed that a verbal berating would follow later tonight unless I defused his fury.

"Listening to a very interesting conversation."

His cheeks reddened as he undoubtedly imagined the tender whispers of an illicit tryst. Even here, in an environment he controlled with guests of his specific choosing, his jealousy knew no bounds.

Speaking quickly to pacify him, I shared the statements I'd overheard about the Schutzbund and Linz. He asked me to point out the men, as I couldn't recollect their names, and requested an exact restatement of their conversation. My theatrical training—with its demanding memorization of lines—came in handy, and I was able to recount the conversation verbatim.

The anger faded from his face, replaced by a slow-blooming elation. "This is exactly what we need." He lifted me off the ground and swung me around. The guests tittered at what they assumed was newlywed affection.

Fritz whispered in my ear. "I married more than a pretty face. I married a secret weapon."

CHAPTER FIFTEEN

February 17, 1934
Vienna, Austria

A RE YOU SAFE?" I ASKED MAMA, BREATHING HEAVILY because I'd raced to the front door the moment my driver dropped me at my parents' Döbling home.

"Yes, Hedy," Mama answered, as if she could never be anything other than perfectly fine. As if even the outbreak of the Austrian Civil War in Vienna proper could not disturb her. What did she gain with her impervious manner?

"Where's Papa?" I asked her as I hung my fur on the rarely used coat stand in my parents' entryway. Where was Inge? Perhaps she'd left the city for the safety of the countryside, as had many. All except my parents, of course, whom I'd begged to join us at Villa Fegenberg, where Fritz, with all his inside knowledge about the political machinations and military operations of this conflict, knew we'd be safe. Mama had refused to leave Vienna, labeling our concerns as "unfounded hysteria," and Papa wouldn't leave her.

"He's lying down in our bedroom."

"Has he been hurt?"

"No, Hedy, of course not. I would have sent word. It's one of his migraines."

I walked past my mother and up the stairs. Not until I pushed open the bedroom door and laid eyes on the body of my sleeping father did I slump in relief. I hadn't realized how tightly wound my muscles and nerves had been until I saw for myself that my parents were unscathed by the battles that had broken out between the Heimwehr and Schutzbund on the Vienna city streets.

Sinking onto the bed next to Papa, I started to cry. What had I done? I'd been so delighted in Fritz's reaction to my sleuthing. Eager to please him so that he'd unlock my gilded cage during the daylight hours, I had begged him to allow me into his larger world. Flattered if a bit wary, he started by giving me a tour of the Hirtenberger Patronenfabrik munitions and arms factories in Austria and Poland, and while I made the appropriate squeals of delight, I was secretly stunned at the havoc his weaponry could wreak on the world. He then allowed me access into his private library with its scientific, military, and political tomes, and he began including me in a few of his business lunches. I started to learn the politics and mechanics of war.

I'd been pleased with my success and thrilled to reengage with the larger world. Sitting at Fritz's side during a luncheon with Vice-Chancellor Emil Fey and Prince von Starhemberg, I'd felt so important. I'd been the only woman in the room, the only pop of color in a sea of dark suits. Thinking about the good I might do helping keep Austria safe from its fascist neighbors—one of the stated goals of my husband and his compatriots—I had felt alive.

"Do we have the evidence we need?" Fey had asked Starhemberg after we'd finished a lunch of schnitzel and niceties.

I had listened, sipping my coffee. The men had ordered brandies after lunch, but I wanted to keep my wits about me. I'd contributed little other than small talk, but Fritz had begun consulting with me after these meetings and seeking my advice. Sometimes he even purposely left the table to speak with another diner, to see if the men would say something intriguing in my presence alone, something they didn't want my husband to hear but that they assumed I wouldn't understand. I needed to absorb every word and nuance so I could offer insights and guidance. I'd found that, on the tightrope I walked, my path was a little steadier when Fritz turned to me for thoughts on these partnerships and business decisions, and I did not want to disappoint.

"Is evidence really necessary? It's not like we're going to allow this action to be adjudicated," Starhemberg had answered.

"True enough, Ernst." Fey had paused, turning to my husband. "What about you, Fritz?"

"My factories have been working overtime to ensure the necessary supplies. Everything will be ready within the day."

What were they talking about? Evidence and action? Overtime at the factories? Fritz hadn't said anything about an "action" or "necessary supplies." I felt stupid but kept my expression alert and knowing.

"Excellent. We will finally be able to put those Jews back where they belong." Fey had lifted his brandy in the air, and the men had clinked glasses. Even Fritz had drunk to this horrific toast. "To the Hotel Schiff."

Papa's eyes fluttered open, and he said, "Oh, *Liebling*, why are you crying? The fighting is over, and Mama and I are fine."

I laid my head on his chest, breathing in the familiar scent of his tobacco and cologne. "I'm so relieved."

"Surely you knew that Döbling hadn't been in the line of fire? Almost all the fighting took place in the *Gemeindebauten*, the city council housing estates."

"Yes, Fritz kept me well-informed." I didn't mention that Fritz had only confessed to his involvement in this "action" after I'd confronted him in the car after the luncheon. In the weeks that followed, he continued to insist that the conflict would be little more than a search for contraband the Schutzbund might be stockpiling at the Hotel Schiff in Linz. Even when it escalated into violent battles between the two paramilitary groups that spread to other towns throughout Austria, he blamed the Schutzbund for not complying with Dollfuss's ban. It was their own fault, he'd said, that they needed to be taught this lesson.

"Then why all the tears, little princess?"

"Oh, Papa, thousands of people have been wounded and hundreds killed. And I feel like it's all my fault."

"Don't be silly, *Liebling*. What could *you* possibly have to do with this? The Social Democrats and the Christian Social Party have been at each other's throats for years. It was only a matter of time before the Heimwehr and Schutzbund turned that verbal warfare into actual bloodshed."

"I think I ignited the fire, Papa," I said quietly, studying the floor. I didn't want to meet his eyes.

His brow furrowed as he asked, "Whatever do you mean, Hedy?"

I explained to him the overheard conversation about the Schutzbund and Fritz's reaction. "I think that after Chancellor Dollfuss banned the Schutzbund, the Christian Social Party had been waiting for some sign of resistance on the part of the Social Democrats so the Christian Social Party could annihilate them. This conversation I overheard—about the Schutzbund amassing weapons and troops in Linz in defiance of Dollfuss's edict banning the group—gave the Christian Social Party the ammunition they needed. So with Chancellor Dollfuss's blessing, the Heimwehr, with Fritz and Ernst in tow, headed to Linz to start this civil war at the Hotel Schiff. And now that they've won, I'm hearing rumors that Austria's democratic constitution will be replaced with a corporatist constitution. Papa, Austria will become an authoritative regime not only in practice but in name."

Wincing in pain, Papa sat up. "Hedy, you cannot possibly blame yourself for this. If you hadn't provided the kindling, someone else would have. It sounds as if Dollfuss and his people have been on the hunt for it. And anyway, I don't think there will be much change in daily Austrian life. The country's been operating as a dictatorship for a while now."

"It's more than that, Papa. You wanted me to marry Fritz because you thought that, with all his power and connections, he could protect me from the anti-Semitism of the Nazis should Chancellor Hitler rise to power in Austria. But the hatred of the Jews doesn't just come from without."

"What do you mean?" Papa's brow knitted not only in pain now, but confusion as well.

He looked so despairing, I hesitated to tell him. How much more could he bear? Could he withstand the news that the man he'd hoped would protect his daughter was in league with racists? I held back. "It's nothing, Papa. I'm just shaken by this fighting and bloodshed. That's all."

A determined glint shone out from my father's eyes, one I usually associated with talk of his work at the bank, and he said, "Don't lie to me, Hedy. We've always been honest with each other, and I don't expect that to change now. Certainly not over something this important."

I sighed. The weight of sharing this news with him was heavy. "I've heard Fritz's colleagues say terrible things that have led me to believe an awful truth. The Christian Social Party—Fritz's people—are anti-Semites too."

CHAPTER SIXTEEN

July 25–26, 1934
Vienna, Austria

T HE SUCCESS OF FRITZ AND HIS COMPATRIOTS IN THE
Austrian Civil War yielded the results I had feared.
Chancellor Dollfuss used the Schutzbund's resistance as a reason to ban the Social Democratic Party altogether, and in May,
the conservative Christian Social Party suspended the democratic constitution. Defying the Austrian Nazi Party's strident
opposition, the Christian Social Party and the Heimwehr
merged into the sole legal political party, the devoutly Catholic
Patriotic Front, and took control of the government. Austria
became a fascist state not only in practice but in name. I clung
to Papa's words that it was a technical change only and what
mattered was the government's ongoing dedication to keep
Nazi Germany at bay. But I never stopped looking for signs
that Fritz and his new government would waver in their commitment not only to stave off the Nazis, but also to thwart the
temptation to become like the Nazis themselves.

In spring and early summer, our homes became the focal
points of celebration for the Patriotic Front. Fritz and I hosted

dinner parties at our Viennese apartment, hunting weekends at Villa Fegenberg, and balls at Schloss Schwarzenau. Hirtenberger Patronenfabrik entered into more new contracts than it had capacity, and Fritz began plans to expand his factories and his staff. His mood was euphoric, and I could do no wrong.

I fostered Fritz's elation by performing the role of perfect hostess to his exact specifications. I dressed more conservatively—wearing darker colors and dresses with a more modest cut—and let my jewels speak more loudly than my body. Unless Fritz was at my side or my hostess duties demanded, I spoke only to women, making whatever banal small talk the other wives offered, and this assuaged not only his jealousy, but also the suspicions of the women too. Always, my priority was listening. I was like an antenna seeking out sounds no one else could hear. Silent harbingers of doom.

Ernst von Starhemberg's ballroom was crowded with luminaries celebrating midsummer, but Fritz and I moved across the dance floor with ease. There was no jostling for position as the band played a slow-tempo classical piece, making the dancers' movements as languid as the July night air. Fritz and I were waltzing around the black-and-white marble surface when a servant tapped on Fritz's shoulder. Fritz opened his mouth to berate the young blond servant but closed it quickly when the boy handed him a note in Starhemberg's hand.

Skimming the words, Fritz glanced up at the balcony. Starhemberg was waiting for him there. "Excuse me, *Hase*. I must go."

What could possibly be happening to take Starhemberg's attention away from his own ball? Particularly during the first dance of the evening? I needed to know. Interlacing my fingers with Fritz's, I asked, "Is it so urgent, Fritz? I was enjoying our dance."

"Yes, *Hase*," he answered firmly, but his pleasure at my reluctance over his departure made him willing to disclose a little more. "Urgent enough for Starhemberg to assemble the council during his annual event."

This unofficial council—consisting of Fritz; Starhemberg, who was currently vice-chancellor and head of the Patriotic Front; Minister of Justice and Education Kurt von Schuschnigg; and a senior general of the Heimwehr—secretly advised Chancellor Dollfuss on any large-scale or troubling development. They would have only broken away from the ball to gather for an emergency situation.

I pointed to a navy silk sofa with a clear view of the balcony and said, "I will wait right there for you, Fritz. Hopefully, the prince will not need you for long, and you can return to me."

He squeezed my hand, then marched over to the curved marble staircase that led to the balcony. As the men assembled, I studied their worried expressions. Brows furrowed, they listened without interruption as Starhemberg explained the mysterious situation. Only then did shock register on their faces, followed by fury. They began gesticulating wildly, seething but not at each other.

A disturbance rippled across the ballroom. At first, I couldn't identify its source, as the guests still danced and the band still played as merrily as before. But then I noticed that, in the dark recesses of the ballroom, in the alcoves underneath the balcony, soldiers had begun to assemble. Within moments, an entire detachment of the Heimwehr lined the room.

What on earth was happening that required military protection here, at Starhemberg's Viennese palace? My heart pounded, and I felt like I couldn't breathe. Still, I kept a half smile fixed on my lips and my posture erect until Fritz walked back down the stairs. I couldn't let my composure slip.

I sprung up as he neared. "Everything all right, my love?"

Drawing me close as if about to nuzzle my neck, he whispered in my ear, "The Nazis have attempted a coup. A small group of German SS officers camouflaged themselves as soldiers in the Austrian Armed Forces and took over the national public radio building so they could broadcast a bunch of lies about that Nazi Anton Rintelen taking over power from Dollfuss. Simultaneously, a hundred or so disguised German SS stormed the Federal Chancellery. Most of the government escaped unharmed, but not before they shot Dollfuss twice."

My eyes widened in horror. No, no, no. Hitler was one step closer, one of my nightmares. I had known that the civil war in February and its aftermath had agitated the Austrian Nazi Party, leading them to clamor for unification of Austria and Germany, but I hadn't fathomed their unrest would serve as a direct invitation for Hitler's own soldiers to act. "Has Hitler invaded Austria?"

I grabbed a champagne flute from a passing tray and drank it down as Fritz explained quietly. "Other than the hundred or so SS soldiers in the Federal Chancellery and national public radio building—who have been killed or imprisoned—there isn't any German military inside Vienna or Austria proper. But German troops have assembled on the Austrian border. We've sent word to Mussolini, who made a public announcement supporting Austrian independence and has agreed to rush military troops to the Brenner Pass at the Austrian-Italian border as he promised he would. The presence of the Italian army should deter Hitler from advancing beyond the border."

His words and the champagne provided a modicum of relief, but the idea of Hitler and his armies precariously close to Austria terrified me. "Did Dollfuss survive?" I whispered. The ball continued on around us, and it seemed the council had its reasons for not informing the guests about the putsch.

"No," he admitted, a tinge of sadness in his voice. Although Fritz was willing to shift political allegiances somewhat when it suited his business interests, he'd forged a real alliance with Dollfuss.

"Then who is in command of Austria?"

"Starhemberg. For now."

The choice didn't surprise me. Starhemberg was vice-chancellor after all and the natural choice for this unexpected succession. Not to mention that Starhemberg's views matched Dollfuss's policies almost exactly.

I looked up at the balcony where the new chancellor of Austria remained in deep conversation with Schuschnigg. "So the Heimwehr is here to protect him from the Nazis?"

"Yes, along with the rest of the council and the other guests." He puffed up his chest. "We are *all* critical to the security of Austria."

"Of course," I said quickly. "Should I warn my parents?

Should we move them from Vienna to Schloss Schwarzenau or Villa Fegenberg?"

"No need, *Hase*. They are in no danger. The Nazi SS officers have been taken out of commission one way or another, and martial law has been declared in Vienna. The streets are completely protected by the police, federal troops, and Heimwehr, and it will only be a matter of hours until they crush the coup entirely. We need only await official word that the putsch is over, and life can resume as normal."

"What do we do while we wait?"

He gave the crowded ballroom a sidelong glance and, with a wry smile, said, "We dance."

I placed my hands on Fritz's shoulders and moved across the dance floor as if I had not a care in the world but this song and this moment. The orchestra played a calming piece by Gustav Mahler, and as we glided, I caught glimpses of the joyous faces dancing alongside us, all oblivious to the cataclysmic events transpiring on the streets below. But I gave them no cause for alarm. I fixed a smile upon my red-lacquered lips and bestowed it upon my husband's beaming face.

I knew then that my fate was forever linked to him and his cause, because it was my husband's weapons and his colleagues' politics that had kept Nazi Germany at bay. For now.

CHAPTER SEVENTEEN

October 4–5, 1934
Vienna, Austria

T HE COUP LAID BARE A CRACK IN THE VENEER OF AUSTRIA. Even though the government proceeded as if nothing had occurred, the financial systems reacted to the uncertainty Austria faced, from within and without. The banks suffered from the instability, Papa's Creditanstalt-Bankverein in particular. Mama and Papa's financial situation declined, and while they refused to acknowledge it verbally or accept help from me in any way, they could not hide it. No servants appeared during a recent visit to their house in Döbling, and their favorite mantelpiece clock, a fixture of my childhood, was noticeably absent. And midway through our afternoon tea, Papa excused himself so he could tend a migraine, undoubtedly triggered by stress.

Even Fritz, whose factories seemed to be minting money while manufacturing munitions, felt the stress of the political upheaval and the strain of maintaining his power base. Shortly after the failed putsch, Schuschnigg was appointed Austrian chancellor, and Starhemberg returned to his role as vice-chancellor. While Schuschnigg shared most of Dollfuss's policies, in particular his top priority of keeping Austria independent, the new chancellor took a very different tack. He adopted a policy of appeasement toward Germany and Hitler, which Fritz found far too soft. So Fritz focused his energies on strengthening ties with Italy, believing that Schuschnigg's actions needed bolstering.

In public, Fritz's visage and allegiance with Schuschnigg appeared unaffected, but at home, he was a mass of nerves and frustration over the new leader. Nothing I did could please him. In fact, I seemed to engage exclusively in enraging behaviors, never mind the social perfection for which I strove. He found flaws in my dress, defects in my banter with the ladies, and failings in my propriety toward our male guests. When he began listing the faults in my features, I knew the problem rested not with me but with Fritz. I started to tune him out, as a radio with a dial, as I couldn't bear the constant harangue.

"I have a special surprise after the meal," Fritz announced to our relatively small dinner party. Our vast Viennese dining table could seat twenty-four, and we often filled it with invitations to a wide variety of people, not only political and military players or royal folk. I'd sat beside renowned writers such as Ödön von Horváth and Franz Werfel, designers such as Madame Schiaparelli, even the celebrated psychologist Sigmund Freud. We always ended with a surprise.

But tonight was business focused, so we hosted only twelve, four of Fritz's senior company aides and eight Italian government officials and financiers with whom Fritz was forging closer relations. Just before dinner, the men had finished a critical meeting at Fritz's city club, hashing out the details of arming Mussolini's Ethiopian campaign. The African country was one of the few remaining independent states in the European-dominated continent, and Mussolini was waiting for an excuse to invade, to expand Italy's deserved rule over larger lands, as he saw it. Italy needed equipment and arms, and the men were ebullient at whatever arrangements they'd made.

What surprise had Fritz planned? I wondered. In the first few months after our wedding, he'd sprung upon me unexpected performances by opera and jazz singers that I'd mentioned liking. Lately, however, the after-dinner surprise was more likely to be a rare vintage wine or a decadent dessert designed to impress his business-minded guests. Not me.

"Some of you may not know that my wife is a retired actress. She was a star on the Theater an der Wien stage before she met me and decided she'd rather be Mrs. Mandl than an actress."

He paused as the guests respectfully chortled, and I held my breath. Where was Fritz going with this? Usually, if the dinner conversation turned to the theater, he changed the subject, wanting to keep any reminders of my former life from me. Fear, I had no doubt, that I'd want to return to the stage and use the precarious balance of our life together plagued him, no matter my assurances to the contrary. No matter that many actors, directors, and writers of Jewish descent were being pushed out of the profession in Germany and elsewhere, forcing them to abandon their craft or flee to places like Hollywood where Hitler had no grip. Why was he affirmatively bringing up my acting career now?

"Before we met, however, Hedy made a film called *Ecstasy*. Unfortunately, the film had a rather limited release and was only screened in one Viennese theater for a week. However, *Ecstasy* is getting a second chance at life. It was recently entered in the Second Venice Film Festival, and it received not only a standing ovation, but also a best director award for Gustav Machatý." Fritz waited until the guests finished making the appropriate noises of appreciation.

"I think my wife deserves to have her award-winning movie seen, particularly by her husband. So I arranged for a screening here, tonight."

I understood the purpose behind Fritz's surprise. Despite his complimentary words about me, the screening wasn't really in my honor. It was yet another means of influencing the Italians and cementing his relationship with them. How could they not be impressed by Fritz if his wife had starred in a film that their own institutions had acclaimed?

Yet Fritz had never seen *Ecstasy*. Of course, he'd read publicity about its scandalous content and knew about the controversy surrounding its release. But reading about scenes in which your naked wife frolics with another man and witnessing her do so were very different matters. My stomach churned, and sweat beaded on my forehead as I braced for his reaction.

We rose from the dinner table and walked toward the parlor, my anxiety mounting with each step. During dinner, the staff had transformed the room into a private projection room. As we settled into our seats, with Fritz and I sitting in the first row, waves of nausea coursed through me about what he would see on the screen.

Was there any way I could stop this fiasco before the film began rolling? What would embarrass Fritz less: the halting of his planned "surprise," or watching me cavort with another man on-screen while his guests witnessed his reaction? I knew what I had to do.

"Fritz," I said, leaning into him. "This might not be the most appropriate film for your business associates to watch. Let's create a different surprise."

"Nonsense," he barked as he craned his neck to ensure his guests were settled into the seats behind us. "It won an *Italian* award. What could be more perfect."

"But you know the movie has some controversial scenes, and I'd hate—"

"Shh," he hissed at me, then lifted his hand to signal for the projectionist to begin.

The lights dimmed, and the camera whirred. The word *Ecstasy* shone on the screen, and I was immobile, thinking about the movie's filming. When I first shot the scene in which I rode out on horseback into the picturesque Czechoslovakian woods with the cameras surrounding me, I'd thought nothing of what was to be recorded next. I simply threw myself into the mind-set of a young wife hastily married to an impotent older man, desperate for a more fulfilling life, and delighted in the escape she must feel in that moment. When the director, Machatý, called out for me to hop off the horse, strip off my clothes, and jump into the lake on my path, his instructions seemed the most natural next step in the world for my character. In the later scenes, when my character has an affair with a young engineer, the directions about our feigned lovemaking, even the simulated orgasm, seemed in keeping with my character and entirely appropriate for the film. Only later, when I saw the horror on Mama's and Papa's faces during the screening in Vienna, did I realize what a mistake I'd made, that a film I'd considered "artistic" had been silly and ill-advised. The awards from the Second Venice Film Festival did nothing to change my regret.

Fritz watched the opening scenes with pleasure, even nudging the Italian general to his right when the film revealed that my character's husband was impotent. Dread did not begin to take hold until I saw myself astride the horse. I knew what scenes came next, and I longed to run from the room. Yet I knew I had to remain at Fritz's side and endure.

As the film progressed, his fingers dug deeper into my arm. I knew his nails drew blood, but I didn't dare move or pull my arm away. The room grew uncomfortably quiet, and I sensed our guests' discomfort. When someone let out an involuntary gasp during the orgasm scene, Fritz could take it no longer.

"Turn it off," he barked at the projectionist.

Fritz stood up. Without looking at me, he walked past me, bypassing the Italians. He stood before his aides and ordered, "Buy up every copy of that film from every filmmaker, movie studio, and owner in the world. I don't care what it costs. And burn them." Then he stormed out of the room.

I spent a sleepless night awaiting Fritz's fury. I guessed that he'd take me roughly, as he'd done that night at the Hotel Excelsior. Or that he would berate me, maybe even beat me, even though his anger hadn't reached that point yet. I braced myself for any of these possibilities. Imagining how he would exact his punishment caused me even more pain than having to undertake my hostess duties—cheeks flaming red—by escorting the Italian government officials and Fritz's company aides to the door after he stormed out and locked himself in his bedroom. I knew the men were imagining me as naked as I'd appeared in the film.

But he hadn't doled out his sentence by the time dawn began to emit a pale-gray light into my bedroom the next morning. I'd begun to think about steeling myself to face the day when the door flew open. I grabbed my robe from my nightstand and sat up in my bed. It was Fritz.

Without a word, he marched over to my side of the bed and pulled me to my feet. He dragged me past the scurrying maids and the butler polishing silver to the entry hall. There, standing before me, was the heavy oak front door, now bearing seven locks instead of one.

"You are in need of protection," Fritz continued, his voice strangely calm and devoid of anger. "I can see from the reprehensible scenes I witnessed last night in *Ecstasy* that you are not capable of making appropriate decisions for yourself. You must have the wisdom and guidance of me or your parents at all times."

My mouth opened and closed as I formed words of protest, and then I thought better of it. Maybe this punishment wouldn't be as terrible as I was beginning to imagine, and speaking might inflame him. I needed to wait a moment longer and hear him out.

"From this point forward, you will be locked safely within

our homes behind seven locks. You will remain inside until I arrive home to escort you to our evenings' activities. If you need to leave the house during the day for a salon appointment, a dress fitting, or a visit to your parents, you will ask my permission first. If I choose to grant it, you will be allowed to go out, but only with the driver and a guard."

Was he serious? Looking at his face, I knew he was. How could this be happening to me? No matter how relentless and vast my imagination, I could have never envisioned this. Fritz was turning me into his prisoner.

A scream welled up inside me, but thinking of Papa and Mama, I knew I couldn't release it. My happiness was the least matter at stake in this marriage. In order to win this power struggle with Fritz, I would have to feign acquiescence, even penitence. Once I built up his trust again, I would change his rules and, with any luck, secure more freedom. But for the first time, I began to think about escape.

CHAPTER EIGHTEEN

February 12, 1935
Vienna, Austria

For months, I gave Fritz what he wanted. Not a typical Austrian society wife exactly, I thought, because those wives were perpetually proper, even invisible. But invisibility meant that you were not seen and not heard. And while Fritz didn't want me to be heard, he certainly wanted me to be seen, as long as I followed his rules.

I let him think he'd broken me and recast me into a mold of his own making, a graceful automaton of a hostess who smiled vapidly and chatted pleasant nothings in the ballroom as well as a compliant, inexhaustible mistress in the bedroom. One who never harbored ideas about returning to acting or conversing with a man other than my husband. Within several weeks, Fritz invited me into his confidences again and began seeking my advice, and I believed that we would soon return to normal, if the irregular life we'd lived before the *Ecstasy* screening could be considered normal, although he had yet to lift the restrictions he'd placed upon me.

But I seethed beneath my composed exterior and bided my

time with small victories. During my approved, escorted shopping outings, I purposefully spent thousands of schillings, even purchasing a wardrobe of fur coats, until Fritz—annoyed by my extravagance but not wanting to appear penurious—decided I would be better off with an allowance instead of unlimited charge accounts at Vienna's best shops. I hoarded every one of those doled-out schillings—far fewer than I'd been charging at the shops, but still a significant amount—in a shoebox in the back of my closet, my savings for the rainy day of the escape I'd begun to contemplate.

Once I amassed my schillings hoard, I wanted more. Not schillings, that was, but leverage. In the past, I'd paid close attention to Fritz's conversations in order to assess the Austrian commitment to keep the German Nazis from our border; after all, I'd married him in large part so he could protect me and my family. But now, I listened for another reason. I sought out conversations revealing flaws in the weaponry systems sold by Fritz, the sort of problems I'd overheard his colleagues hint at over dinners. If I could secure a vital piece of information about problems with his munitions or weapons components, perhaps I could blackmail him into letting me leave. He wouldn't want me to reveal to his clients or his manufacturing and political competitors that he sold them flawed weapons, would he? Maybe this would be my means of fleeing this marital prison.

Four months after the fateful *Ecstasy* screening, we hosted a relatively intimate meal with only Prince von Starhemberg and his younger brother, Count Ferdinand von Starhemberg, who joined us occasionally, as guests. During post-dinner drinks, an opportunity to gather more information presented itself.

"Do you really believe this Hellmuth Walter's supposed solution will work?" Prince von Starhemberg asked Fritz, to whom guests always deferred in matters of munitions. Although the prince blurted this question out in the midst of a discussion about a play we'd seen earlier in the week, I immediately understood the context.

Several luncheons and dinners had been devoted to two primary problems endemic to submarines and ships and their launching of torpedoes, for which Fritz manufactured significant components: the issue of supplying enough oxygen underwater to sustain combustion while maintaining speed, and the trickiness around developing a remote-control system for torpedoes instead of launching them with a thin insulated wire to allow for human guidance. I'd filled in any gaps in my understanding with a couple of key volumes from Fritz's library collection.

"I think he's already come up with a solution to the oxygen problem by using an oxygen-rich fuel that could be chemically decomposed to supply its own oxygen and use that reaction to drive a turbine. It still needs some testing, but my German spies tell me it has tremendous potential and that the Nazis plan on using it when they launch their attacks. I'm hoping to get my hands on some plans so I can get something similar in development at my own factories."

What did Fritz mean his "German spies"? Since when did my husband have a secret intelligence network within the Third Reich? Weren't the Nazis his enemies?

"No, Fritz." The elder Starhemberg sounded irritated. "That's not what I'm worried about. My concern is the remote-control problem."

"I hear that Walter has actually come up with something that might move his stubborn Germans bosses off their love of wire guidance. If my spies are to be trusted, the rumor is that he has crafted a system that allows torpedoes to be launched simultaneously using a number of set frequencies, with pairs communicating on one radio signal. It's got bugs, of course."

"Let me guess. The radio signals are jammable."

Even *I* knew that most countries—including Germany—were reluctant to switch their torpedo systems from wire to remote control because the latter relied on a single-frequency radio technology that could be intercepted and jammed by enemies. Military men had discussed the problem around and around with Fritz for years, and I'd surprised myself by not only understanding their discussions but developing a keen interest in the subject.

Fritz nodded, then launched into a highly technical description of radio frequencies. I was following along when Ferdinand glanced over at me, his lips curled in a half smirk undoubtedly to indicate his boredom at the deeply scientific conversation and his assumption that I was bored too. Starhemberg's younger brother, notorious for riding on his elder sibling's coattails, shared neither his drive nor his intellect. Nodding in false solidarity, I turned back toward Fritz, as I didn't dare anger him by making eye contact with another man, even one as familiar to us both as Ferdinand.

The next morning in the library, the butler interrupted my reading of a tome on radio frequencies. "There's a phone call for you, madame."

For me? No one called me save Papa, and never during the daytime, as he'd be busy at the bank. My heart started pounding, and I raced to the phone.

"Hello?"

"Hedy, you need to come." It was Mama. "There's something terribly wrong with your father. I've sent for the doctor."

"I'll be right there."

I turned to Müller, who lingered in the library pretending to dust the books but was eavesdropping on my conversation, as Fritz had undoubtedly instructed. Even before the screening of *Ecstasy*, I knew he'd ordered the servants to listen. In fact, he'd recently brought the prickly maid Ada to our Vienna apartment from Villa Fegenberg, and I guessed the purpose was to add another set of eyes and ears—belonging to an individual predetermined to dislike me—to this watchful task. "Have Schmidt bring around the car."

"Madame, the master did not leave word that you had an appointment today."

In my concern over Papa, I hadn't even thought about Fritz's oppressive rules. Would Müller really dare stop me from leaving my own house? I'd abided by Fritz's edicts because I felt certain they'd be relaxed after I played the desired part for whatever period of time he deemed necessary. That way, I could still keep my commitment to Papa about our family's security.

But I was not going to allow Fritz's commands to stop me from reaching Papa if he was mortally ill.

Normally, I'd circumvent all this nonsense with a call to Fritz at his office, as I knew he would never prevent me from seeing Papa. But he was traveling to his factory in Poland today. "This is not a request, Müller. It is a command from the lady of the house." I started for the entry hall, calling back to him, "Have Schmidt bring the car around."

The clip of Müller's efficient step echoed throughout the entry hall, and he reached the front door before me. Blocking it, he turned to face me. In a quivering voice, he said, "I apologize, madame, but I cannot allow you to leave. I have not received word from Mr. Mandl that you have an appointment today."

Taking four more steps, I brought my face so close to Müller's that I could smell the tobacco on his breath. In my heels, I was at least two inches taller than him, and I stared down into his eyes. "You will give me the key," I seethed. "I know you have one."

"The master would be most disappointed in me if I did so, madame."

"The master would be *more* disappointed in you if you blocked me from seeing my sick father. If you do not hand over that key, I will reach into your pocket and tear it from you."

His hand shaking, he reached into the inner pocket of his black servant's jacket and pulled out a copy of Fritz's key. One by one, he sprung the locks that sequestered me from the rest of the world. Before I strode out into the bright light of day, I called back, "Send the car around for me."

The dazzling February morning was at odds with the

darkness mounting within me as we approached Döbling. What was wrong with Papa? His migraines had increased in number and intensity in recent months, but we'd attributed it to the stress he'd shouldered in the wake of the financial difficulties faced by the banks. He'd always been unshakably strong and dependable, and I prayed to a nebulous god—for the first time in a long time—that he would remain stalwart and very much alive.

Schmidt drew the car alongside my parents' house, and before he even stopped the engine, I hopped out. Running down the walkway, I threw open the front door, calling for my parents.

Mama stepped out of the parlor. "Hush, Hedy. The doctor is upstairs with your father, and I don't want you to disturb the examination."

"What happened?"

"He looked pale over breakfast this morning. In the middle of his eggs, he stood up from the table and excused himself. I thought perhaps he'd forgotten about an early work meeting and was rushing to the office, but he started to walk up the stairs. I asked him what was wrong, and he looked at me with strange, glassy eyes and said that his chest hurt. I helped him into bed and immediately rang the doctor and then you."

Heavy footsteps clunked down the staircase, and Mama and I both rushed to hear the doctor's diagnosis. Dr. Levitt, who lived in Döbling not too far from Peter-Jordan-Strasse, set his black medical bag down on the bottom step and took our hands in his. "I believe that the chest pain he suffered today— and on other days as well, although he might not have told you—stemmed from a severe attack of angina."

Mama and I glanced at each other, unfamiliar with the term. Brow furrowed, Mama asked, "Emil had a heart attack?"

"Angina is not a heart attack, Mrs. Kiesler, but pain resulting from an inadequate supply of blood to the heart. It can signify that the heart is under stress and indicate that the sufferer is at higher risk for a heart attack."

"Oh no." Mama extricated her hand from Dr. Levitt's and lowered herself down onto the tapestry bench in the entry hall.

"Will he be all right, Dr. Levitt?" My voice sounded panicky.

"Yes, for now. But he needs rest." He paused, as if loathe to bestow his next piece of advice, then said, "And to reduce his anxiety, although I know that's a hard prescription to fill these days."

"Can I see him?"

"Yes, if you're quiet and don't excite him. I'll stay here with your mother. I have some instructions about his care."

I tiptoed up the stairs and into my parents' bedroom. From the doorway, my father, over six foot four inches tall, appeared huge sprawled across his twin bed. As I approached him, however, his large frame appeared to hang off his bones, and he seemed shrunken.

The mattress creaked as I sat down next to him. His eyes opened at the noise, and he smiled at me. Stretching out an index finger, he wiped away the tear trickling down my cheek and said, "No matter what happens to me, Hedy, promise me you'll protect yourself and your mother. Use Fritz as a shield. Leave him only if you have no other option."

When I didn't answer, he said again, "Promise me, Hedy."

What choice did I have?

"I promise, Papa."

CHAPTER NINETEEN

April 28, 1935
Schwarzau, Austria

I STOOD BEFORE THE LAKE AS IF BEFORE AN ALTAR. THE evergreen mountains near Villa Fegenberg, impervious in their constancy, stared back at me. With the undulating, evergreen hills as its backdrop, the lake was utterly still. So still, in fact, that its surface acted as a mirror, reflecting the mountains and sky almost photographically.

I glanced around the empty shoreline of the lake. Did I dare? I longed for the purity of the lake's waters. It was a mighty risk, but I might never have the chance again. Fritz had not relaxed his rules, no matter my strict adherence to them, no matter my grievous loss. I was still his prisoner.

With a final survey of the landscape, I dared. Stripping off my black riding clothes, I dove into the exhilaratingly cold water, shattering the perfect reflection. Much as my life had been shattered.

I swam the breaststroke until I tired, and then I stopped and simply floated. In the stillness, the reflected image of mountains and sky rejoined, and I lingered in the image of the dip between two mountains, as if nesting in nature's own arms. The sun caught the tips of tiny waves until they glimmered. It was beautiful. *No*, I thought. *Not beautiful. Pure.*

For a moment, I felt free and complete. No mask, no subterfuge, no grief—just me and the water. As I floated, I wondered: Could I ever be made whole again?

Over two months ago, just a few short days after Papa's initial angina attack, our chauffeur had driven me to Döbling so I could check on Papa, with Fritz's permission and forgiveness for the earlier, unauthorized visit. When the car pulled into Mama and Papa's driveway, the house was dark, and the blinds in my parents' bedroom were drawn. Why, in the middle of a surprisingly bright winter morning, were the blinds still down? Mama was fanatical about throwing open the curtains as soon as the day began, and even though they now had only one part-time servant, she strode through the house freeing the windows from their nighttime coverings every morning. Perhaps Papa hadn't been well in the night, and Mama was still sleeping, tired from caring for him. I crept into the house, careful to prevent the front door from slamming behind me. After tiptoeing throughout the first floor and finding it empty, I mounted the stairs to my parents' bedroom, opening their door just a crack.

Although the room was dark, I saw that Mama, still in her bedclothes, was lying on Papa's chest. His eyes were closed, as were hers. Yes, I'd been correct; she'd fallen asleep caring for him in the night. Pushing the door open a bit wider, the hinges creaked, and Mama looked up. Our eyes met, and before I could whisper my apology for wakening her, I understood that her face was wet from tears. She hadn't been sleeping, and neither had Papa. I sunk to the floor, realizing that the heart attack that the doctor had promised was only a "remote" possibility had happened.

How could my strong, infallible Papa be gone? Who would anchor me in his absence, love me unconditionally? Only with Papa did I remove all the masks. The grief had been like a hammer, splintering my true self and my many masks into countless pieces, and over two months later, I was still broken. Perhaps I would always be shattered.

The rumble of wheels over gravel disturbed the silence, and I froze. *Please*, I thought. *Make it not be Fritz.* Without making a single sound, I listened. A car door slammed. *Please*, I prayed. *Let it be a delivery truck.* But voices travel over water, and soon, a familiar, if muffled, voice called out my name, and when the gravel crunched with the pace of his distinctive stride, I knew my prayers hadn't been answered.

Keeping my arms and legs submerged to reduce any noise, I swam as quickly and quietly as I could to the shoreline. Scrambling onto the rocky beach, I winced as I tiptoed over the jagged rocks to the pile of my clothes. Just as I was about to shimmy into my slip, the scraping of gravel grew quite loud, and I realized that I'd misjudged how long I had before he found me.

An arm shot out from thick branches of evergreen and grabbed me. Fritz appeared in full and slapped me across the face. Stumbling to the ground with the force of the blow, I clutched my cheek with one hand and the top of my slip, only half on, with the other.

"What is this? Some reenactment of *Ecstasy*?" he yelled, his furious voice echoing across the still lake.

I flinched.

"No, no, Fritz. Nothing like that. Just a dip in the lake on a warm day."

He crouched down next to me, bringing his angry face within an inch of mine. "A naked dip? For the benefit of the servants?"

"No," I insisted as I struggled to free my arm from his grip. "Nothing like that at all. I would never do that. I just didn't want to get my riding clothes wet, as I knew that I'd be riding home in them."

"Oh, was it for the benefit of some guest I might have brought with me then?" He seethed, spraying spittle on my cheek. "I will never let another living person lay eyes on your naked body. You belong to me."

"No, Fritz, I swear. I thought no one could see me." Still holding my cheek, I shifted my position so that I was on my knees, the rough rocks of the beach ripping into my skin. Sobbing, I begged him, "Please don't hurt me."

His hand froze midair. His expression shifted, as if awoken from a deep slumber, and the menace slipped away. "Oh, *Hase*, I'm so sorry. That damn *Ecstasy* movie still tortures me, and when I saw you naked in the lake, it brought those awful scenes back. I lost control of myself."

He reached for me, but instinctively, I recoiled. Scrambling away across the rocky surface, I grabbed my heap of black clothes. Shaking, I stood up and rushed the pants and jacket back over my body. I felt him approach, and I wondered whether he'd embrace me or hit me next.

His muscular arms wrapped around my body from behind. I stiffened at his touch, and a chill passed through me, and not from the cooling mountain air. The monster who'd lurked in the shadows, lurked behind the flowers and the presents and the jewelry and the many houses, had emerged in full. And there was no hiding him again.

CHAPTER TWENTY

June 20, 1935
Vienna and Schwarzenau, Austria

H E NEEDS YOU," STARHEMBERG WAS INSISTING. "HOW will Schuschnigg maintain strong Italian ties without you? Mussolini was always *your* associate."

"Then why is he being so damned pigheaded?" my husband asked, the volume of his voice rising alongside his irritation.

"He's a neophyte, Fritz, utterly unaware of what it actually takes to keep Austria safe. I mean, he thinks the politicians do the heavy lifting," Starhemberg responded to Fritz's largely rhetorical outburst.

Fritz practically snorted. "Imagine if relationships between countries were, in fact, dictated by the politicians alone. Schuschnigg thinks he can protect Austria from German invasion by not angering Hitler. You can't appease a madman."

Starhemberg snorted back. "All this cooperation that he's planning with Hitler will backfire. It just gives Hitler time to prepare for an Austrian invasion while we sit idly by, politely abiding with the Treaty of Saint-Germain by keeping our troops to an emasculated thirty thousand."

"Why can't Schuschnigg see that the only thing that stopped Hitler in the putsch was Italian troops? What if the rumors are true that Hitler and Mussolini are moving toward alignment in Ethiopia, in public support anyway? It will just be a matter of time before Il Duce and Hitler reach a general accord that includes Austria."

I had been listening to a version of this conversation since the solidity of the Austrian leadership between Starhemberg and Schuschnigg had begun to dissolve. Starhemberg thought Schuschnigg was too soft on Germany, thereby making Austria vulnerable, and Fritz agreed. My husband and his cohort, who had controlled the fate of Austria behind the scenes for years, worried that if independent Austria faltered, so would their power. The two men had no real ideology; their only real belief was in the infallibility of their own power. They'd shift their positions as needed.

"Unless you intervene," Starhemberg pronounced.

Fritz took a long drag on his cigarette before echoing Starhemberg. "Unless I intervene."

Four weeks later, this overheard conversation ran through my mind as I sat across the dinner table from Mussolini himself. I'd met Il Duce before, during trips to Italy, but always in passing. Brief bows and curtsies constituted the totality of our exchanges. Until now. Now, I was his hostess.

With Fritz in tails and me in a gold-lamé gown custom designed by Madame Schiaparelli, a previous dinner guest, Fritz and I had greeted Il Duce in the entry hall of Schloss

Schwarzenau. We'd considered inviting him to our Viennese apartment or Villa Fegenberg, but in the end, his security needs and the meeting's privacy requirements necessitated the castle.

In the weeks leading up to the dinner, Fritz even enlisted my help in readying the castle for the occasion, something he'd never permitted before. I purchased new table linens and napkins for the dining table, met with florists on the decor, sampled cakes to assess which would best please Mussolini, and listened to various musicians to determine their suitability for the after-dinner performance and dancing. I rejected three groups because their renditions of several classical pieces were a touch too jazzy for the traditional Mussolini, finally settling on an impeccably trained and highly recommended orchestral group from Vienna. The quest for perfection, usually Fritz's bailiwick, was never so important to me; our guest was critical to the ongoing independence of Austria from Germany.

Three days prior to Il Duce's arrival, Fritz and I did a dry run of the entire evening, complete with all five courses in our evening attire, and we felt as prepared as we'd ever be. The mounting pressure of the occasion united me with Fritz in a way that hadn't happened since the early days of our marriage, though naturally, I remained wary of him. He was, of course, still mercurial.

Nerves aflutter, we stood at the base of the grand staircase in the entryway of Schloss Schwarzenau to meet Mussolini. He arrived, dressed in full military regalia as if leading a parade, with a platoon's worth of soldiers and military officers in tow. Fritz greeted the dictator of Italy with a bow and a handshake that turned into a hug, and I lowered myself to the floor in a curtsy as Fritz had instructed, but that too ended differently than it started—with a kiss on my palm.

We entered the castle and, after a welcoming conversation, retired to the dining room, where the decadent five-course meal awaited His Excellency and his more prominent entourage members. We'd planned the meal carefully to be heavy on the vegetables he favored but with a spectacular veal dish at its center. All the preparation Fritz and I put into the dining room showed. The freshly cleaned Gobelin tapestries on the wall framed the exquisite table display; the long table, extended fully for the occasion, was covered by a violet-blue silk tablecloth, and scattered deep-blue orchids set off the gold table setting that Fritz had shipped in from the Viennese apartment.

As we settled into our seats, the servants circulated around the room with the wine; among the Viennese staff we had imported for the occasion, only Ada, the maid who'd been inexplicably moved from Villa Fegenberg to Vienna, had been kept at the apartment, as I couldn't risk a mishap she might orchestrate to reflect poorly on me. Our most senior servant, Schneider, whom we'd assigned to serve only Mussolini, held a carafe over Il Duce's crystal goblet. But Mussolini shook his head to the proffered wine. Fritz and I shot each other a look; we'd forgotten to instruct the servants that Mussolini did not drink alcohol. How could we have made such a gaffe? My heart pounding, I glanced over at the dictator, who was busy chewing on the garlic-laden salad we'd heard was his favorite. He didn't appear to be offended.

While I kept my eyes lowered demurely as Fritz preferred, through my lashes, I glanced at Il Duce. His square jaw

reminded me of Fritz's, although Fritz did not jut his out with
as much punctuation as Mussolini. Both men exuded power
and confidence, although the dictator's wattage was somehow
higher.

As befitted the host, Fritz raised conversational topics,
although, of course, he allowed Mussolini to direct the path of
the discussion. Talking about politics was strictly *verboten* at the
dining room table, unless the dictator raised the matter himself,
so Fritz and I had fashioned a list of acceptable subjects, honing
in on the many cultural projects advocated by Il Duce.

Fritz raised a question about a vast undertaking in Rome,
in which streets would be redesigned from their medieval, cir-
cuitous routes and transformed into wide, straight "modern"
roads. This project also encompassed the creation of new buildings with hard lines and blank cement walls. We'd heard that
the rush to create as many buildings and public works as possible made the projects inconsistent architecturally and rather
slapdash, but we'd never share anything but praise with Il Duce.

"Ah yes," Mussolini answered in a booming voice. "The
road construction and the building expansion proceeds apace.
Simultaneously, we are excavating and preserving many
ancient Roman sites. We must glorify all things Roman—
ancient and modern."

"Of course," Starhemberg agreed, interjecting himself into
the conversation. "It's necessary for the unity of your people."

Il Duce nodded vigorously. "Precisely. When a leader does
not have this noble heritage and future upon which to base
a strong government, he must rely upon other less effective
and often unsavory means to fortify his state. Take Chancellor

Hitler. The Germanic people don't have the illustrious history of the Italian people, so Hitler has been forced to create a state around this fiction of the Aryan race and his hatred of the Jews. This is an unfortunate basis for a new regime, even if his loathing is understandable."

I flinched at the way he blurted out "Jews" and described Hitler's "loathing" of them as "understandable." Italy had no restrictions on Jews, unlike Germany, and as a result, I'd believed that Il Duce wasn't anti-Semitic. No longer. I couldn't believe this was the man upon whom I was pinning all my hopes for an independent Austria free of government-sanctioned anti-Semitism.

The dictator wasn't quite finished. He continued, "Culture is, of course, the best vehicle to inculcate the people with the fascist ideology, which is the proper system for all countries."

Fritz and I froze, as did our other dinner guests, all Mussolini invitees except for Starhemberg and his wife, who rarely attended any occasions with her husband save critical ones. We had constructed the evening to avoid a political conversation, and here, Il Duce was plopping it on the table during the first course. The dictator continued chewing his salad, but the rest of the room was immobile. No chatter, no eating, no sipping.

I needed to salvage the moment. "Your Excellency, on the topic of culture, I have heard that Ottorino Respighi's *Pini di Roma* is your favorite musical piece. Is this true?"

Mussolini stopped chewing and took a long drink of water. My heart beat wildly as I waited for his response. Would he take offense at my interjection? I knew from Fritz that he preferred women to be round, maternal, and, most importantly, at home. Except for his mistresses, of course.

Finally, his face grew lively, and he said, "You have done your homework, Mrs. Mandl. I do find *Pini di Roma* particularly moving."

"Mr. Mandl and myself have arranged for the finest musicians in Vienna to play for you after dinner. Would Your Excellency mind if we had them perform *Pini di Roma*?" I asked casually, although Fritz and I had spent several hours with the musicians we'd hired for the evening making certain they could perform *Pini di Roma* perfectly.

"That would be delightful," he answered with a broad smile, and then he launched into a discussion of Italian composers.

Silently, I exhaled in relief at his response, along with the successful change of topics. As did the rest of the room. Fritz shot me a conspiratorial glance and then smiled. He was pleased with my efforts, a rarity these days.

"Shall we retire to the ballroom?" Fritz asked after the guests finished their last bites of the massive Sacher torte and colorful *Punschkrapfen*, fanciful fondant confections.

The ballroom was arranged in two sections: one with gilded chairs arranged in a semicircle around the orchestra and another leaving the black-and-white marble dance floor bare. Fritz and I took our seats alongside Mussolini to listen to the orchestra perform his beloved Respighi piece. The dictator's eyes closed, and he swayed to the inspiring symphony. When the violinist drew the last note across his bow, Mussolini jumped up and applauded. And the rest of the guests followed suit.

The musicians transitioned to a classical piece suitable for dancing, and the guests gathered around the periphery of the dance floor. I was expected to take the first dance with our honored guest. Since Mussolini hadn't brought his spouse, Fritz invited Starhemberg's wife to the dance floor, and Il Duce extended his hand to me.

He slipped his hands down my sides, resting on my hip bones. I, in turn, gingerly placed my gloved fingers upon his shoulders. We stood nearly eye to eye; thankfully, I stood no taller. Fritz had instructed me to wear flat shoes under my gown, as Il Duce was only five feet seven inches tall, my height exactly, and loathed women who towered over him.

His eyes were steely and his skin rough in close proximity. I couldn't help thinking that my hands lay on a man who'd gained power through gangs of former soldiers who beat, killed, or jailed anyone who stood in their way. And he didn't just issue orders advocating violence. His hands were dirty with the blood of those he'd beaten himself.

Before I could engage in the usual innocuous pleasantries I trotted out for every conversation with one of Fritz's colleagues, Mussolini asked a question of me. "You were once an actress, were you not, Mrs. Mandl?"

How had he known that? Rumors, I guessed. Hopefully not from the Italian visitors the evening of the *Ecstasy* screening. "Yes, Il Duce, although that was years ago. My only role now is wife."

"Of course, Mrs. Mandl. That is every woman's greatest role, is it not?"

"Indeed, Il Duce."

"I believe you were a tremendous actress before your marriage," he persisted.

I was confused. Had the dictator seen me onstage? Surely someone would have mentioned seeing Il Duce in the audience of one of my shows. I'd never even heard gossip about his attendance. Then I knew.

"I saw you in *Ecstasy*," he whispered, drawing me closer to him.

I was horrified, and a wave of nausea overtook me. I couldn't stand the thought of this man, who'd seen me naked, with his hands on me. But I kept dancing, speechless, as I didn't know what to say, and praying that the song would end and partners would change. What other choice did I have? The stakes were too high.

"I enjoyed watching you in the film so much that I purchased my own copy. I've watched it more times than I can count."

I was no longer simply repulsed. I was terrified. Was I the reason he'd finally accepted the invitation Fritz had been extending for years? I kept the smile plastered upon my face, but the ill feeling intensified.

"You are a lovely woman, Mrs. Mandl. I would like to get to know you better."

This was no invitation to tea. This was an invitation to his bed. Did Fritz know? Had he already colluded in the pimping out of his wife as part of his sordid negotiations with Mussolini? No, he was so insanely jealous, I found the notion unconceivable. I did not believe that Fritz would relax his possessiveness of me even for Mussolini.

Mercifully, the song concluded, and one of Mussolini's aides rushed to his side. He cocked his head to one side to better hear the man's supplications over the din of the crowd, and then said, "My apologies, Mrs. Mandl, but I must tend to an urgent matter."

I nodded, and as soon as he disappeared from sight, I raced across the crowded ballroom floor and up the stairs to my bedroom. Locking the door behind me, I stood before my full-length mirror. I stared at the beautiful woman in the mirror—arched brows, buoyant raven hair, deep green eyes, and full, lacquered red lips—and did not recognize her as myself. Whose face was this? All the features painted over with layers of artifice looked unfamiliar. I raked my fingers over my cheeks, over and over and over, until they were bright red, almost bloody. Papa would not have recognized this person.

Who had I become?

CHAPTER TWENTY-ONE

May 21, 1936
Schwarzau, Austria

T HE YEAR THAT FOLLOWED MUSSOLINI'S VISIT TO SCHLOSS Schwarzenau brought to Austria threats from within and without. How could I even think of mentioning Mussolini's proposition to Fritz? Austria needed to cling to the last vestiges of Mussolini's protection, and I could not do anything that might cause Fritz to resist—or reject—Il Duce, if the solicitation had not been approved by my husband. And if, unbelievably enough, the overture had been sanctioned by Fritz, well then, I didn't want to discuss it with Fritz, because I couldn't bear to know that truth. It would have been impossible to maintain my role as Mrs. Mandl.

The barricade Fritz and his compatriots had built around Austria on the basis of Italy's military strength began to show rifts. Armed by Fritz, Mussolini marched into Ethiopia in a display of fascist power that Fritz initially celebrated, particularly because of the financial benefit it brought us. But when Hitler offered his unconditional support of Mussolini's invasion in the face of condemnation and economic sanctions by the League of

Nations, the wariness with which Mussolini typically regarded Hitler began to soften, and our collective worry about Austria's fate increased. Would Mussolini begin to favor the Nazis, with their unquenchable thirst to "reunite" Austria and Germany into one Aryan land? And although I would never dare broach my worries to Fritz about the impact of an Austrian and German unification on me personally—my Jewish origins were a well-kept secret, and Fritz liked to forget I'd ever been a Jew—my anxiety was compounded that fall by Hitler's enactment of the Nuremberg Laws, which stripped Jews of their citizenship and civil rights. It was an act that made real all Papa's fears.

But Fritz and I danced on as if the world wasn't crumbling around us. In public, anyway. In the privacy of one of our homes, when all the guests had departed and the servants had retired for the evening, there was no dancing. There were only rules and locks and fury. By imprisoning me, it seemed he hoped to cage the rampant virus that was Hitler. I became the unspoken emblem of the evil within and without whenever he needed a place to vent his anger.

Mama occasionally saw the results of his outbursts during our regularly scheduled teatime visits, one of the few outings Fritz still permitted. A bruised arm where he'd grabbed me to whisper a scathing critique during a dinner party. An abraded neck left by his rough ardor, if his nocturnal visits to my bedroom could even be called by so pleasant a name. She never commented upon them, and when I tried to address the artifacts of his anger, she changed the subject or made oblique references to "duty" and "responsibility." I knew I couldn't look to her for support, and my visits with her became fewer and fewer.

I found it unbearable to sit in the Döbling home I had once considered a refuge and feel nothing but despair.

Even the dancing slowed by March. Emboldened by the inaction of the League of Nations upon Mussolini's invasion of Ethiopia, Hitler marched troops into the Rhineland, the former German territory west of the Rhine River that the Treaty of Versailles had made off-limits to Germany. Schuschnigg informed Starhemberg that Austria needed to reach some kind of accord with Hitler, that Mussolini had, in fact, instructed him to do so or lose Italian support. Starhemberg opposed this quite vocally, which led to his ousting as vice-chancellor in May. With Mussolini busy with his Ethiopian campaign and his burgeoning relationship with Hitler, he had less and less time for Austria—and Fritz. The power of my husband and Starhemberg slipped away, and I wondered whether I'd reached the point past where I'd promised Papa I would stay. If my husband had become an opponent of Austrian leadership and his power to keep our country independent had waned, had he become a liability rather than a source of security? If I hadn't vowed to Papa that I'd keep Mama safe too, I would have left the moment the question occurred to me.

It was after midnight. The dinner service had been cleared, and the servants had retired but not before restocking the alcohol on the sideboard and placing a tray of candied violets and *Trüffeltorte* on the center of the table. Fritz and Starhemberg had wanted a respite from Vienna and the political machinations, so we decamped to Villa Fegenberg with only Starhemberg's brother Ferdinand in tow. The two men had wanted to plan without risk of listeners, and Ferdinand and I didn't count.

I wished that Fritz wanted my presence for this crucial exchange because he trusted my opinion, but that wasn't the reason I hadn't been banished to my bedroom. Fritz allowed me to remain at the table because I'd become like one of the Rembrandts on the wall or the antique Meissen porcelain on the sideboard. Simply another priceless, inanimate decoration for Fritz to display, a symbol of his wealth and prowess.

"Sole dictator of Austria. What a joke," Starhemberg said, interrupting my maudlin musings with a swig of brandy and a slurred declaration. He was drunk. I thought I'd never see the staid aristocrat in such an inebriated state, but then no one ever expected Schuschnigg to proclaim himself sole dictator of Austria either, and he'd done just that two days before.

Fritz seethed. "The audacity." I wasn't certain whether he was referring to Schuschnigg's self-proclaimed dictatorship or his recent hints that the Austrian government might take over the country's munitions works, including Fritz's factories and company. Both developments had sent him into a tailspin the past few days.

"We launched him into that position. How dare he try to oust us from power?" Starhemberg swayed as he spoke. His brother reached out to steady him, but Starhemberg swatted him away like a fly.

"Of course, he's trying to marginalize us. We're the only ones left who'll challenge this damned German-Austrian agreement he's considering." Through channels still loyal to Fritz and Starhemberg, they'd heard that Schuschnigg had begun to negotiate an agreement with Germany in which, in exchange for Hitler's pledge to keep Austria independent, Austria would make its foreign policy consistent with Germany's and allow Nazis to hold official posts. Fritz and Starhemberg lamented that the agreement would isolate Austria diplomatically and encourage other European countries to view Austrian-German relations as a purely internal affair of the German people. More than anything, they believed it was a ploy to weaken Austria for Hitler's invasion. Hitler would have men on the inside of the Austrian government after all.

"What political or economic capital do we have left to pressure Schuschnigg now that Hitler and Mussolini have reached some sort of understanding? I hear they're about to formalize their friendship into something they're calling the Rome-Berlin Axis. Axis of what? Another one of Hitler's made-up phrases signifying his power."

Fritz snorted in derision at this "Axis" nomenclature. "Our greatest strength was always the ability to deliver Italy to Austria's side. We can no longer do that if Hitler and Mussolini have crawled into bed with one another." I'd never heard Fritz sound despondent before. He'd always been bullish and self-confident in the extreme.

Weaving over to the sideboard, Starhemberg grabbed a full bottle of schnapps and placed it between himself and Fritz. He poured them each a snifter full of the amber liquid until it nearly spilled over the brim. No one offered to refill either my glass or Ferdinand's. It was as if we weren't in the room.

"I think we have no other choice," Fritz said with an air of resignation.

What was he talking about? About what did he and Starhemberg have no choice? "It's against everything we've worked for."

"I know, but what are the options? If we continue our efforts to promote independence, then we will lose whatever influence we still have. Not to mention assets. But if we shift our liquid assets out of Austria before the Anschluss while pursuing a new outlook on Austrian-German relations long in advance of the invasion, we avoid seeming motivated exclusively by our own interests, and, well…" Fritz trailed off, letting Starhemberg fill in the blanks. Whether he even realized that I was filling in the blanks as well, I didn't know. Maybe he didn't care. Certainly, Ferdinand didn't seem to have registered the magnitude of what Fritz and his brother were saying—that they were considering switching sides and becoming advocates of a unified Austria and Germany to retain their power base.

"It might work, but only if you're allowed to sell arms…" Starhemberg said, then trailed off. Both Fritz and I knew he was referring obliquely to Fritz's Jewish heritage.

Starhemberg knew Fritz's secret—that he was half-Jewish—perhaps even before I'd learned it. Aside from one reference to his father's conversion on our engagement trip to Paris, Fritz had kept this fact hidden even from me during the first year of our marriage. Only then did he reveal that his Jewish father had a premarital relationship with his Catholic mother while she served as a maid in one of the Mandl family homes. After Fritz was born, his father relented and converted to Christianity in order to marry his mother and legitimize Fritz.

"Under the Nuremberg Laws, I could be granted the

status of 'Honorary Aryan,'" Fritz announced, addressing Starhemberg's concern without ever saying the word *Jew* aloud.

"What the hell is that?"

"It is a special designation created by General Goebbels for Jewish people who serve the Nazi cause directly."

"So even if they deem you to be a Jew"—Fritz winced at the word, but Starhemberg continued—"you'd be allowed to sell arms."

"Yes."

Starhemberg sat back in his chair, nodding. "Well, that changes things, doesn't it?"

The men clinked their snifters before draining their glasses of every drop of the gleaming liquor. I sank back into my own chair, astonished at what I was hearing. On some level, I supposed it shouldn't have shocked me, but it did.

Papa and I had banked on the force of Fritz's will for our security, and it seemed inconceivable that with all his power, wealth, and drive, Fritz could not keep Hitler at bay. Yet Fritz had finally come to the conclusion that he couldn't win this fight, and when Fritz couldn't win a battle head-on, he wasn't ashamed to switch to the side of the victor.

I was now in bed with a man who was in bed with Hitler.

CHAPTER TWENTY-TWO

November 28, 1936
Vienna, Austria

THE PLAN SEEMED EASY AT FIRST. SLIP ON A MASK—ONE I hadn't worn in a long while but that still felt familiar—and say the lines of my character. The lines I'd speak were not by some unknown playwright but ones I'd written. Otherwise, the plan resembled the opening night of a play. Or so I told myself.

I waited to raise the curtain on my performance until Fritz left for a business trip. His travels to the remote reaches of eastern Europe—the "peasant terrain," as he called it, in Poland and the Ukraine where some of his factories were located—had become far more common than jaunts to the glamorous destinations we used to take for pleasure or business. From overheard conversations, I knew the purpose of these trips was to consolidate his less productive holdings and liquidate them when possible, squirreling away the proceeds in South America, a place far away from the pending war. He kept chugging at full capacity those factories that churned out munitions and arms components pursuant to contracts with Austria, Spain, Italy, and South American countries and those he believed the Third

Reich might utilize if he could persuade them to come to the negotiating table after he'd advocated Austrian independence for years.

I selected as my costar a man known for his vapidity and lack of foresight. This trait was necessary for the role I'd assigned him. Fortunately, fate had provided me with a perfect, ever-present pawn, one even Fritz wouldn't suspect of wrongdoing or capable of much at all and, more importantly, one to whom I had easy access: Ferdinand von Starhemberg, Ernst's brother.

The first scene opened in the drawing room of our quiet, fully locked Viennese apartment on a bright November morning. I sat before my art nouveau writing desk and, from the window framed over it, watched the golden leaves of the trees lining the Ringstrasse lift and twirl in the breeze. The clear autumnal light and liberating nature of my plan made me feel free, almost giddy.

Picking up my fountain pen, I inked a letter upon my heavy stationery, embossed with my initials.

> *Dearest Ferdinand,*
>
> *I find myself with some free hours this afternoon and the desire for company. Might you be available as well? If so, please join me for tea in our parlor.*
>
> *Yours, Mrs. Mandl*

Signing the letter "Mrs. Mandl" felt stilted, given my intentions, but I didn't think Ferdinand had ever addressed me by my first name, even though I certainly called him by his. Fritz was far too proprietary for such familiarity with my first name, even with Ferdinand, whom he considered a harmless fool, one with only his title and his brother's reputation to recommend him. Still, I couldn't risk punishment should my letter be intercepted or my plan foiled.

I sent Auguste, the youngest, most pliable servant, to the task of delivering the letter to Ferdinand's residence, a mansion Fritz described as a mass of tasteless opulence. I couldn't risk entrusting the usual servant in charge of such deliveries, Ada. I'd never uncovered evidence of an older or current affair between Fritz and the pretty maid, but for whatever reason, Ada loathed me and delighted in my prison sentence, as her hateful, furtive glances proved. I could not trust her with the letter, as I could imagine her peeking at its contents, desirous of uncovering any damning information she could obtain about me. I suspected she'd like nothing more than to report some wrongdoing on my part to Fritz. Or had I begun to imagine conspiracy everywhere?

Ferdinand's response arrived far more quickly than I'd expected, as he had slit open my letter and read it on the spot. I had guessed that he'd be lounging about at this hour, and Fritz often muttered that Ferdinand's primary occupation seemed to be attending social gatherings. Entreating Auguste to stay while he scribbled out his reply, the servant trotted home with an acceptance to my invitation. All I had left to do was order the tea, busy the servants with tasks that would take them well into the evening hours, and ready myself.

The long, silken train of my most formfitting dressing gown trailing sinuously behind me, I left the safety of my bedroom suite for the parlor, site of the second scene. The mantelpiece clock chimed a quarter to four, and my nerves chimed along with it. Would my script work? To steady myself for the performance to come, I laid my fingers on the piano keys and lulled myself into calmness with Mozart's Serenade No. 13, *Eine kleine Nachtmusik*. For a moment, I was transported out of my gilded prison into freedom.

A clearing of a man's throat interrupted my reverie. My fingers froze, and I looked up. It was Ferdinand, appearing mesmerized and uncomfortable all at once.

Leaping up, I raced to his side and clasped his hand a little too long. "Ferdinand, you have rescued a damsel in distress. Fritz is away for two days, and I find myself with long stretches of time on my hands and nothing to do."

"It seems you've filled them with lovely music. I had no idea you played so beautifully."

I smiled at him coyly. "There are many things about me you don't know, Ferdinand."

As a scarlet flush crept from his neck to his cheeks—the precise reaction I sought—I gestured for him to join me on the sofa, before which the servants had arranged tea, petit fours, and a crystal carafe of sweet schnapps. I allowed my hand to linger on the handle of the teapot before switching to the carafe. "Do you mind if we start with a small drink rather than tea, Ferdinand?"

"Of course not, Mrs. Mandl. I'm happy to follow your lead, as always."

I knew that he'd follow my lead in more than the drink

selection, of course. Along with being completely empty, Ferdinand was utterly transparent, and he'd never been able to hide the longing he felt. Not from me, anyway. Fritz couldn't see it beneath the vacuity.

We downed our drinks and made small talk about the fine autumn weather. I poured him another and another while I sipped upon mine slowly and waited for a sheen of mild intoxication to appear on his face.

"I'm guessing you're wondering why I invited you here. Without Fritz." His confusion over this encounter had been apparent from the start, probably from the moment he received my letter this morning, but I knew his uncertainty wouldn't be outweighed by his desire and curiosity.

"Yes."

As if overcome by emotions and shyness, I kept my eyes lowered while I said, "I've had feelings for you, Ferdinand. For some time."

"I-I-I," he stammered. "I had no idea you felt this way, Mrs. Mandl."

"Please call me Hedy," I purred. "I'd love to hear the sound of my name on your lips."

"Hedy," he said, never taking his eyes off my face.

I leaned in to kiss him. Stunned, he didn't react at first. His lips were as immovable as Fritz's resolve. But they quickly softened and began to respond in kind.

"I've longed to do this," I whispered, allowing my breath to linger on his neck.

"Me too," he whispered back. "You have no idea," he said as he lunged toward me.

Even though I found it rather repugnant, I kissed him for another moment before breaking away and feigning breathlessness. "Not here, Ferdinand. The servants spy for Fritz."

The mention of Fritz made Ferdinand's posture stiffen but didn't dampen his ardor. "Where then?" he asked, pulling me close to his chest again.

"I have a friend in Budapest with an empty house. If you can help me out of this apartment, we could take the train that leaves in an hour. We might be there before midnight."

He didn't answer. I could see that his face was aghast at the prospect of stealing away with Fritz Mandl's wife. He'd probably been hoping for a quick tryst at a local hotel.

I pressed myself to him, running my hands along his shoulders, chest, and finally grazing my knuckles along the front of his trousers. "We would have two days and nights together. For uninterrupted pleasure."

The balance had been tipped. "Let's go."

"Truly?"

"Yes. How will we get you out of here without alerting the servants or"—he could hardly bring himself to say the name—"Fritz?"

I recited the plan I'd concocted, pushing aside the slight guilt I felt at utilizing my mother in this manner. "Leave here now, but call the home line from the nearest phone you can access. To whichever servant answers the phone, say you're calling from Vienna General Hospital on behalf of Gertrude Kiesler, who has just been admitted and who would like to have the company of her daughter. Then drive to the hospital, and I will meet you at the admitting desk. From there, we will go to Budapest."

"Clever," he said with an appreciative smile.

I made him repeat the words he would say on the phone to the servant. Then I rose from the sofa, feigning reluctance to leave his arms. "Go. I will see you shortly."

The third scene took place precisely as I'd scripted in my mind. The call, my hysteria, the driver's race to the hospital, the secret reunion with Ferdinand. I giggled with delight at the ease of it. All escape had taken was mustering the bravery to take the plunge. If only I'd known, I might have left Fritz sooner, the moment I realized he could no longer protect me.

Before I could second-guess my plan, Ferdinand and I were sitting in a first-class train car to Budapest, with my bag of hoarded *schillings* and some minor jeweled necklaces sitting atop the rack overhead. I rewarded myself with several glasses of champagne, which nearly took the edge off my irritation with my costar, until he became overwhelmingly physical with me. I feared that I'd actually have to consummate my ruse right here on the train, when the conductor opened our car door to admit an elderly woman with a small poodle. I'd been rescued temporarily.

I'd planned the final scene to culminate quite differently from Ferdinand's expectations. We would hire a cab to take us to the home of my childhood friend—that part remained true—but the house would not be empty. She would be there with her husband and small daughter, not expecting me but pleased to see me nonetheless. The invitation was always open, she'd told me when I saw her the past spring during a trip taken with Fritz. But the presence of my friend and her family would make impossible the amorous dalliance, I would tell Ferdinand,

and he would have to return to Vienna unfulfilled. I would then be free to take flight wherever my fancy took me. Beyond that, I hadn't yet planned.

Ferdinand stepped off the train in the Budapest station, holding his hand out to me for assistance down the steep stairs to the platform. As I descended, I gave him my winningest smile, which he returned along with a tight squeeze of my hand as we walked along the platform toward the station exit. We took only a few steps before we saw him.

Fritz.

Fire turns not red or orange when its flames are hottest but white. That terrifying white, the shade of a thousand-degree fire, was the color of Fritz's face, a hue I'd never seen on his—or anyone else's—face before. Not the red of rage but the white of unspeakable fury.

Ferdinand and I released each other's hands, but no one spoke. What could either Ferdinand or I possibly say? That the scene wasn't as it appeared? That I actually hadn't planned on sleeping with Ernst's brother but rather only abandoning Fritz?

"You will come home with me, Hedy," Fritz said in a tone of eerie calmness.

"Of course, Fritz," Ferdinand said in a tremulous voice, even though Fritz hadn't acknowledged his presence in any way. My husband had only spoken to me.

Fritz pivoted back to the station exit, where a black Rolls-Royce waited. Without a backward glance at Ferdinand, I followed him at a clip. As the chauffeur closed the car door behind me and began driving toward Vienna, we sat in silence until Fritz turned his white-hot face toward me.

"Did you really think you'd get away from me, Hedy? I flew here to make certain I'd beat your train." He was seething, his spittle flying over my cheeks.

How did he find out? I wondered. Was it Ada, finally uncovering a damaging nugget of information about me to proffer to Fritz? Or did one of the servants tell Fritz about the supposed call from the hospital regarding my mother? I had no doubt Mama would forsake me if Fritz inquired about that call with a follow-up visit to her.

He slapped me full across the face and then pushed me back into the car seat. Ripping my dress from my body, he took me. I'd known he was a monster. I'd always known. But as he took me over and over, I *saw*. And seeing was so much worse.

CHAPTER TWENTY-THREE

July 12, 1937
Vienna, Austria

I WOULD NOT BE SO FOOLISH THE NEXT TIME. THERE WOULD be no hastiness, no reliance on others. Alone, I would play the long game.

While I planned, I retreated into the persona of Mrs. Mandl. But the mask no longer fit. The edges had grown gritty, rough, even slippery in parts. I'd find myself mid-conversation at a party or dinner, and the mask would slip off. I'd find myself unmoored, uncertain of who I was and how I was meant to act. But the freneticism in the air—the bubbling up of worry and frantic energy due to the unstable political situation—meant that no one noticed. As long as my face was painted and my body swathed in a gown, no matter what personas vibrated beneath the surface, I was Mrs. Mandl.

Since people perceived me only as Fritz's vapid wife—if they discerned me at all—I garnered a sort of invisibility. It allowed me to listen, unnoticed or perhaps ignored, to the legions of builders, weapons developers, foreign politicians, and military buyers who now populated my homes instead of royals and dignitaries. Fritz manufactured shells, grenades, and military aircraft among other munitions, so I often overheard discussions of military plans and suitable weapons, including talk of the strengths and weaknesses of Germany's systems. These covert maneuvers allowed me to see—or perhaps accept—the inevitable Anschluss future that most still denied, and that my husband would help in this annexation of Austria into Hitler's Germany.

Only to Fritz was I visible. My attempt at escape, it appeared, had done nothing to diminish his desire for me. He seemed to believe that, as long as he conquered me physically, he still owned me. So by night, my body became a country over which Fritz constantly asserted dominion.

One unseasonably brisk summer morning, I proceeded as I did every day, the routine identical regardless of which home I inhabited. After wakening alone in my bedroom, I scanned myself in the full-length mirror for signs of the warfare exacted upon me by Fritz. A long soak in my deep marble tub came next, where I scrubbed my skin with pumice to scour away evidence of my husband. Sitting before my dressing table, I painted on the face of Mrs. Mandl and dressed the part of a wealthy lady of leisure. And then, after nibbling on breakfast and lunch, scanning scientific volumes, and playing the piano, I waited for instructions from Fritz.

On this particular day at Villa Fegenberg, however, no instructions came, either in person or by missive. But judging from the constant slamming of the heavy front door, people were arriving, a fair number of them. The creaking of the ancient entryway staircase and the thud of trunks being hoisted up the stairs by the servants told me that these were overnight guests. Who were they? Fritz had said nothing to me of hosting a party or ball, and even though he handled the details of such events with the staff, he always informed me so that I could ready my gown and face and arrange for my jewels to be taken out of the safe.

I sensed a frisson of fear and anticipation among the servants, who resisted all my efforts to pry information from them. Fritz must have issued strict orders about the secrecy of our guests, and on this occasion, I guessed he'd even named me specifically as one from whom details must be kept. What was going on in the villa?

I couldn't ask Fritz outright. Such questions would trigger his suspiciousness, already on higher alert than usual because of my botched escape with Ferdinand. Unsubstantiated rumors that I intended to return to the theater had recently surfaced in the local paper, all the more ridiculous in light of the many Jewish performers flooding Vienna from Berlin where the Nuremberg Laws banned them from the profession, including my friend Max Reinhardt, and these had heightened his fears about another possible flight. When I finally encountered Fritz later that afternoon in the hallway, I sought information obliquely.

"Fritz, I sense a certain flurry among the servants, as if they're preparing for a dinner or party. I want to make certain I'm dressed properly for your guests whose arrival I heard rather than saw. What gown would you like me to wear this evening?"

He scanned me, searching for signs of rebellion. Finding none, for I'd clung to a pleasant memory of a Sunday walk in the woods with Papa to ensure that innocence imbued my features, his face relaxed.

"No need to ready a gown, Hedy. The guests are here for business only. You will be not expected at the dinner."

"Thank you for letting me know. I'll have the cook prepare a plate for me to take in my suite so I will be out of your way."

He nodded his approval and continued down the hallway. Before he passed from view, he turned toward me and said, "Be ready for me around midnight."

Something unpleasant was afoot. Fritz had never hosted a "business dinner" where he didn't want to show off his trophy. Even after the unpleasantness with Ferdinand, Fritz kept me on his arm for countless dinners and parties and dances. And he had never worried about my exposure to his business and political conversations, including the recent machinations in which Fritz had secretly armed both sides of the Spanish Civil War earlier that year. In fact, he often solicited my opinions on those conversations. So he could not be shielding me from sensitive information. What on earth was transpiring in Villa Fegenberg that Fritz did not want me to see or hear? Machinations involving the Nazis—considered treasonous even in these days of Austria's chancellor's collaboration with Hitler—were the only thing I could imagine he'd try to shield me from.

Later that evening, I took a great risk. As I'd informed Fritz, I did indeed have the cook prepare a dinner plate for me, to be served in my bedroom suite. When a maid knocked with my tray, I answered the door in my robe, looking tired and ready for bed even though the hour hadn't reached nine o'clock. Yawning, I requested that I not be disturbed for the rest of the night.

I waited until the clock indicted ten thirty before I donned my lightweight overcoat to cover my dressing gown. Cracking my door open a sliver, I peered down the hallway for evidence of any staff members. Finding none, I crept to the wide balcony that wrapped around the north corner of the villa. Cigarette dangling from my lips, as if I'd stepped out on the balcony for a smoke, I strolled casually until I reached another set of doors that led to the ballroom, smaller dining room, and study in which I'd guessed Fritz was holding his meetings.

Did I dare proceed? No excuse could be proffered for my presence in this area of Villa Fegenberg except spying on Fritz and his guests. If I was discovered, the punishment from Fritz would be worse than any I'd suffered yet. Still, I needed to confirm my greatest fear and suspicion—that Fritz's "business meeting" was with the highest ranks of the German Nazi Party. So I pushed open the door.

The hallway was empty, save for voices drifting in from the smaller dining room. I knew that a small, little-used butler's pantry connected to that particular dining room. With any luck, it would be empty, as the servants would be tending to Fritz and his guests via the half kitchen on the opposite side of the dining room instead of the butler's pantry. The servants preferred using the half kitchen because it also housed a dumb-waiter, thereby eliminating trips up and down the stairs.

I took my chances and tiptoed down the hall. After exhaling in relief that my guess proved correct, that the servants had chosen to use the half kitchen to serve, I hiked up my robe and squatted in the empty, pitch-black butler's pantry. I settled down to listen.

"How can we be sure that you will provide us with the necessary items in advance of the invasion? Your past actions don't reflect the unification goals of our country," a gravelly voice said in a hard-edged German accent, quite different from our softer Austrian German. The speaker must have hailed from Germany itself.

"You not only have the contractual documents outlining the promised delivery of arms, munitions, and weaponry component, but you have my ideological commitment. I see now that fighting against the inevitable union of our two Germanic countries was a foolish and false endeavor. Please believe me, Reichsminister," Fritz said in a pleading tone I'd never heard in his voice before. My husband commanded others; he was not commanded *by* others. Until now.

"I cannot make that decision, Mr. Mandl. Only our führer can absolve you of your past actions against the Reich and your alleged Jewishness. He will assess whether you are deserving of our trust. I must leave that decision to our führer," the Reichsminister answered my begging husband.

The room grew quiet, as if awaiting someone. It could only be Hitler. I held my breath, fearing that one deep inhale might be loud enough to give me away. A full minute ticked by on my wristwatch before anyone spoke or made any kind of sound.

Finally, a mild, commanding, yet even-keeled voice started speaking. I knew that it must be Hitler—after all, the Reichsminister opened the floor only to his "führer," his leader—but the speaker's words were so soft, I could hardly make them out. Where was the forceful, almost hysterical yelling that Hitler used in his famous rousing speeches?

Once I became used to the volume and accent, I could make sense of some of Hitler's words. "I believe that you understand that we Germans are one people separated by an arbitrary boundary line and that our destiny will not be fulfilled until we are reunited. I also believe that your Jewishness stood in the way of that understanding until now—"

I heard Fritz try to interject, to protest his Jewish label. Someone must have restrained him, because he suddenly stopped, and Fritz was not known for silencing his views. But apparently, no one interrupted Hitler.

Hitler continued on as if the attempted interruption had never occurred. "I alone decide whether someone is Jewish. I have decided that you will be granted the title 'Honorary Aryan,' which means that whatever Semitic blood stains you bear have been washed clean. You are no longer a Jew. I feel certain that, without the besmirchment of that blood, you can, and indeed have, fully adopted our faith in one Germanic country."

"Thank you, Führer," Fritz said quietly. His use of the word *führer* itself sent me reeling. Had my husband just called Hitler his leader? Had he pledged his allegiance to the enemy?

"As an Honorary Aryan, you will, of course, be exempt not only from the Nuremberg Laws when they go into effect upon the reunion of Germany and Austria, but also from any future plans I may make to permanently remove Jews from German society. As will your wife, who I understand is also a Jew."

My whole body began shaking as I listened to Hitler label

me a Jew. I suddenly felt naked and threatened, here in my own home. How did the Third Reich know about my Jewish heritage?

"Permanently remove Jews from German society?" Fritz asked the question I was wondering myself. What did Hitler mean exactly?

"Ah yes." Hitler's voice relaxed as explained. "The problem of the Jews is one that must be solved. They simply cannot be allowed to exist among the German people. The Nuremberg Laws are only the first step in a plan that I hope, one day, will be comprehensive, particularly as the Reich overtakes the entire continent."

I gasped and then immediately froze. Had anyone heard me? I listened for any break in the conversation or advancing footsteps indicating my impending exposure. When the discussion continued, I crept out of the room, down the hallway, and onto the terrace.

I couldn't believe what I'd heard. My husband—the Merchant of Death—was living up to the moniker bestowed upon him years ago.

And he would be hand-delivering that death to Austria and its people.

CHAPTER TWENTY-FOUR

August 24, 1937
Vienna, Austria

I COULD WAIT NO LONGER, AND IN TRUTH, THERE WAS NO need. The elements of my plan—two months in the making—were largely in place. I'd mapped out the method of escape, an unexpected but not overly complicated route. I'd deposited the items critical to my new life in easily accessible safekeeping after lingering for long hours over my other possessions—exquisite bejeweled couture gowns, handmade shoes and purses of the finest leather and silk, and especially jewelry laden with emeralds, diamonds, pearls, and countless other precious stones—culling only those essential to my next steps. And most importantly, I'd secured the lynchpin, an unsuspecting servant critical to the entire scheme, my new lady's maid, Laura. I needed only to select the right moment to set the events in motion.

Before I could proceed, however, I needed to fulfill the final piece of my promise to Papa.

"Mama, if I were to leave Vienna, would you come with me?" I asked my mother over tea at her home during a visit to Döbling. The once-grand house now seemed small and my mother even smaller. And though it was still cluttered with all my parents' belongings and scattered with memories, including the evocative smell of my father's pipe tobacco, it felt empty without Papa.

She stared at me, her eyes brimming with judgment. I could almost see her pondering the reasons I was asking this question, and I began to wonder: Had Fritz told her of my flight to Budapest? Had he shared how I had invented an alibi based on a fabricated hospital stay for her? Mama had never mentioned my failed escape, and of course, I would never dream of informing her about it myself. But she likely had a myriad of reasons for keeping the knowledge from me, if indeed she knew.

Her teacup steamed in her hands, and I heard the summer rain tap on the parlor window during the long minute she waited before bringing the cup to her lips to sip. Only then did she answer me. "Why would you leave Vienna, Hedy? Your husband is here." Her tone was unexpectedly inscrutable.

I had to tread carefully with Mama. No matter my attempts to explain the strictures of my life with Fritz, she either chose not to hear me or always sided with him. Even when a bruise was blooming on my cheek, she urged "commitment." *A wife's duty is to her husband*, she was prone to announcing whenever applicable. I wondered, not for the first time, whether this proclamation was borne out of jealousy and a modicum of rage. That because she herself had made the sacrifice of a promising career as a concert pianist to become a hausfrau and mother, she believed I should be bound to make similar renouncements and commitments. No matter the cost.

"I meant if my husband and I left Vienna, because of the political situation." I almost said "because of the threat of Hitler" but caught myself. Knowing that my husband had just entered into an agreement with Hitler, I couldn't bring myself to utter the boldface lie, even if it was for a good reason. "Would you come with *us*?"

I needed to know whether to include her in my final scheme. Whether the planning and risks I'd committed to take for one needed to be expanded for two. I hadn't dared to broach my plans with her, but if I had to guess, she wouldn't be amenable to fleeing Vienna, particularly if we were going alone, against Fritz's wishes or knowledge.

"Of course not, dear. This is my home. And anyway, your father was always excessively overwrought about the damage Hitler might do. Vienna is—and will remain—perfectly safe, whether or not Hitler's threats become real." She tsked a little and then added, "He always included you in his political musings and worries. He should have never troubled you with all that nonsense. It's not as if you were his son."

Anger surged in me. How dare Mama speak ill of Papa? And how could she even suggest that I meant less to him because I was born female?

Her words prodded me to speak thoughts long buried. "You never did care for my relationship with Papa. And you never did like me, did you? I wasn't the daughter that you hoped for."

She arched her eyebrow, the only nod to surprise she ever allowed herself. But her voice remained even. "How could you say that, Hedy?"

"Mama, when I was growing up, you never once

complimented me. You only issued critiques and instructions on how I could alter myself to become more like the other Döbling girls."

Her expression didn't change. "It isn't that I didn't—or don't—like you. I had other reasons to be sparing in my praise."

My voice rose along with my fury. I couldn't bear the calm certainty in her tone, the continued withholding of anything save judgment. "What reasons, Mama? Why would a parent choose to 'be sparing' in their praise and affection?"

"I can see that you wouldn't believe me, Hedy, even if I explained it to you. You've become entrenched in your manner of thinking about me. No matter what I say, what explanations I offer, you will only think the worst."

"That isn't true. If there *are* reasons, I'd like to know them."

Mama rose, straightening her skirt and smoothing her hair as she said, "I think our time together is over. Our teatime, I mean." And she left the room.

I had been dismissed. Just as my mother and I had begun to embark on the most intimate discussion of our lives. But I had received the answer to the question for which I came. Mama had no intention of leaving Vienna with me.

As I buttoned up my lightweight raincoat and readied to leave, I felt conflicted. Part of me felt honor-bound to race back into the study to which Mama had retreated and tell her about the conversation I overheard about Hitler's plans for the Jewish people. Would she then consider joining me? I doubted that this information would change her mind, and I wondered whether she'd even believe me. In fact, I worried that worse might result from my disclosure. I suspected that she'd report my plan to Fritz, thereby ending my best chance at escape. I decided that the safest route, for now, was silence.

Mama had made her decision, and I'd never been able to make her waver. I had fulfilled my final promise to Papa.

CHAPTER TWENTY-FIVE

August 25, 1937
Vienna, Austria

THE LATE AFTERNOON SUN IMBUED THE CARAMEL SILK walls of my Viennese bedroom suite with a warm glow. From my vantage point at the bench before my dressing table, I glanced over at my husband. He was half-asleep in my bed, satiated with the carnality I'd instigated after luncheon, a tactic to quell his constant jealous vigilance. For a moment, I was a newlywed again. A young girl, enamored of her powerful, older husband and grateful for the protection he offered her family.

Fritz's eyes fluttered open, and I met them with my own. I was an innocent girl no longer. Feigning a coy smile, I walked toward the bed, utterly naked, and stood before him. He ran a finger between my breasts, down past my navel, resting on my right hip bone. I tried not to shudder with disgust at the sensation of his traitorous finger touching my body.

"I wish we had time for more," he said in a sleepy voice.

I whispered, "Me too," although I secretly prayed this would be our last time. Ever.

"But duty calls, and we must prepare for dinner. Guests will be arriving for cocktails before too long."

"Will the navy gown suit the occasion?" I said the words I'd rehearsed.

"Yes, it looks well on you."

With practiced nonchalance, I said, "I was thinking that the Cartier set would complement it well."

"The one from our engagement trip to Paris?"

"The very one." Did I sound casual enough? As if my plan didn't hinge on wearing my most expensive jewelry?

"The gown would enhance the sapphires and rubies, wouldn't it?"

"That's what I was thinking." I didn't say what I really thought. That Fritz had purchased all my other jewels for Mrs. Mandl the hostess, not me. The Cartier jewels were the only ones that Fritz actually bought for me, the Hedy I was before I became his wife. They belonged to me.

"I'll take them out of the safe for you."

By the time Fritz delivered my Cartier necklace, earrings, and bracelet, I was already dressed in my navy gown, sitting patiently while my new maid, Laura, tended to my hair and makeup. In the mirror, I watched as Laura hooked the necklace around my neck and bracelet around my wrist and screwed on my earrings cautiously to preserve my coiffure.

How long and hard I'd searched for her—a highly credentialed lady's maid who resembled me—after pretending to *finally* acquiesce to Fritz's longstanding suggestion that I hire a servant dedicated to me exclusively. Similar in height, weight, and general coloring, Laura looked like me as long as the inspection kept its distance. Upon closer scrutiny, her eyes were brown while mine were green, and her features didn't have the symmetry and grace of mine. Still, from across a room and in similar attire, we could be mistaken for each other. It was the key reason I'd chosen her from among the ocean of candidates.

"Please tend to the darning in my closet while I'm at the dinner, Laura. I will rejoin you here afterward."

"Yes, ma'am."

After the usual cocktails and small talk, Fritz invited the guests to the dining room. I took my seat at the head of the table and smiled down at my husband while he gave a toast. Our guests were unknown to me before this evening. Not the royalty, artists, and Austrian businessmen of the early days of our marriage, and not the political and military types who frequented our homes in the calmer political days that followed. I suspected that I sat at the dining table with the next wave of politically minded Austrian industrialists who'd soon be running my country at Hitler's behest.

Midway through the second course, I began to wince periodically, as if I were experiencing discomfort. Nothing intense or of long duration, but by the time we reached the dessert course, I kept my hand cupped on my low belly.

After Fritz invited the guests to retire to the ballroom for some music, I approached him and whispered, "I'm not feeling terribly well."

"I noticed." He paused, then his face lit up. "Could it be?" Nearly a year before, Fritz had ordered one of the many bedrooms at Villa Fegenberg to be converted into a nursery. He had no idea that I used a diaphragm whenever I could get away with it.

"Who knows?" I said with a wan smile, one that I hoped conveyed excitement and anticipation.

"Should I call for Laura to help you to your room?" His unexpected solicitousness made me feel uncomfortable. I wasn't used to kindness from Fritz.

"No, no, I'll be fine walking down to my room. And I will ask Laura to stay with me in case I need anything." I gestured to the people milling around, waiting for Fritz to lead them into the ballroom. "I don't want to alarm the guests."

"Of course." As if reminded of their presence, he turned back to them and began shepherding them in the direction of the ballroom.

I strolled slowly back to my bedroom, careful to keep up my ruse of ill health.

Laura jumped when I pushed open my bedroom door. "You're back early, ma'am."

"I'm feeling a bit peaked. Shall we have tea, Laura?"

I'd started the little ritual of sharing tea with Laura at day's end—an unusual practice for a lady and her maid but necessary for my plan—as soon as I'd hired her, six weeks before. As she did most evenings, Laura readied the tea for us both, and I waited on the caramel silk sofa for her to join me. Just as she set the teacup-laden tray down on the table before me, I said, "Oh, Laura, I brought some honey back from the market yesterday. Do you mind fetching it from my closet? It's in a bag sitting alongside my shoes."

"Of course, ma'am," she answered, scurrying off to the

closet. As she hunted for the honey that I'd placed in an obscure location in my closet, I pulled the sleeping draught powder I'd procured from the local pharmacist a few weeks earlier for this purpose out from underneath the sofa cushions. Into Laura's tea, I poured three times the recommended dose of the powder, enough to knock her out but not enough to harm her.

When she returned with the bag, I patted the sofa cushion beside me and said, "Let me spoon the honey into your tea. It's completely pure and supposedly much sweeter than the usual honeys." I hoped that the honey would mask or at least explain the syrupy sweetness of the powder.

"Thank you, ma'am. That's very kind."

While we sipped our tea and chatted about the outfits I'd need for the next day, Laura started to yawn. Her eyes began to droop, and within a few minutes, she fell asleep sitting up on the sofa.

I froze. Although I'd planned Laura's somnolence and all that followed, I suddenly felt shocked. Was my plan really happening? Might my escape succeed this time? What would happen if I failed again?

Think, Hedy, think, I told myself. What came next? I closed my eyes and recalled the checklist I'd written out weeks prior before tossing it in the roaring fire in my bedroom.

While Laura slept, I tore off my gown and threw it on the back of my dressing room chair. From the darkest corner of my closet, I pulled out a shoebox containing the elegantly embroidered Alpine boots I wore only in the harshest winter weather, slipped my hand down into the boots, and pulled out my hoarded schillings. Digging out my cross-body black leather purse, I loaded it with my identification papers, my schillings, and the Cartier jewelry set. Lifting the top off a Chanel hat box, I reached underneath the small, feathered cloche hat and fished out a maid's uniform that matched Laura's exactly. After unwinding my coiffure and styling my hair into Laura's simple bun, I placed a lace maid's cap over it and tied on a pair of plain black brogues.

I glanced at myself in the mirror. The resemblance to Laura was uncanny. I felt ready to inhabit another mask, albeit temporarily.

I stepped out into the hallway. Keeping my eyes fixed on the marble parquet floor, I adopted Laura's gait. Using her quick, small steps, I reached the kitchen in record time. That room, I knew, presented my biggest challenge. I hadn't been able to map out my route from the entrance to the servant's door because I couldn't predict which servant would be where at the moment of my entry. But when I pushed open the swinging door, no one was present, except for the cook, who was preoccupied with pouring warm *Bowle* from the stove to a serving bowl for our guests' after-dinner drinks.

I raced across the tiled kitchen floor, keeping my footsteps light. Grabbing the bag of clothes—a couple of daytime dresses and jackets, one evening gown, and two pairs of shoes—and toiletries I'd stashed in the pantry earlier behind a row of jarred pickles, I reached for the door. The doorknob turned easily, and I stepped out into the black, sultry night.

Laura's battered Opel, which we'd purchased for her to run errands and bring items back and forth among our homes, as she alone among the servants was meant to travel with us from house to house, sat in the farthest corner of the servant's lot. Stones crunching underfoot, I was thankful for the lack of moonlight. If anyone spotted me—even me in the guise of Laura—in the servant's parking lot at this hour, Fritz would certainly be alerted.

Using the key I'd filched from Laura's pocket, I opened the car door. Key in the ignition, the car rumbled to life, and although I knew it was premature, I felt elation as I pulled away from my Viennese home. As if I'd escaped from prison, which, in a sense, I nearly had.

I drove directly to the train station, the *Hauptbahnhof* on the Mariahilfer Square. From there, I could get the Orient Express to Paris, one of the few cities in which Fritz had no spies and limited power. The platform was deserted when I bought my ticket from the agent, who informed me that there was a twelve-minute wait before the train's arrival into the station. The intervening seconds and minutes passed as slowly as the honey I'd dripped into our tea not an hour earlier, and I kept looking over my shoulder for Fritz to appear. When I finally heard the tracks clatter with the arriving train, I exhaled deeply. I might just reach Paris and, from there, a train to Calais and a boat to England.

In London, I hoped for a fresh life and a new history.

PART II

CHAPTER TWENTY-SIX

September 24–30, 1937
London, England, and the SS Normandie

T HE HEAD OF MGM STUDIOS WAS OFFERING ME A CHANCE at a second history.

I'd been envisioning this transformation and building to this moment for weeks—months, really, considering how long my flight had been in the planning—yet it still didn't seem real. Could I really be deserving of this fresh beginning?

"What about Lamarr?" the voice chirped over the sounds of the waves crashing against the hull of the enormous ocean liner. Mrs. Margaret Mayer always made certain her distinctive tone was heard.

Her husband, Mr. Louis B. Mayer, lifted his paddle away from the Ping-Pong table and turned toward her. "Say that again," he commanded rather than asked. The founder and head of MGM Studios, the most prestigious film studio in Hollywood, was used to giving orders, even to his wife. She rarely accepted his barks without some form of protest.

"Lamarr," she answered with authority, addressing Mr. Mayer and his cronies, all Hollywood men like himself, who had stopped playing or watching Ping-Pong and turned toward Mrs. Mayer as well. Alone among women, she commanded their attention and, sometimes, their respect.

"That's got a good ring to it," Mr. Mayer said, puffing on his ever-present cigar. His bespectacled, usually dour face brightened.

"Sure does, Boss," one of his men echoed. Were these men ever allowed to think their own thoughts? Or better phrased, were they ever allowed to voice them?

"Why does it sound familiar?" Mr. Mayer asked, mostly to himself.

"Because of Barbara La Marr, the silent film star who died of a heroin overdose. You remember her, don't you?" She answered his question with a loaded question of her own, accompanied by a lift of her right eyebrow and a knowing glance.

I'd seen this same expression on her face when her husband was chatting with a beautiful woman near the swimming pool on board the *Normandie*. It wasn't a stretch to guess that there'd been a relationship between Mr. Mayer and Barbara La Marr. The rumors about Mr. Mayer's philandering—some called it preying—had reached all the way to the Viennese acting community.

"Right, right," he answered with the closest to a sheepish expression I'd seen on his face in the four days we'd been at sea.

During the exchange, indeed during the entirety of the men's Ping-Pong game, I hadn't moved from my position next to Mrs. Mayer, leaning against the deck rail, even though the wind was whipping my hair. I knew the safest place on the ship was at the side of the most powerful man's wife, and I had no intention of leaving it. Listening carefully to the men, I realized that I was being discussed as if I weren't present, as if I were chattel—which, after the deal I'd struck, I now was.

The first stage of the deal had been negotiated in London, although Mr. Mayer might not have realized it. To get as far away from Fritz's reach as I could, I had fled Paris for London, just according to my plan. It was a place where my resourceful, connected husband had no reach. Only once I reached the British capital did I stop peering behind me to see if Fritz was stalking me. Until that point, I kept seeing his square jaw and angry eyes in the face of every new man I saw on every train and on every street—just waiting to exact his vengeance for my escape.

Once in London, I knew I'd have to find a way to support myself. The schillings I'd brought and the money I'd get for selling my Cartier jewels would only last so long. Acting was the only profession I knew, but I needed to steer clear of Fritz's influence, and with Hitler on the move and the Nuremberg Laws in place, the only safe place for a Jewish émigré to work as an actress was Hollywood, even if no one knew that émigré was Jewish. From my old acting grapevine, I'd been hearing rumors about the quiet exodus of Jewish theater folk to America for nearly a year.

I'd finagled an introduction to Mr. Mayer through Robert Ritchie, an MGM talent scout I knew through my old mentor Max Reinhardt, who was already working in America himself. According to Mr. Ritchie, Mr. Mayer held his meetings in his suite at the Savoy Hotel. I loathed to enter the space on my own—I could imagine what a "hotel suite meeting" might entail—so I entreated Mr. Ritchie to come along. I said it was for translation purposes, which was true in part. My English was rudimentary, but Mr. Ritchie could translate if I needed, as he had some basic understanding of my other languages. But I also needed him as security.

To my great relief, when the suite door swung open, the meeting was not between Mr. Mayer and myself alone. I was greeted by a phalanx of dark-suited men lining the walls of the meeting room like wallpaper, including Benny Thau, a man Mr. Mayer described as his "second," and Howard Strickling, his press representative. Mr. Mayer gave me a thorough apprising, even asking me to spin around several times and saunter. Then he asked me about *Ecstasy*. "We make wholesome films in America. Films the whole family can see. We don't show parts of the female body that are only meant for a husband's eyes. Understand?"

I nodded. I'd prepared for this question. I knew *Ecstasy* would follow me. "I don't want to make immodest films anymore, Mr. Mayer."

"That's good." He stared at me long and hard, then added, "And no Jews. Americans won't tolerate Jews on screen."

America was a more lenient land, I'd thought. Through my contacts, I'd been told that Mr. Mayer himself was a Russian Jew who was in London, in part, to scoop up Jewish émigré artists to bring back to Hollywood. Not as a savior but because Jewish talent—banned from performing due to the Nuremberg Laws—could be bought for a song.

Did he know I was Jewish or just suspect?

He hadn't really asked me a question, so I thought it best not to answer.

"You're not a Jew, are you?"

"No, of course not, Mr. Mayer," I answered quickly. What else could I say? If my survival in this new life depended on lies, then lies it would be. I was no stranger to them.

"That's good, Mrs. Mandl. Or do I call you Miss Kiesler?" He turned to the other unnamed men lining the back wall of the hotel room. "What the hell are we going to call her? Mandl and Kiesler are too damn German," he yelled.

"Could go with a good American name like Smith," one of them called out.

"Does she look like a Smith?" He screamed at his now redfaced colleague and turned back to me. "If we can come up with a name for you, we'll give you a contract. Standard. Seven years. One hundred and twenty-five dollars per week."

I arched my eyebrow but otherwise kept my face impassive. "One hundred and twenty-five dollars per week? For seven years?"

He puffed on his cigar. "That's the going rate."

I glanced over at Mr. Ritchie with a quizzical expression. He translated "going rate."

Squaring my shoulders, I looked directly through Mr. Mayer's glasses into his dark, cold eyes. He was as ruthless and mercurial as his reputation, but I'd dealt with far worse than him. To get what I wanted, I'd have to be just as tough.

I took an enormous risk, but it was the only gambit that might catapult me to a stratum beyond a low-paid, backup actress who might be easily forgotten. Men never forgot expensive things or people. "That may be the 'going rate' for some unknown. But that's not *my* 'going rate.' I will only accept what

I think I'm worth." With my most penetrating gaze, I stared at each man in the room. Then I pivoted away and left the room.

Mr. Ritchie trailed behind me as I marched out into the hotel hallway. "What the hell are you doing, Hedy? You're blowing your chance," he yelled at my back.

I wasn't certain what "blowing your chance" meant exactly, but the reason for Mr. Ritchie's ire was plain. He believed I'd jettisoned my sole opportunity for a Hollywood career. But Mr. Ritchie had it all wrong. I wasn't done with Mr. Mayer; this was only the first phase of our negotiations. Even though Mr. Mayer didn't realize it.

Turning to face Mr. Ritchie with my staunchest expression, I said, "I'd hoped Mr. Mayer and I could reach an accord today, but I knew we might not. I will get far more than a pathetic one hundred and twenty-five dollars a week. Just watch."

"You don't know what you're doing." He shook his head at me. "You've just refused the most important movie producer in the world, and you won't get a second chance."

I gave him an enigmatic smile. "I have a plan, Mr. Ritchie."

I sold the bracelet from my Cartier set and purchased a ticket for the *Normandie*, which I'd learned would be taking Mr. Mayer across the Atlantic and back home to America in a week's time. I figured several days at sea with the movie tycoon would give me plenty of opportunity to persuade him to grant me a larger contract.

It didn't take days. It took exactly one night.

On the very first evening at sea, I poured myself into my sinuous dark-green gown—a dress that matched my eyes and the only one I'd brought from my vast collection as Mrs. Mandl because I knew its effect—and strode toward the ballroom. Before I stepped inside, I closed my eyes for a moment, reaching deep within myself. I summoned all my power to command attention, much as I'd done before stepping onstage as an actress, and then pushed open the ballroom door.

Standing at the top of the dramatic, winding staircase that led to the dance floor, I waited until all male eyes, including those of Mr. Mayer, lingered on me before I descended. I took my time with each step, making certain that the Hollywood kingpin witnessed the effect I had on the other passengers. I then walked directly over to the Mayers.

I greeted Mrs. Mayer deferentially but only nodded in Mr. Mayer's direction. Having experienced firsthand the demeaning manner in which the wives of powerful men were treated, especially by attractive women, I'd vowed to never behave in such a manner. In any event, Mrs. Mayer could be far more beneficial to my career as a friend, and I wanted to make my allegiances clear.

Mr. Mayer let out a low whistle. "Nicely done."

"Thank you, Mr. Mayer."

"If you can work a room like that, no doubt you can work a camera. I underestimated you—you *are* worth more than the going rate." He puffed on his cigar, looking me up and down. "What about a seven-year contract at five hundred and fifty dollars a week with all the usual escalators? It's the most I've offered any starlet."

"I'm flattered, Mr. Mayer." I kept my voice businesslike, trying to suppress my mounting excitement. "The terms are agreeable."

"Is that a yes?"

"Yes."

"You drive a hard bargain for such a lovely young woman."

"As I said before, I settle for only what I think I'm worth. And if I do not ask, you will not give."

He gave me an appreciative glance, and Mrs. Mayer nodded approvingly. He said, "I like that. I want my family—and anyone who's signed a contract with me and my studio *is* family—to have strong opinions of themselves."

Could this Mr. Mayer actually value powerful women? I suspected this was a statement he bandied about when it suited the occasion but that he didn't really feel. He was too domineering himself to make room for anyone, let alone a woman. Still, since it suited my position at the moment, I'd take his comments at face value.

"Good."

"The deal comes with a caveat," he said, ever the shrewd businessman, making an agreement and then sneaking in one more term.

"What is that?" I could not prevent the irritation from slipping into my voice.

"We need to find you a new name. And a different past."

I returned to the present moment, where the men were still discussing my new name. Stepping away from the deck railings, I drew closer to Mrs. Mayer, in solidarity with her suggestion. She was my ally among these men.

"Hedy Lamarr," Mr. Mayer said, turning to stare at me, hands on hips. "It suits."

A chorus of "sure does" and "yes" sounded out from Mr. Mayer's colleagues.

"Nice. Nothing German-sounding there. Mysterious. A little exotic, like our Hedy here." Mr. Mayer walked over and gave my arm a squeeze.

Mrs. Mayer squeezed my other arm. "Yes, like *our* own Hedy Lamarr." Clearly, she did not want me to belong to him alone; she wanted his hands off me. Her squeeze signaled to him that I was his chattel for movie-making purposes only.

"All right then, we'll rechristen her Hedy Lamarr," Mr. Mayer declared.

*Re*christen? I almost laughed, as he assumed I'd been christened before. The conversion to Christianity in advance of my wedding had been a sloppy, rushed affair, forced upon the Karlskirche priest by Fritz and his promise of a sizable donation. It had required only a verbal formation of faith but no pouring of symbolic waters.

I tried on my new name. "Lamarr," I whispered to myself.

To me, it sounded like the words *la mer*—French for "the sea." Standing as I was on the deck of a vast ship, sailing across the endless ocean waters, I found the name auspicious, even a good portend. From the sea, my new history would be born.

CHAPTER TWENTY-SEVEN

February 22, 1938
Los Angeles, California

I LOST MYSELF FOR A SHORT TIME. THE SEARING SUN OF California, the blue Pacific waters, the newness of the buildings, the parade of men for the taking, and the abundance of smiles burned away the old Hedy and all her tired masks. I forgot—or perhaps pushed to the recesses of my mind—my life as Mrs. Mandl and the threats to Vienna and the people of Döbling at the hand of the German madman, including Mama. After all, California offered a bright, blank canvas upon which I could paint a fresh narrative about my life, and it was so simple to pretend.

Then one day, I awoke, craving the sepia tones of the Austrian buildings, the history abundant under every cobblestone, the smell of apples baking for strudel, and the sharp German edges of my home language. And I felt the stirrings of guilt. For leaving. Alone. Without Mama or anyone else.

Only then did I realize that in accepting a second history, I could never really leave the first history behind. My past life would seep into my new world like water through cracks in a

dam that had never been properly shored—until I faced my
original history square on.

"Come on, Hedy. Get ready, or we'll be late. You know how
highly Mr. Mayer values punctuality. I don't want to risk a role
just because we turned up past the appointed time," my roommate scolded me. Upon my arrival in Hollywood, Mr. Mayer
had assigned me an apartment and roommate, the Hungarian
actress Ilona Massey. She'd also been swept up in Mr. Mayer's
collection of émigré performers. Ilona and I got along famously,
laughing as we tried to perfect our English and adopt a more
American appearance, as Mr. Mayer had instructed.

"Can't we just go to see *Bringing Up Baby* again tonight
instead?" I begged. Ilona and I haunted the local movie theater, where we watched the same movies over and over to learn
proper diction and inflection, and we'd enjoyed *Bringing Up
Baby*, with Katharine Hepburn and Cary Grant.

Ilona laughed but stood firm. "Hedy, we've come too far to
relinquish our chances over a party."

The party, hosted at the Hollywood home of a director
friend of Mr. Mayer, was a command performance. This soiree
wasn't the first required appearance that Ilona and I had made
in the almost six months since we had arrived in California,
although I wished it were the last. These gatherings primarily
functioned as a means for every filmmaker, director, writer, and
studio executive in Hollywood to watch the parade of young
women vying for roles and to make a selection for themselves.
We were like carousel horses on a merry-go-round, each of us

meant to jump higher than the next or catch the eye with more fanciful sparkles than the others, and I hated it. But what other choice did I have at the moment?

Ilona and I zipped each other into the machine-made dresses we'd purchased at Broadway, the local department store, for these sorts of occasions. We then hopped in a cab to the mansion where Mr. Mayer and the Hollywood folks awaited. While the Tudor-style house probably impressed most of its visitors, to me, it seemed a sad, paltry approximation of the true Bavarian schlosses and villas that I'd not only visited but once owned. For a fleeting moment, I felt a longing for the luxurious life I'd lived with Fritz as Mrs. Mandl.

Fritz. Where was he at this moment? Hosting a ball at Schloss Schwarzenau for the Nazi officials now firmly implanted in the Austrian government? Did he have a blond Germanic maiden on his arm as he negotiated the terms of a weapons deal with one of Hitler's emissaries? Through a lawyer I'd met in London, I'd initiated divorce proceedings, and I knew my lawyer had sent Fritz notice of the action. I'd expected to receive word from him via my lawyer's address— not mine, of course, as I'd given instructions to keep it from Fritz at all costs—but I'd heard nothing. Not even the angry ravings of a jilted husband, the monster who hid behind banal pleasantries when others were in the room. And Mama never once mentioned Fritz in the curt letters she wrote in response to mine.

Ilona and I sauntered into the gathering, drawing lascivious attention that we did not seek. As we grabbed cocktails from a passing waiter, we mapped out the room. We tried to be strategic about these parties, ensuring that we spoke to the most prominent filmmakers, the ones preparing to hire their casts, and making certain that Mr. Mayer saw us in order to receive credit for attending. But we tried to work as a pair to avoid compromising positions with any of the men present. We'd heard too many stories about aspiring starlets—usually girls without a contract, connection, or financial means—being preyed upon in empty bedrooms and dark hallways.

As we squeezed past a group of men I recognized as RKO Pictures studio executives, I heard one of them jeer at the other, "You can look at those two, but don't even think of touching. They're Mayer's property."

I whispered the man's phrase to Ilona and asked, "What does that mean?" But for his suggestive tone, I assumed he meant that we were under contract to MGM Studios.

"That Mayer owns us. On and off the set," Ilona explained with a disgusted look in her eyes.

I felt sick to my stomach. I'd sworn when I left Fritz that I'd never allow another man to own me.

Seeing the expression on my face, Ilona linked her arm in mine. She pulled me toward the lounge chairs near the pool, upon which hundreds of bobbing candles floated. I might have found the sight lovely but for the RKO executive's comment. Had I just traded ownership by Fritz for another sort of possession?

"Listen, Hedy," Ilona said once we sat down. "We don't have to allow that ridiculous talk to touch us. Not really. We're not going to succumb to the sort of behavior those men intimated, and we don't have to dignify it by listening to it either."

I raised my eyebrows, wondering if I should broach my real worry. Deciding that I must, I asked, "But does Mr. Mayer think it's true?"

Before she could answer, the director Reinhold Schünzel approached us. Ilona had been hoping to speak with him tonight, as she'd heard a rumor that he was casting for *Balalaika*, a musical romance that would suit her talents well. When he asked if she'd like to get a drink at the bar to "discuss a project," she glanced over at me excitedly, and I gave her a nod. This sort of connection was the reason we subjected ourselves to these parties, although we both knew she must be careful. A drink at the bar could mean many things.

I was at loose ends for a moment and had begun to think about grabbing a taxi home when Mr. Mayer appeared as if from thin air. He settled his girth next to me on the narrow lounge chair. "Miss Kiesler. Oops, I mean, Miss Lamarr," he said in a deliberate reminder that he was my creator.

"Hello, Mr. Mayer. Are you enjoying your evening?" I used my best approximation of an American accent. I'd been gobbling down English hungrily, happy to leave behind the language of my husband's Nazi dinner table. Neither the German language nor a German accent went down well in Hollywood these days. Or anywhere in America, for that matter.

"I am, Miss Lamarr. How are you liking Hollywood so far?" he asked.

"Would you like the truth?" I guessed that Mr. Mayer was used to fawning starlets, eager to flatter him into any opportunity. I wanted him to know that I was different from those girls, that I wouldn't do *anything* for a role, as those dirty men suggested. Something he should already know from our first meeting at the Savoy Hotel.

"Of course."

"Well, the truth is I'm rather let down."

"What?" He seemed genuinely surprised. "How could all this"—he gestured to the pool and the mansion—"let you down?"

"Don't forget from where I came, Mr. Mayer. Real castles and villas were my everyday life. But the opportunity to act is worth the sacrifice." I paused for effect. "Assuming I have that opportunity?"

His eyes narrowed behind his round glasses, and I recognized the hard, possessive glare staring out at me. I'd seen it on Fritz's face many times before. "Well, hopefully, *you* won't let *me* down, Hedy. Especially not now that I've made you part of my MGM family."

"Why do you mean, Mr. Mayer? I've been practicing my English and working on my appearance, just as you asked." I thought but didn't say that he knew precisely how I'd been spending my time. Mr. Mayer hired security folks to keep Ilona and me under regular surveillance.

"I mean, I hope you understand that if you're *nice* to me, those opportunities could be available sooner rather than later. In fact, I have a role I've been considering you for," he said, reaching out to stroke my knee in the safety of the dark night.

I'd been right about Mr. Mayer's expectations.

Still smarting from the RKO executive's offensive comment and brewing over Mr. Mayer's assumption that I belonged to him, I said, "No man owns me, Mr. Mayer. And no man ever will. Not even you."

Unmistakable rage appeared on his face. He started to sput-
ter vitriol toward me when we both heard his name being called.

Mrs. Mayer appeared on the periphery of the pool and
made a beeline for me and her husband. "Hedy," she said, then
gave me a warm hug and sat down on the lounge chair across
from us. "I had no idea you'd arrived."

She glanced over at her husband with obvious suspicion.
"Why are you keeping Hedy hidden away in the corner? Aren't
you always screaming at your actors and actresses to mingle at
these awful parties?"

A laugh escaped me, quite against my will and my mood.
So Mrs. Mayer thought these parties were awful too? I wasn't
surprised, but I was astonished to hear her admit it. Although
she was a bright woman with a strong will, I could imagine
that these parties were intolerable for her. It was comforting
to know that I wasn't alone in suffering through these long,
painful evenings.

I decided to use the appearance of Mrs. Mayer to my
advantage—to force Mr. Mayer's hand. "Your husband has
good reason for this quiet corner, Mrs. Mayer."

"He does, does he?" Her hand slipped onto her hip, and she
looked ready for battle.

"Yes, he was just telling me about the movie role he's secured
for me. Apparently, it's quite hush-hush."

"How exciting," she said to me, leaning forward with
another squeeze. But she chastised her husband, saying, "I've
been telling you that it's time to get Hedy off the bench."

I wasn't familiar with the English phrase "on the bench,"
but I guessed it meant not working.

"It's only been a few months, Margaret. Anyway, she needed to polish up her accent. We couldn't have her barking out German on the set. What would the audience have thought? That we hire Krauts? Doesn't seem too American."

"I suppose that's true. But her English sounds quite polished now. It only has that hint of European around the edges. Nothing too specific, just as you like."

"And that's why I found a role for her *now*," he snapped, undoubtedly irritated at the position in which I'd placed him.

"Do you mind telling us about it, Mr. Mayer?" I asked, all deferential smiles now in Mrs. Mayer's presence.

I'd boxed in the studio head. He was fuming but knew he had to behave in front of his wife. "I think I've found just the vehicle that will exploit your on-screen appearance while utilizing your differences—your otherness—to best advantage. You're going to become Gaby, a French tourist visiting the Casbah, the labyrinthine native quarter of Algiers. In the film—we're calling it *Algiers*—your character inadvertently draws out a notorious French jewel thief, Pepe le Moko, sparking the movie's action."

"It sounds ideal," I commented, and I meant it. "Who will play Pepe?"

"A French actor called Charles Boyer."

"I'm familiar with his work. He's excellent."

"Then it's all settled," Mrs. Mayer pronounced. "You'll make sure that all goes well on set, won't you, L.B.? That no one gives Hedy any kind of trouble?" She arched her eyebrow, intimating that I shouldn't be subjected to harassment from anyone, including him.

"Of course, Margaret."

She turned back to me. "Come, Hedy. I have some lovely women for you to meet."

CHAPTER TWENTY-EIGHT

March 4, 1938
Los Angeles, California

Y OU'RE WANTED ON SET IN FIVE MINUTES, MISS Lamarr," the runner yelled into my dressing room. Susie raced to finish my eyeliner and zip up my gown. I didn't want to be the one holding up filming, as the director, John Cromwell, was notoriously punctual. This role had been too hard-won from Mr. Mayer to risk.

Once she finished, Susie stared at me in the mirror over my dressing table, crowded with pots of ruby-red lipstick and nail polish, black eyeliner, and pale face powder. The bubbly young woman assigned to be my dresser was the antithesis of my chilly Theater an der Wien dresser, Mrs. Lubbig, whose reticence I sometimes missed. She squealed, "You look gorgeous."

I stood up and studied myself in the three-way mirror at the back of my dressing room. My heavy makeup looked lurid in the bright light of the dressing room, but I knew it would work well for the cameras. My costume consisted of a black silk sheath topped by a luxurious white silk jacket, gleaming pearls, and light-catching diamond earrings. All fake, of course, but glittery. The director and costume designer Irene Gibbons deemed this to be the appropriate attire for a wealthy Frenchwoman touring the rather impoverished tangle of alley-ways of the Casbah. It was ridiculous to think that a rich tourist would even travel through Algiers' underbelly, especially in this ensemble, but this was Hollywood.

The one decision the costume designer got right was the bold black-and-white palette of my costume. It was striking, in the same way my Mainbocher wedding dress had been. The limited color scheme enhanced my dark hair and pale skin, made even paler with powder, and I knew it would make for a dramatic impression on film. The many, many movies Ilona and I had watched to perfect our English had taught me more than the appropriate accent; I'd learned about light and shadow from the American films as well.

I was giving my appearance a final once-over when Susie's hand appeared on my shoulder. I nearly jumped. Americans were so familiar with one another, almost from the moment they met. Mrs. Lubbig would never have dreamed of touching me unless necessary to dress me for a role, apply my makeup, or style my hair. But I was trying to be an American now, and I stifled my Austrian impulse to squirm away from Susie's touch.

"Actually, Miss Lamarr, you look glam," she said with a giggle. "Wait until they get a load of you out there on the soundstage."

What did Susie mean by *glam* and *get a load of*? From the expression on her face, I guessed that they were compliments of some sort, but I sometimes had trouble making sense of her colloquialisms.

I nodded at Susie, deriving a bit of what she called moxie from her praise, and opened the door of my dressing room. The hallway leading to the soundstage felt unnaturally long, and my black satin pumps clicked with uncommon loudness. Or was it just my nerves?

The clanking of equipment and the low hum of chatter soon drowned out the sound of my heels. I arrived on set to little fanfare. Industry of all sorts surrounded me—carpenters and grips and property masters and actors and extras appeared frenzied from their tasks—bringing to life a North African city right here on a soundstage in America. I was no stranger to theatrical scenery, but somehow, this elaborate construction was different from any stage or movie set upon which I'd performed. This felt vast and real. And I felt overwhelmed.

Why did I ever think that my short time as a European actress qualified me for Hollywood?

When no one gave me a second glance, I summoned my courage and walked toward a stern-featured man with graying hair who seemed to be at the center of this beehive of activity. Perhaps he could give me some guidance. He looked up from a rather heated debate with a cameraman and stared at me. Finally, he exclaimed, "Why, you must be our Gaby!"

I stretched out my hand to shake his, relieved to have been identified. From his authoritative manner of speech, I guessed at his identity. "I am, sir. Are you Mr. Cromwell?"

As we shook hands, he said, "I am indeed. But please call me John."

"And please call me Hedy. I appreciate the opportunity to be your Gaby."

Mr. Cromwell looked me up and down. "You're every bit as stunning as Mayer promised. And it's a good thing, as we've got big plans for you in this scene."

His announcement about "big plans" for Gaby both delighted and relieved me. The storyline of *Algiers* was chockfull of action and intrigue, but those scenes were off-limits for my character Gaby, who functioned as forbidden fruit for the main character, the jewel thief Pepe. The ornamental nature of my character didn't surprise me—most roles for women in Hollywood were decorative only—but the chance to give texture and heft to Gaby was an intriguing, if unexpected, opportunity. I'd thought about scenes in which Gaby joined in the chase instead of sitting by ornamentally. Still, no matter the scope of the role, the scale of the set and staff reminded me to be grateful for the opportunity.

"I'm excited to hear that, Mr. Cromwell, I mean John. I have many ideas about how we can enliven Gaby, and I'd love to talk to you about them."

John's brows knitted in confusion, but he didn't respond directly to my offer. "Well, let's introduce you to our cinematographer, James Wong Howe. He has something special in mind for you."

We strode across the soundstage to a corner of the set where a narrow alleyway, dwarfed by faux clay buildings, had been built. There, a short Chinese man, sporting a beret and a cravat around his neck, was issuing orders to two cameramen about equipment position and to three grips, stationed on top of the clay buildings, about lighting angles.

"Jimmy, I've got our Gaby here," John called.

Mr. Howe pivoted toward us. "Ah, we've been waiting for you, Miss Lamarr. The scene has been set for your arrival."

"You know what to do, Jimmy. I will leave her in your capable hands," John said, then marched off across the soundstage.

"Are you ready?" Mr. Howe asked. He hadn't asked me to call him Jimmy.

"I know my lines for this scene, Mr. Howe, but I'm afraid I haven't had the opportunity to rehearse with my fellow actors. And John mentioned you have new plans for this scene, but I don't know what they are."

"Don't let that worry you," he said in the calming voice one might use with an anxious child. "The plans we have for you won't require a lot of rehearsal."

"All right," I answered slowly. I still wasn't sure what Mr. Howe wanted from me.

"Before we film the scene with all the extras, we're going to make sure we have the cameras and lighting just right." He took me by the hand and situated me on an alleyway step where tape marked an X. "I've created a signature lighting for you, one that will illuminate you from above and cast precise shadows on your symmetrical features. I've toyed with this idea for years, but I've never had an actress with a countenance as perfect as yours."

"Thank you, Mr. Howe," I said, although he hadn't said it as a compliment but as a simple observation.

He lifted a finger under my chin, studying my face from several perspectives.

He stepped back and directed me. "Stand perfectly still. And open your lips just enough to tantalize, but not enough to show your teeth."

Positioning myself as he'd asked and remaining immobile, I waited. Mr. Howe ordered the cameramen and grips to make slight modifications to their equipment, and then the cinematographer stared at me through the lens of the central camera. I hadn't moved, so I couldn't imagine what he found interesting.

Long minutes passed, and I wondered what Gaby would be doing next. What were the "big plans" to which the director had referred? Surely this wasn't the entirety of my scene.

"Should we block Gaby's next actions?" I asked after I'd estimated that ten minutes had passed.

"What do you mean, Miss Lamarr?" Mr. Howe answered from behind the lens.

"John Cromwell mentioned 'big plans.' Shouldn't we practice the movement we're inserting into the scene?"

"Miss Lamarr, this extended shot—with its carefully plotted lighting and camerawork—is the 'big plan.'"

"But I'm not doing anything." I was confused.

"You don't need to *do* anything," Mr. Howe said, the irritation unmistakable in his voice. I could almost hear him think, *Why is she asking these inane questions? Why isn't she just doing as she's told?* "The director's vision is to present you, an emblem of womankind, as a cypher, a mystery that Pepe, and the audience along with him, needs to unpuzzle. And you must know that the best way a woman can inspire mystery is with her beauty and her silence."

Silence. Once again, silence was required of me. I'd left Fritz and his world behind in part because all he wanted was a mute, compliant shell. Although I knew it had been fanciful thinking, I'd hoped for more here. But it seemed that Hollywood sought exactly the same.

CHAPTER TWENTY-NINE

March 13, 1938
Los Angeles, California

S USIE BEGAN HELPING ME OUT OF THE BLACK EVENING
gown and pearls required for the *Algiers* scene I'd just
reshot—the moment Gaby and Pepe first laid eyes on each
another. This scene, like many of my scenes, required me to sit
stock-still for long moments while the camera lingered on my
face. I'd begun to feel more comfortable on the set, but for these
awkward interludes, when the rest of the cast had to recede quietly and wait while Mr. Howe's lens finished with me. During
those endless minutes, I tried to summon the power I'd felt
onstage to bring texture and interest to Gaby, and I hoped that
energy showed on-screen. Still, I couldn't help but feel that I'd
been relegated to nothing more than a shop mannequin.

The thin walls of my dressing room shuddered with a loud
knock. As Susie cracked open the door, I tied my silk robe
around me tightly. On set, business could be conducted anywhere, at any moment, and I knew—with *Ecstasy* in my past—I
needed to maintain my modesty.

My former roommate, Ilona, peered through the open

door, rolled-up newspaper in hand. A couple of weeks ago, we'd decided to get our own places, and I'd rented a small six-room house high in the Hollywood Hills with enough yard for a few animals to keep me company. But Ilona and I were still quite close, particularly since we'd made friends with a sympathetic group of Hollywood émigrés like ourselves, including directors Otto Preminger and my old mentor Max Reinhardt, and Jewish Americans, such as producer Walter Wanger. Over dinners, we kept each other abreast of European developments that weren't making their way into the American newspapers. And even though the man I'd begun to date, the actor Reggie Gardiner, was English and not continental like the rest of us, he supplied the group with information from his contacts as well. Of all my suitors, I'd chosen him to date because of his kindly nature and nonthreatening manner. No more Fritz Mandls for me.

From Ilona's expression and the newspaper she carried, I understood that she wanted us to talk alone. "Susie," I said, "do you mind getting us some coffees from the commissary?"

"Of course not, Miss Lamarr," she answered brightly. I understood Susie's English well enough but not her perpetually effervescent personality. It was as unnerving as the constantly sunny California weather.

As she closed the door behind her, Ilona handed me the newspaper. Closer to me now, I saw that the rims of her eyes were red from crying. Before I could glance at the paper, she asked, "Have you seen this?"

"No, I've been on set all day. Is it about—"

She didn't need me to finish to know what I asked. "Yes."

We had been waiting for news about Austrian political developments, about which Mama seemed to remain blissfully ignorant in her correspondence, perhaps intentionally so, knowing her. A few days earlier, in response to rioting by the Austrian Nazis and German insistence that Nazi sympathizer Arthur Seyss-Inquart be named minister of public security with unbridled control, we'd heard that Chancellor Schuschnigg—the man who'd ousted Ernst von Starhemberg for pronouncing him too soft on the Germans—called for a referendum on the issue of Austrian unification with Germans. In response, Hitler threatened Schuschnigg with invasion. Ilona was Hungarian, not Austrian, but she looked at Hitler's actions as a blueprint of what might come to pass for Hungary. Could Hitler really overtake Austria? What would the world community do if the Germans tried?

Ilona couldn't wait for me to read the article. The news was bursting from her. "Hedy, it's unbelievable. Yesterday, the German army crossed the border into Austria as we feared. Do you know what they faced when they arrived?"

"No," I said, even though I'd already envisioned the Austrian troops battling against Hitler's forces at the key security points I'd toured with Fritz over the years. I wondered if, once again, Fritz would be outfitting both sides of the skirmishes. Or had he finally been unsuccessful at playing both ends against the middle, as was his wont, and been forced to flee?

"The sight of cheering Austrians waving Nazi flags—and no military resistance. None at all. Incredibly, the Austrian government had ordered the army not to fight back. Hitler just drove in."

"What?" I was shocked. Sitting down at my dressing table chair, my legs shaking, I asked, "No opposition? Nothing?"

"No. It seems that in the days before the actual takeover, the SS had secretly rounded up all potential dissenters. Even still, Hitler was surprised at the welcoming reception he got. He had intended to demolish the Austrian military, leaving it as a puppet state with Seyss-Inquart as head of a pro-Nazi government, but he didn't need to take those measures. The Austrians were so supportive, he just absorbed Austria into the Reich."

"And just like that, Austria became part of Germany." My voice shook as I said the words.

"Just like that," Ilona answered, the incredulity apparent in her tone.

The Anschluss, the invasion and conquest of my home that Papa and I had feared and that had served as the impetus for my marriage, had happened. Even though I knew Ilona was telling me the truth—in fact, I knew better than almost anyone else that this event had been inevitable—the news still astonished me. Part of me had never believed that this day would actually arrive, and I'd prayed that it wouldn't, even though I didn't have a specific god to whom I prayed.

In the days just before and following my escape from Fritz, I'd begun to acknowledge that the Nazis might well conquer Austria. I'd presumed that Hitler's military might and the fanaticism of his followers would be hard for Austria's forces, ill-equipped under the weak Schuschnigg, to beat. But I never expected the Austrian people to welcome the madman into their midst.

Where was Mama when the Nazi troops marched down

the Viennese streets to the sound of welcoming cheers? Surely she wouldn't have waved a welcoming flag. But she'd probably sat in her parlor sipping tea while the tanks rolled down the streets, pretending that she couldn't feel her house vibrate. Was she safe?

I needed to get her out of Austria before her intentional obliviousness damned her. But would she allow me to try, now that Germany controlled Austria? If so, how would I go about extricating her? I didn't even know what the Austrian emigration rules would be under German control or the nature of America's immigration laws. I'd entered the country on Mr. Mayer's arm and influence, the sticky web of paperwork and approvals smoothed out for me.

I started to cry, and Ilona knelt by my side, hugging me. "Your mother is still there, isn't she?" she asked.

I nodded but spoke nothing of the thoughts that plagued me. What would happen to the Austrian Jews now? Would the Nuremberg Laws be applied to them, to Mama? Having listened to Hitler's plans to remove Jews from German society from his own mouth, I was fairly certain of the answer, although I couldn't speak the words aloud to anyone.

To utter such words would have been tantamount to admitting that I was a Jew myself and that I'd been privy to this event before it happened.

And in Hollywood, there were no Jews.

CHAPTER THIRTY

January 14–15, 1939
Los Angeles, California

*A*LGIERS CHANGED EVERYTHING AND NOTHING.
The fame I'd sought came. I walked down red carpets for the premiers of *Algiers*, fans lining the streets and calling my name. Women everywhere adopted what the newspapers called the "Lamarr look"—dark hair, often dyed, with a center part and cascading waves; symmetrical, arched eyebrows; pale skin; and full, glistening lips. The look I'd thought was so American, one cultivated at Mr. Mayer's insistence, now became associated with the "exoticism" of Hedy Lamarr, the irony of which gave Ilona and me a good chuckle.

The money came as well. While holding Mr. Mayer at bay, who persisted in his advances, I insisted on more compensation than I'd originally negotiated. The "cult" of Hedy Lamarr gave me the courage and leverage to insist on higher salaries to accompany the box office profits everyone believed my future films would garner.

On the heels of the *Algiers* release, my lingering terror of Fritz dissolved as well. My divorce was granted. Even when the legal proceedings provided Fritz access to my address and he began to send letters, his words were oddly conciliatory now that he had no legal control over me and his own power had waned. He'd been ousted from Austria when his allegiance with the Nazis frayed, and he'd retreated to South America, where he'd begun squirreling away most of his assets during our marriage. By reconnecting with me, he seemed only to want the borrowed fame that came with having a well-known ex-wife, nothing more, but I gave him nothing. The divorce not only freed me from my fears, but also gave me liberty to date whomever I chose. This license gave me renewed hunger to bounce from man to man, seeking a safe haven in their arms but never surrendering my autonomy, and men other than the kindly but ultimately dull Reggie Gardiner followed.

But no matter all these men, a deep loneliness trailed after me like an abandoned dog, barking into the silence whenever the noise of the crowds or the whispers of a man stopped. Sometimes, as a sort of balm for my loneliness, I allowed myself to follow in the rapid wake of the Americans—who moved quickly, as if they feared slowing down might cause history to encrust upon them like a barnacle—but then the memories I tried to evade overtook me, and guilt took hold. How could I justify living in such abundance when terrors and deprivations were happening daily in Austria? When Jews were subjected to brutal attacks on the streets by swastika-wearing thugs and stripped of their rights by the Nuremberg Laws? When an anti-Semitic frenzy ignited November pogroms in which Jewish stores were looted and vandalized and Jewish synagogues were burned, including those in Döbling? All horrors about which

I had foreknowledge, in a general way. My American life seemed folly against the mounting darkness, and the lightness it required grew ever harder to muster.

So I cleaved myself in two. By day, I painted on the lips and eyebrows and enigmatic glances for the camera, assuming the mask of Hedy Lamarr. By night, I became Hedy Kiesler again, a woman beset by worry about my people, both Viennese and Jewish, even though I'd never really thought of myself as Jewish until I left Austria. I began to understand that in fleeing Austria without forewarning anyone about the seriousness of Hitler's plans, I owed the Austrian people—particularly the Jews—a tremendous debt. But I didn't know how I could help anyone. Except Mama.

It sickened me to think that I didn't persuade her hard enough to leave during our last meeting together. Over teatime, I'd allowed myself to become angry over her criticism of Papa, and I'd permitted myself to experience a frisson of fear over what she might reveal about my plans to Fritz. And those emotions took hold, causing me to shut down any efforts at persuasion the moment Mama expressed an unwillingness to leave Vienna. I should have tamped down my feelings and told her what I knew about the Anschluss and Hitler.

Before, I'd given up too easily. I wouldn't let that happen again. I would find a way to extricate Mama from Austria.

Her most recent letter told me that I no longer needed to focus my efforts on convincing her to leave her precious Vienna. Not that Mama wrote in her letters directly about the horrors occurring there; she was justifiably worried that Nazi government officials might scan letters heading abroad and exact retribution. Instead, I sensed her dread over these horrific events in every cautious turn of phrase and every word she *didn't* write.

Dear Hedy,

I hope your new life in Hollywood continues to treat you well. Your success is something you have always sought—

I took a deep breath as I read these words, trying not to let the backhanded compliment bother me. Mama was constitutionally incapable of praise—god forbid that she congratulate me on my work in *Algiers* instead of just saying film success was something I "sought"—but I couldn't allow her natural negativity to deter me from my course. I continued reading.

I think often of our conversation over tea before your departure. I realize that I should have heeded your advice, Hedy. But mothers often fail to credit their daughters' knowledge, and I am no exception. I wonder now if it is too late.

In the event that it is, Hedy, I want to correct a misunderstanding that arose between us over that same tea. During our conversation, you shared with me your belief that I'd long withheld affection from you out of spite or an innate dislike of you. Nothing could be further from the truth. I sought only to temper your father's unmoderated adulation and indulgence of you. I worried what might happen to

a very pretty child, already adored for her beauty by
society at large, who is told that everything she does
and thinks is perfect by both her parents. It was not
a practice I found easy, but contrary to your belief,
I did it out of love.

Tears streamed down my face at these words, the closest
Mama had ever come to an expression of sentimentality toward
me or an apology. Her letter almost made clear another thing:
Mama was ready, even desperate, to leave. I needed only to
figure out how to get her to America.

The next evening, a chance conversation pointed the way. At a
Hollywood party, two of my European friends scampered off
to chat with a director with whom they hoped to work, abandoning me to a rather dull, mousy fellow who'd been hovering
around the periphery of our conversation. I almost walked away
without bothering to excuse myself when I recalled something
he'd said to my friend—that he was an attorney.

"You mentioned that you're a lawyer?" Given that he'd
been invited to this party populated primarily by movie folks, I
guessed that he didn't practice immigration law. Still, I figured
it didn't hurt to inquire. At the very least, perhaps he could give
me the name of an attorney expert in the field.

His eyes lit up when I turned my gaze upon him, as if he
couldn't actually believe I was talking to him. I almost couldn't
believe it myself. He stammered for a second and then said,
"Y-yes, yes, I am."

I didn't see any point in making unnecessary chatter, so I was direct. "Do you know anything about getting people admitted to America from Europe?"

"A l-little," he said, still stammering. Was I making him nervous, or was his speech an unfortunate habit? "It's not my area, but I know the laws generally. Can I assume you're asking about someone in particular?"

I nodded.

"Where is he or she coming from?" The more comfortable he became, the more the stammer disappeared.

"Austria."

"Hmm," he said. His forehead, partially hidden by his large glasses, furrowed. "Well, to start, America doesn't have a refugee policy, only an immigration policy. We have a strict quota system where only a certain number of people from each country are given permission to immigrate each year. As soon as the quota is met, applicants are rejected—whether it's early in the year or late."

"How do I find out whether America is still accepting people from Austria or whether the quota has been filled?"

"Well, I think Roosevelt merged the quotas for Austria and Germany now that the two countries have unified—"

I almost screamed that the countries weren't "unified" but that Germany forcibly took over Austria for itself. But the lawyer was talking, and I needed to hear him out.

"Still," he continued, "I'm sure I could find out the quota number for you. But you should know that it's more complicated than just the question of whether slots remain. Has this person started the paperwork?"

I hadn't thought of the administrative piece of this puzzle yet. I shook my head.

"Well, America has made immigration quite the bewildering process. On purpose. The government uses the hoops of its onerous application as a deterrent."

"Why?"

"So as few immigrants as possible can enter the country, of course," he went on, oblivious to the dreadful nature of his statement. "Here's the gist of it. The applicant first registers with the American consulate and gets on the waiting list for an American visa. While they're biding their time, they have to a collect a long list of documents to submit, things like identity papers, police certificates, exit and transit permissions, and a financial affidavit, because the applicant has to prove that they can support themselves. The trick of these papers is that they all have expiration dates, so you've got to obtain them and get off that waiting list to submit them before they expire. Or you've got to do it all over again. The timing of this paperwork is so complicated—nearly impossible—that they call it the 'paper wall.'"

I nodded, my mind spinning at all the requirements Mama would have to meet to hurdle this "wall." I couldn't even guess at how long the process would take. Could she stay safe while we waited? I couldn't take the chance. "Is there any way to shortcut the process?"

"Well, it would take some pretty high-up connections. But if you knew someone with ties in the federal government, you might stand a chance at moving someone up the waiting list—or at eliminating some or all of the paperwork."

I knew what I had to do. Without even catching the lawyer fellow's name—and worse, without even thanking him for his advice—I disappeared into the throngs of partygoers. I ran toward the one person I knew with precisely the sort of "ties" I needed—Mr. Mayer.

CHAPTER THIRTY-ONE

January 28, 1939
Los Angeles, California

S HOULD WE RUN AWAY FROM HERE AND GET MARRIED?" A
voice asked from the shadows of the pool deck.

I jumped, nearly dropping my cigarette. I came outside to
be alone and hadn't spotted another soul. If I'd known a man
was out here on his own, I would have avoided the area and
sought a different sanctuary away from the terrible gathering.

The crowded party was precisely the sort of Hollywood
soiree I despised, but Mr. Mayer insisted on my attendance
and, given that he'd agreed to help with Mama's situation, I
didn't dare refuse. This celebration of a doleful film premier
consisted of gossiping about the latest Hollywood contracts,
jostling for roles in upcoming films, and enduring the leers of
drunken studio executive and filmmakers. I would have much
preferred to spend the evening chatting about political and cultural developments in the homes of my like-minded European
friends or alone in my new house, playing the piano or tinkering with a few scientific creations inspired by the years sitting at
Fritz's dinner table and listening to men discuss inventions. But

here I was, listening to Mr. Mayer make self-congratulatory pronouncements about me to the sycophantic "boys" always in tow: "The old man isn't such a bad judge of talent, wouldn't you say? I looked at this dame once and said to myself, that girl's a star. And in a very short time, I made her into one."

Normally, I'd flee before I had to make conversation with a stranger, especially an unknown man. But something about the tenor of this gentleman's voice was familiar, even compelling. Not to mention he was amusing. His entirely inappropriate and overly friendly question made me laugh. No mean feat these days.

"Did you bring the wedding ring?" I called back into the darkness. How would this fellow's banter fare with a bit of a challenge?

"Of course. Assuming you like diamonds?"

"I prefer emeralds, but diamonds will do."

"I was thinking of an emerald necklace as a wedding present after the ceremony."

"You know your bride all too well." I nearly giggled.

"After all these years, darling"—his voice grew louder—"I better."

A figure of a man emerged from the shadow of the terrace. As the man drew closer, I realized that he was quite tall, perhaps six foot three inches. Just like Papa.

"Yes, you better," I said quietly, wary of who was about to materialize.

Although I still couldn't make out his features with any specificity, the dim light from the party inside began to illuminate his face, as it must have illuminated mine. "Oh my god, you're Hedy Lamarr." He sounded surprised but not cowed. I liked that. Since *Algiers*, men were shy around me, or overly aggressive.

"Oh my god, I am," I said in mock surprise, then took a long drag of my cigarette. Ash dropped from the tip, and I realized that my fingers were quivering from my proximity to this attractive older man. His fastidiously combed hair and immaculate suit contrasted with his easy smile, warm eyes, and comfortable manner. I felt like I knew him, and no one else had roused that sensation in me since I'd arrived in Hollywood.

"I guess I should apologize for being presumptuous," he offered, but I didn't hear any contrition or discomfort in his voice.

"Please don't. If you do, I'll have to banish you back to that corner so we can carry on a normal conversation."

He laughed, a deep, hearty chuckle. Again, just like Papa.

"What brings you outside on a chilly January night when a warm party brews indoors?" he asked.

"I'm Austrian. This is hardly chilly weather."

"You didn't answer my question."

"I guess the conversation is better outdoors than inside."

The white of his teeth flashed as he smiled. "A compliment from Miss Lamarr? I'm flattered."

"Who said I was talking about *your* side of the conversation? Maybe I was talking about mine."

He laughed again. "No one told me that your wit matched your beauty."

"Flattery will get you everywhere and nowhere, Mister..." My voice trailed off, realizing that I didn't know who he was. Although if he'd been invited to this party, he must be in the movie business, which made me like him less.

"Markey. Gene Markey."

I knew the name. He was a screenwriter, but I remembered that he'd also been married to the actress Joan Bennett and had a young daughter with her. He wasn't a notorious womanizer, but he wasn't *not* a notorious womanizer either. The knowledge left me slightly off balance.

With his smooth conversational skills, he filled in the pause. "Shall we leave this wretched party? I know a little bar just around the corner that might just suit."

It went against my personal rules to join him. After all, I didn't really know this man, and Hollywood was full of predators. But I was drawn to him. For once, I let go of the reins and took a chance.

Nodding, I linked my arm in his, and together, we stepped off the terrace and onto the road. Walking alongside him, I felt unexpectedly calm and safe, sensations I hadn't experienced since Papa's death. His presence left me wondering whether I'd finally met a man with whom I needn't play a part.

CHAPTER THIRTY-TWO

July 10, 1939
Los Angeles, California

M Y BASKET LADEN WITH WILDFLOWERS, I PUSHED OPEN
the back door of our one-story white farmhouse on
Benedict Canyon Drive, which we'd dubbed Hedgerow Farms,
a cocoon of calm with its white walls and white furniture, the
only splashes of color found in rugs, art, and flowers. I walked
into the living room. Gene was sprawled over the white sofa,
fast asleep, with pages of his script scattered about the red carpet. Donner, our Great Dane, had attempted to curl his enormous body into the tiny section of cushion open by Gene's feet.
The twosome radiated contentment, a deeply rooted happiness
in which I'd just begun to trust. When my private demons slept,
that was.

I crept into the kitchen, not wanting to disturb them. I
pulled out a simple white porcelain vase from the cupboard, filling it with water. After trimming the ends off the colorful spray
of flowers, I slid them into the vase and began arranging them.

Suddenly, I was swirling in the air in Gene's arms. The full
skirts of my dirndl spun in circles, and I giggled. Placing me

down upon the ground, he said, "My little hausfrau, how fetching you look in your homely garb."

"Thank you, kind sir." I curtsied as he wrapped me in his arms.

I would have never guessed that our chance meeting on a stranger's pool deck would lead to a marriage less than eight weeks later. I supposed the familiarity and comfort I'd felt with Gene from the very start had made the decision surprisingly easy. But I couldn't stop wondering, in the midst of a European war from which I'd just managed to extricate Mama, why I deserved this slice of happiness. If I'd stayed in Austria, my reality would have been very different.

"Penny for your thoughts?" he asked.

But I didn't want to tell him what I was really thinking. I'd never shared with Gene the secret of my Jewish heritage or that my ex-husband sold weapons to Mussolini and Hitler. He knew that I'd been married before, of course, but nothing more. I didn't dare tell him the secrets I kept buried deep within myself.

"I was remembering our wedding day," I answered instead of speaking the truth.

We'd been sitting over the remains of a delicious seafood dinner at a favorite beachside restaurant. It was early March, and it'd been a long Friday on set for us both. I'd been rehearsing for *Lady of the Tropics*, and Gene was working on a script rewrite. We'd both be back at it on Monday morning, and I looked forward to the rare weekend respite. My directors often demanded I work on weekends.

"Let's get married tomorrow," Gene said, taking my hand and planting a kiss on my palm.

I laughed. A lively conversationalist and ardent practical joker, Gene never failed to get a chuckle out of me, much as Papa might share a silly riddle or leave a mysterious wrapped figurine for me on my bedside table. At almost twenty years older than me, having lived whole lives as a decorated naval officer in the Great War and a novelist before he met me, his experience and unflappability made me feel secure.

Gene's dark eyes were serious. "I'm not joking, Hedy. I want us to start a life together, and I don't want to wait."

I stopped laughing. "Is this a proposal?"

Gene appeared as though he'd surprised himself. "I suppose it is."

I was flabbergasted. While I felt closer to Gene and safer with him than any another man, including Fritz in our early days, we hadn't even been together for two months. And I'd promised myself that I'd never let another man possess me, as Fritz once had. But would marriage to Gene resemble marriage to Fritz? I couldn't imagine this worldly, affable man, with his singular ability to make me feel secure, treating me as Fritz had. But I worried that I'd be jumping into the marriage largely as a way to feel settled in a world that otherwise left me rather unsettled.

I stalled for time by lobbing back a joke at him. "Are you finally going to give me that diamond ring you promised me on the first night we met?"

It was Gene's turn to laugh. "I was hoping you'd forget."

I held out my bare hand. "A wife needs a ring."

He smiled. "Does that mean you're saying yes?"

Was I? I couldn't imagine exchanging vows with Gene—or anyone else for that matter—but I couldn't fathom saying no. Gene had made my life in Hollywood real instead of the fanciful stage front I'd found it to be. Should I really say no only because I was scared to say yes?

Against all odds and against my better judgment, I said, "I suppose I am."

That evening, we drove to the northern state of Baja California in Mexico, the only place where we could get married within twenty-four hours. The next afternoon, Gene waited for me on the top step of the Mexicali Governor's Palace. He held a bouquet of purple flowers in his hands for me. The afternoon sun gave the structure an ethereal air, almost as if it glowed from within.

I stepped out of the limousine—we'd decided to arrive separately, for propriety's sake—and mounted the steps to the palace. When I reached the last one, I took the bouquet from Gene with a nod and, with my free hand, intertwined my fingers in his. But we did not talk. We'd been told that the Mexican tradition required that the bride and groom not speak until the ceremony ended, and we did not want to incur the bad luck rumored to afflict couples who broke the rule.

We stood before Apolonia Nunez, the Mexican civil magistrate, and next to the three required witnesses, Gustavo Padres Jr. of the Mexican Consul, Raul Mateus of the Central Police Department, and Jimmy Alvarez, manager of a local tavern. It felt like a stage set until Mr. Nunez began speaking. Neither of us comprehended the Spanish vows, but we understood the magnitude of the words.

I glanced over at Gene, handsome in a simple gray business suit. He chose it to complement my dark plum dress, one that my dear designer friend Adrian had made for me, although not for this occasion. The service called for decorum, but Gene couldn't stop grinning, and I couldn't prevent myself from grinning back. How different this wedding day was from my first.

"Hedy?" I heard my name from the reaches of my reverie, and it snapped me to the present.

"Shouldn't we be getting ready?" Gene asked.

"Ready for what?" I was genuinely confused. I thought we'd decided to have a traditional Austrian meal at home, then spend the rest of the night reading by the fire.

"For the party at the Trocadero, of course. I hear it is tie and tails for men, so you better pull out one of your gowns."

I'd remembered the Trocadero event but didn't want to go, and anyway, I thought we'd determined not to attend. I'd only pretended to forget to extend our time together—alone.

I drew close to him, whispering, "I thought we'd have nice evening in." I kissed him lightly up and down his neck, as I knew he liked. Gene was a skilled, ardent lover and usually very easy to sway with my ministrations.

Wrapping his arms around me, he kissed me back hard. I ran my fingers up and down his back, drawing intricate circles until he groaned softly. Then I said, "It's decided."

Extricating myself from his embrace, I entwined my hand with his and began leading him toward the bedroom.

Gene pulled away from me. "No, Hedy, let's go out. We stayed in twice this week."

"And went out the remaining five nights." My voice betrayed my irritation. How could he want to venture out to those awful parties nearly every night of the week? I'd grown to adore evenings at home with Gene, playing the piano or tinkering with ideas I had for scientific creations—whether they were sketches or models from clay and wire—while he read or worked on scripts. Wasn't the wonder of having a spouse you enjoyed staying home in their company, whether before the fire or in bed? I hadn't had that with Fritz.

"Come on, Hedy. You know how the game is played. Positions in films—whether as an actress, writer, producer, whatever—come from power. Power comes from relationships. And you cannot create and maintain relationships without making the rounds of parties."

Gene delivered this superfluous monologue about the way Hollywood worked—which I knew as well as anyone—as a smokescreen for his real concerns. He'd been working as a producer on the new film *Lillian Russell,* and he'd been having problems with his colleagues at 20th Century Fox. He seemed to believe that a little schmoozing would smooth over the bumps, just as he believed that a stunning appearance by me at the Trocadero would fix my unsettled dispute with Mr. Mayer over money for the movie I was currently filming, *I Take This Woman* with Spencer Tracy. I'd taken a hard line with my boss over the percentage of profits I felt due to me. For a sophisticated man, Gene was surprisingly naive sometimes. It would take a lot more than an evening at the Trocadero.

I looked into my husband's pleading eyes, wondering precisely who I'd married. And I wondered who he thought his wife was.

CHAPTER THIRTY-THREE

October 14, 1939
Los Angeles, California

HUMIDITY SAT LIKE A BLANKET ON THE CITY, MAKING heavier our hearts. Fans spun on the ceiling, and the violet curtain of evening blotted out the sun, but still my clothes were slick and wet. I longed for the icy forests of Vienna but knew I could no longer go home. Not now, maybe never.

Newspapers were scattered across the table at the private room of the Brown Derby, damp with the rings of sweating drinks. The papers hailed from far-flung destinations, and many copies were hard to come by. No matter the language, the letters bled horrific news across the front page. Europe was at war.

My European friends and I assembled not to drink away our distress, but to share information. We'd learned that little of the truth was reported in the newspapers. Certainly, details about the Nazi invasion of Poland were described in detail, as well as the ultimatums issued to Germany by the United Kingdom and France. But as I liked to remind our group, when Hitler invaded Austria, the Nuremberg Laws were put into effect, and few newspapers reported on this. Our European network was our source of the stories that the homes and stores of Austrian Jews were plundered; that Jews could no longer attend schools and universities and were prohibited from practicing professions; that Jews were beaten on the streets whenever and wherever the Nazis pleased; and, terrible to some of my more vain friends, that Jewish actresses were forced to clean toilets. Only the overt violence in November 1938 of Kristallnacht seemed to merit the attention of reporters. Headlines decried the Nazi ransacking of Jewish businesses, homes, hospitals, and schools, the burning of over a thousand synagogues, the killing of over a hundred people, and deportation of more than thirty thousand Jewish men to the recently constructed concentration camps. We'd been heartened by the worldwide outrage that Kristallnacht sparked and thought it would stomp out Hitler's anti-Semitic rage, but the reports soon faded from view. And we were once again left to our own network, particularly when it came to news of the Jewish citizens of Europe.

Word of the truth passed hand to hand, as if we were the first people inhabiting the earth, bound to an oral history alone. When whispers began to grow about an organized program to segregate all the Jews into city quarters separated from the rest of the population, called ghettos, our collective worries mounted. But I worried that the ghettos, although horrific, were only one step in Hitler's seemingly escalating plans to solve what he called the Jewish "problem." How far, I wondered, would Hitler go to remove Jews from German society, especially as Germany spread across Europe like a plague?

The gravity of my crime had become clear. Could I have helped the European Jews if I'd made known that the

Nuremberg Laws were not the limit of Hitler's plans? I bore blame for keeping this secret. My silence and selfishness had allowed the floodgates to open, but what was I going to do to make amends?

Peter Lorre, an actor friend who hailed from Hungary, asked, "Has anyone heard anything new from their families about what's happening on the ground?" We'd learned that firsthand accounts gave the most accurate, detailed information.

Ilona answered first. "I got a telegraph confirming all was well. But then Hungary hasn't been affected. Not yet."

Otto Preminger, a director and actor also from Austria, nodded in agreement.

"As most of you know, I was able to move my mother from Vienna to London early last spring, so I don't have any new information from her," I chimed in, not mentioning that Mr. Mayer's connections helped expedite her move. To secure his assistance, I'd had to back down from some of my salary demands, along with a vow that I wouldn't ask for his help with any other refugees. "I haven't heard anything recently from my extended family in Austria. We were never terribly close to my parent's siblings."

Part of me wanted to move Mama closer, perhaps to America, even though it had proven much easier to get her quickly to England than here. I didn't know if the government would allow me to move her here, even with the power of my celebrity and the backing of the studio, particularly after what happened with the MS *St. Louis*. Nearly three months ago, in May, the *St. Louis* sailed from Germany with almost a thousand people on board desperate to flee the Nazis, eventually landing in Cuba, where the passengers begged for admission into the United States. The Cuban and American governments denied the refugees entry, forcing their return to the dangerous European shores. Why did I think Mama would—or should—fare better than those nine-hundred-plus souls?

My Austrian American costar from *Lady of the Tropics*, Joseph Schildkraut, echoed my words. "Most of my immediate family is here, and we haven't gotten any word from more distant relatives."

The others just shook their heads. No one had family in Germany or Poland, where we were likely to glean the most critical details. As I stared at the newspapers and the dejected European faces that surrounded me—Gene didn't join me tonight; more and more, he chose Hollywood parties over any other evening plan—I thought for the millionth time how selfish I'd been. I'd taken my foreknowledge of the Anschluss and my suspicions about Hitler's plans for the Jews away with me to America and hidden it. Like Pandora's box, I'd kept the dark, terrible secret closed within, more fearful of what sharing the truth might divulge about me than what help disclosure might bring the victims of Hitler's rage. How many lives could I have saved if I'd kept that box open and invited the world into my terrible secret? Would I be held culpable for knowing what was likely to occur and not acting?

Peter slammed his empty glass down upon the newspaper-strewn table. "I hate feeling helpless. I wish there were something we could do." He echoed my own feelings.

"What can we do from here? Join the military? Raise money for the war effort? America won't get involved," Ilona responded to his largely rhetorical comment. "And going back to Europe is not an option."

"I hear Canada might join the fight soon," Joseph said in an attempt to add something to the conversation.

"What good will that do us?" Peter asked in an irritated voice.

"Maybe it'll encourage America to declare war too?" Joseph ventured.

The room grew quiet, everyone lost in their own musings about the war and its impact on their family and friends. Smoke from our many cigarettes rose to the ceiling, swirling around the spinning blades of the fan. Behind the closed door leading to the whimsically arched restaurant, I could hear the gentle roar of Brown Derby diners, mostly movie industry folks. They were oblivious to the distress within these walls, oblivious to the terror that might soon be afflicting their own people if Hitler's plans came to fruition. Denial and the smokescreen of entertainment was the language they spoke.

"I have something that one—or some of you—might do," a familiar-looking woman said. I didn't know her except by sight from a previous dinner with this revolving door of friends, always switching out one for another as people passed from one movie set and location to the next. I thought she had come with Joseph Schildkraut, but it was too late to politely ask for her name.

"Oh?" Peter asked, then took a long drag on his cigarette. Not bothering to hide the skepticism in his voice, he said, "What's that?"

"You could adopt a child."

"What on earth do you mean?" I asked. The woman's suggestion took me aback. "What does that have to do with the war?"

"Everything." She glanced around the room. "There are three women—Cecilia Razovsky and Frances Perkins in America and Kate Rosenheim in Nazi Germany—secretly working to get at-risk children out of the areas controlled by the Nazis and into this country. Mrs. Razovsky is the chair of the Advisory Committee to the Secretary of Labor, Mrs. Perkins, on the topic of immigration legislation reform. She keeps the secretary of labor apprised of the refugee situation around the world, and together, they attempt to effectuate flexibility in the administration's policies. When they aren't successful—which is the case more often than not—they turn their attention to individual cases. Mrs. Razovsky works with Mrs. Rosenheim, who is head of the Department of Children's Emigration in Germany and undertakes this work at great personal risk, to identify children in danger, and then Mrs. Razovsky and Mrs. Perkins try to secure visas for the children and partner with private organizations to sponsor the children's journeys to America."

"Without their parents?" Ilona asked.

"Their parents cannot leave or have been killed," she answered. She didn't need to say the words plainly for us to understand her meaning—the children were Jewish or offspring of those resisting the Nazis. Otherwise, they'd have parents who could accompany them.

The silence in the room was oppressive. The woman filled the void with a plea so plaintive, I wondered how anyone, even these world-weary entertainers, could remain unmoved.

"Will anyone take a baby?" she pleaded, sliding a folded

piece of paper across the small part of the table left uncluttered. "We don't know much about the child except that his parents were deported in the first wave. Please understand that this wouldn't be official, of course, because the Americans don't want to dirty their hands in the war. Not yet anyway, as some of you have pointed out. But we would find a way to legitimize the adoption. Please."

My friends averted their eyes and busied themselves with cigarettes and drinks. No one reached for the folded piece of paper. No one except me.

CHAPTER THIRTY-FOUR

July 8, 1940
Los Angeles, California

WERE MY SECRETS WEIGHING DOWN MY RELATIONSHIP with Gene? Or was the distance between us an honest one? We'd each married someone we hadn't really known, after all. And we'd married each other for very different reasons.

The pattern Gene and I had established in the early days of our marriage had worked at first. Free and as unmonitored as a bird, I left the house every morning for the working world of Hollywood filmmaking, while he stayed home, working on scripts. I would return home in the hopes that we'd spend a quiet evening in. I soon learned that while I craved quiet evenings in the tranquility of Hedgerow Farms, Gene adored prowling through the parties and nightclubs of the Hollywood scene, making connections and gathering material for his writing. He liked having his beautiful movie-star wife on his arm, and initially, I obliged.

In time, though, I stopped playing the role of the famous Hedy Lamarr every time Gene requested. I found his desire for the false, public Hedy instead of the real one upsetting. He began leaving for the night before I arrived home from the movie set. I started finding myself alone at home in the evenings more often than not, and if I wanted to communicate with my husband, I took to leaving him notes or surprising him on the Hollywood scene. Our only evenings at home occurred if we invited people over, principally our dear friends Arthur Hornblow Jr. and Myrna Loy. Otherwise, we were never alone.

Sometimes, I wondered if a new sort of intimacy would grow between us if I told him about my secrets. Or if he'd run. I was too scared to take the risk, and the gap between us grew into a chasm.

"Ready?" Gene asked.

"Ready," I answered, although I felt anything but ready.

We traded sheets of our writing paper, engraved with our elegantly intertwined initials, a monogram we'd carefully crafted in the days after our wedding. My stomach churned as I looked down at the paper Gene had handed me. What would I find on Gene's list? Why had I even agreed to this exercise, one suggested by an actress friend who swore it saved her own marriage?

But I knew why I was willing to list the attributes I cherished most in Gene as well as enumerate my thorniest problems with him. And vice versa. It was a last-ditch attempt to stave off the inevitable: the end of our marriage.

Before I read, I rocked the sleeping Jamesie in his bassinet, ensuring he was settled. I glanced over at Gene, then down at our chubby baby. The chance to adopt the refugee child wasn't one Gene had jumped at. Nor, if I was truthful with myself, had I. I'd felt compelled to pick up that piece of paper off the table at the Brown Derby. My compulsion stemmed not out of maternal longing—my own upbringing was bereft of warm, motherly role models—but from a sense of guilt and my subsequent inaction. Perhaps, I'd thought to myself, if I saved this child, it would serve as penance for all the others I didn't save.

I'd never explained to Gene about Jamesie's likely heritage or the circumstances behind his adoption, but then he had no idea about my own Jewishness either. Would the truth have made him feel more connected to me? More attached to Jamesie? What Gene did understand about the adoption was that it was a possible means of knitting us together. His very willingness to move forward with the adoption *for me*—even when he already had a daughter of his own—made me feel closer to him, and when I held Jamesie in my arms, I gazed at Gene with a sense of completeness. But when bringing a baby into our home didn't yield the close family unit for which I'd hoped but instead the usual two separate lives, the reality of our alienation became inescapable.

I read Gene's words. I heartened a little at the qualities he admired: my European charm, my beauty, my skills as a homemaker and mother, and my intellect. Glancing up at Gene, I gave him a small smile that he didn't see. He was lost in my words.

Then I braced myself for my flaws. But the list was blank.

My brows knitted, and I looked up from the page into Gene's waiting eyes. "You didn't list any problems."

"No."

"Why?"

"Because they're not your problems, Hedy. They're not your flaws. They're mine."

"What do you mean?"

Gene's eyes grew soft, almost sad. "You married me hoping for something entirely reasonable: a husband, a home, a family. But what you want, I cannot give to you. I don't have it in me to be a parent to another child. Not now anyway."

I nodded, understanding at last. This marriage to Gene would never improve, never progress. It was over.

Gene braved the silence, saying what both of us thought but neither wanted to say first. "Shall we meet with a lawyer?"

I nodded. There was really no other way.

"What about Jamesie?" Gene asked, tilting his head toward the sleeping baby.

What was he asking? Was he asking who would get custody? Or was he asking the unthinkable? Whether we would return him?

I lifted my son from the bassinet and squeezed him close. Jamesie squealed a little but didn't waken. "I will keep him," I said, knowing that Mrs. Burton, Jamesie's nanny, would spend far more time with him than me because of my work demands. Still, I supposed, his life here in America was far better than the fate he had left behind in Europe.

Gene nodded, reaching out to touch my free hand gently. "I'd still like to see him from time to time."

"Of course, Gene. You are his father, after all. Whatever role you'd like to play."

I'd clung to Gene as a safe haven, a version of Papa that he couldn't possibly fulfill, and he'd married the glamorous movie star who partied nightly. But I was only simple Hedy Kiesler, and he was a Hollywood bon vivant. I carried a heavy secret for which I needed to atone, and Gene sought the light, shunning even the hint of darkness. We were opposite, and we were strangers.

CHAPTER THIRTY-FIVE

September 19, 1940
Los Angeles, California

I BOUNCED JAMESIE IN MY ARMS AS SUSIE READ ALOUD from the newspaper. How I loved having my cherubic son visit my dressing room during the breaks in my workday, although I constantly doubted my ability to properly mother him in the few short hours I had available for him each day as I shuttled between soundstages, working simultaneously on both *Come Live with Me* with the kindly Jimmy Stewart and *Comrade X* with the convivial Clark Gable. Still, Jamesie, the only vestige of my short-lived marriage to Gene, brought a chunky ray of golden sunshine into my busy, often tense adult world.

"Torpedoed as they clutched their teddy bears," Susie clucked, tears welling up in her eyes.

"What are you talking about?" Surely I'd misheard Susie over Jamesie's sweet gurgles. Why on earth would she possibly mention torpedoes and children's toys in the same sentence? Perhaps my English was to blame. Or Susie's slang.

She didn't answer my question, unusual for the

ever-responsive Susie. Her eyes were fixed on the newspaper. The tears began to stream down her face.

"What is it, Susie?"

Still, she didn't speak. Mrs. Burton, who'd been sitting in the corner knitting Jamesie a cap while I held him, rose from her chair and peered over Susie's shoulder. She let out an audible gasp.

Jamesie squirming in my arms, I sidled up to the women and read the newspaper alongside them.

I read aloud the horrific headline: "'Nazis Torpedo Mercy Ship, Kill Children.'"

Susie whispered snippets from the terrible news story. "'With German air attacks mounting and the threat of land invasion becoming real, private households in Canada spontaneously offered the British government hospitality and sanctuary for British and refugee children. On September 12, 1940, the SS *City of Benares* was packed with 197 passengers and a 200-person crew, among them 90 children headed to Canada for safety from the Blitz and the threat of German invasion. The ship, sailing from Liverpool to Canada, was struck down on September 17, 1940, by German torpedoes when it was six hundred miles from land. The SS *City of Benares* sunk, claiming the lives of 134 passengers and 131 crew members—including 83 of the 90 children sent by their parents to Canada for safekeeping.'"

"No!" I cried out. How could this have happened? Surely even the Nazis wouldn't target a ship full of children?

Susie read aloud other details about the children on board the SS *City of Benares*. They came from British families bombarded by the Blitz as well as refugee families who feared for their Jewish children's lives should Hitler successfully invade England, although I had to read between the lines to reach that understanding, as the paper only described the Jewish children's situation euphemistically. Regardless of their backgrounds, they all sought the same thing for their children—security. The very thing that the Nazis stole from them.

I stared into my year-and-a-half-old son's eyes. But for the vagaries of chance—some unknown factor in the efforts of Misses Rosenheim, Perkins, and Razovsky—Jamesie could have been one of the children on that boat. Only the whim of timing had placed him on a ship to America last October instead of a boat this month to Canada. Having nearly lost my son to the child welfare system when Gene and I separated in July—the American judicial system seemed unable to fathom a single mother continuing to raise an adopted child alone—the possibility of loss was too fresh to bear. I felt the visceral pain of the grieving parents of the SS *City of Benares* victims.

The runner peeked in the door. "It's time, Miss Lamarr."

Mrs. Burton held out her arms and said, "I'll take him home for his nap, ma'am."

Reluctantly, I handed my son to her. She settled him securely in his pram and wheeled him out of my dressing room. *Poor thing*, I thought. Jamesie probably thought Mrs. Burton was his real mother. He had a busy working woman for one parent and a blank space for the other, as Gene's tether to James was gossamer thin, near to snapping since the divorce.

Without my beloved son in my arms, I felt unsteady, and the awful weight of loss bore down upon me. Never mind the ball gown I wore for my next scene, I crumpled like a sheet of discarded paper onto the floor, pulled down by my grief and guilt. Could I have done something to prevent all this loss? If I had told the American government or perhaps the British about my fears over Hitler's plans, would those children have even needed to embark on their fatal voyage? Could the enemies of the Nazis have stopped some of Hitler's terrible machinations so that parents needn't have bundled off their precious children and set them to sail across the vast, dangerous Atlantic Ocean alone? Would anyone have believed me? Was I exaggerating my own role? The emotions I carried weighed so much, I needed somewhere to put them.

"Come now, Miss Lamarr." Susie wrapped her arms around me and gently tried to lift me from the floor. My body was like a dead weight, and she could not move me. Defeated, she took a seat next to me on the floor, and we sat in silence. For once, the bubbly Susie had nothing to say. The language of grief was unknown to her as of yet.

The runner knocked again. They must have been waiting for me on set. When no one answered, he cracked open the door. "Miss Lamarr?" He nearly jumped when he saw Susie and me sitting on the floor, slumped against the wall. Once he recovered himself, he raced to our sides and asked, "Shall I fetch the doctor, ma'am?"

I looked into the blue eyes of the man—really, he was little more than a boy, trying to climb the Hollywood ladder—and realized that this was the moment everything would change. My personal history and every path I *could* have chosen in my past had shaped my present. It steered my thoughts and actions like the unseen wheel of a ship. But nothing wrested my present from its course like the SS *City of Benares*.

I would not wallow in my guilt and grief any longer but instead perform the penance for my sins. I would take everything I knew about the evil that was Hitler and hone myself into a blade. And I would take that blade and slice deep into the Third Reich.

CHAPTER THIRTY-SIX

September 30, 1940
Los Angeles, California

To Robin Gaynor Adrian." Gilbert Adrian, known simply as Adrian, lifted his glass in toast to his newborn son.

Only the celebration in honor of the new child of my dear friends, the Adrians, could have drawn me from my house in the days after the sinking of the SS *City of Benares*. How could I not join a party commemorating the birth of a healthy baby when so many had recently perished? I clinked my champagne flute with my dining companions to my right and then my left, realizing for the first time that I had never been properly introduced to the man sitting to my left, small and blond, with the wide blue eyes of a child.

I almost didn't bother with the nicety of introductions, so dark was my mood and focus on my work. Since the news of the horrific *Benares* tragedy, I'd followed a fixed regime. When I returned home from the set of a silly movie I was working on called *Boom Town*, I spent my time with Jamesie until he went to sleep. Thereafter, I'd spend the rest of the night trying to capture all my recollections from the dinner parties as Mrs.

Mandl where military and weaponry matters were discussed, furiously scribbling them down in a notebook. In those notes, I hoped to find a path to atonement, a way to use the secret information I'd learned to help the people I'd left behind.

When the Nazis burned Jewish and intellectual books after the Anschluss, charred fragments of book pages floated through the air for days afterward, or so I'd been told. The Viennese people might have found a few words by Albert Einstein, Sigmund Freud, Franz Kafka, or even Ernest Hemingway, among others, on sidewalks or on coat sleeves. They'd spent evenings trying to place those snippets in context or make sense of them. As I tried to assemble and parse through my memories of military conversations overheard while presiding over the Mandl dinner table, I felt like my fellow Viennese after the Anschluss, joining together lost puzzle pieces, trying to make sense out of chaos.

I'd made long lists of military plans and weaponry flaws about which Fritz had lamented. Of all the munitions, armaments, and weaponry components Fritz had manufactured, torpedoes had presented the trickiest problems. Their accuracy proved to be challenging, as did their susceptibility to signal jamming by enemy ships. Along with every eavesdropped phrase I'd heard about torpedoes, I'd written down every nugget of information I'd gleaned from my brief conversation with Nazi torpedo expert Hellmuth Walter in Fritz's Hirtenberger factory just before I escaped. It seemed that my best chance of undermining the Third Reich—and ensuring that a German submarine or ship never again harmed a ship full of refugee children—might be to somehow use the knowledge I'd gathered to capitalize on the weakness in the German torpedo systems.

The solution to this problem—how to improve accuracy for the torpedoes of the Nazis' enemies while finding ways to prevent signals to them from being jammed by Hitler's men if a radio solution was to be utilized—was somewhere out there or somewhere within me. Fragments of solutions teased me in half sleep and nightmares and haunted me even during my wakening hours. Inspiration eluded me as I tried to hone my weapon against Hitler.

Adrian brought me back to the present. He hadn't completed his toast. "Robin was a long time coming." He paused for the laughter he knew would result from his double entendre. Most of the friends of Adrian, the dress designer and costumer, and his wife, the actress Janet Gaynor, suspected that theirs was a lavender marriage, that although Janet and Adrian loved each other dearly, they sought romantic love in partners of their own sex. Not that this undermined the strength of their infallible union and their delight in becoming parents. This bright, sophisticated couple hosted the only sort of Hollywood evening I actually enjoyed.

Glancing at Janet, Adrian said, "We thank you all, dear friends, for urging us on and celebrating with us now."

Janet lifted a glass to the table of fourteen friends who gathered around them, the women outfitted beautifully in Adrian's dresses, myself included.

Adrian swung his wife around, declaring, "Now we dance."

Most of the diners jumped up to dance to the gramophone record selected by Adrian and Janet, but I stayed seated, not feeling in the right frame of mind for dancing. As did my tablemate.

In a few minutes, he began to stammer. "I must apologize for not introducing myself. I know, of course, who you are, and I've been frozen with nerves over presenting myself to the famous Hedy Lamarr all through the first course. I could hardly eat," he said, pointing to his undisturbed plate of oysters.

I laughed at his delivery. How could I not? Most people who didn't already know me seemed to feel the way he did but didn't have the moxie to admit it outright, especially men. I found his honesty refreshing.

I stretched out my hand to shake his and said, "I am the one who should be apologizing. I'm afraid I haven't been feeling very sociable lately, and it's hampered my manners."

He looked alarmed. "Is everything all right, Miss Lamarr?"

"Please call me Hedy," I said, then thought about how to answer his question as I lit a cigarette. "It's the war, you see. It's made daily life here in America seem"—I searched for the word—"trivial. I've been reluctant to go out into society. It feels strange making films and money here in Hollywood when the rest of the world is in such a…" I trailed off, fearful that I wasn't making any sense to the American and wondering why I was blurting out my intimate thoughts to a stranger.

He filled in my gap. "I understand. My wife is European, and to her, the war seems far more real and imminent than it does to me, even though my brother, Henry, was killed in June while stationed at the American embassy in Finland, in the aftermath of the Finns' short-lived war with the Soviet Union."

My hand flew to my mouth. "I am so sorry about your brother."

"Thank you for your condolences. It is a terrible loss. But these are terrible times, even if it doesn't seem like it in Hollywood." He pointedly glanced at the merriment of the dancers.

"You *do* understand."

Relief coursed through me at making a connection instead of the usual banal small talk. We sat in companionable, thoughtful silence for a moment watching the dancers, and then he asked, "Here I am, sitting next to Hedy Lamarr, and I've not asked you to dance. Would you care to?"

"Would you be offended if I declined?"

"Actually, I'd be relieved. I've never been much of a dancer. I'm more of a musician."

"A musician? How wonderful. My mother is a retired concert pianist. Is the piano your instrument as well?"

"Yes, although I compose now rather than perform."

"You're a composer," I echoed, intrigued now. "I'm sorry, I don't think I ever caught your name."

"George Antheil."

"The composer of *Le Ballet mécanique*?" During one of our family trips to France in my youth, I'd heard of this rather infamous piece that consisted, in part, of the synchronization of nearly a dozen player pianos—rumored to be an onslaught of erratic meter and chords in a radical style—and the musical riot that had ensued in Paris and Carnegie Hall in New York City when it had been first performed over a decade before. Mr. Antheil was quite a well-known composer and performer of modern, avant-garde pieces, as well as a writer of well-regarded magazine and newspaper articles about the war in Europe and the political regimes behind it, and just about the last person I'd expect to encounter in commercial Hollywood.

"You've heard of it?" He sounded astonished.

"I have indeed. And you are the composer?"

"The very one."

"What brings *you* to Hollywood?"

He laughed at my emphasis. "I'm working on a couple of musical scores for movies."

"That's quite a departure from your earlier work."

"Well, we all need to make money sometimes. And *Le Ballet mécanique* wasn't paying the rent," he said without enthusiasm.

"You should be proud of your piece; I hear it's quite inventive. I should love to hear you play some of it."

"You would?"

"I wouldn't have said so unless I meant it." I gestured to the empty piano.

We rose, and as we walked toward the piano, I realized that George was significantly shorter than me. Perhaps five foot three inches to my five foot seven inches. But our height disparity became irrelevant when we sat down at the piano bench, and, in fact, he seemed to gain in stature once he began to play.

While *Le Ballet mécanique* was as unusual as described, it was also as alive as anything I'd heard for ages. I felt invigorated by the discordant chords and expressed my disappointment when it came to an end.

"I'm guessing that with a concert pianist for a mother, you play piano quite well yourself, Miss Lamarr," George commented.

"It's Hedy, and I do play, although I wouldn't describe it as playing 'well.' Or at least my mother wouldn't." I could imagine Mama's horror at the well-known composer George Antheil asking about my proficiency on the piano. She'd be the first to criticize my technique to him.

"Would you care to join me in a duet?"

"As long as you don't mind my lack of skill."

He smiled an impish grin at me and began playing a tune, one that seemed familiar but I couldn't place. I followed along, as the melody was simple enough, and then he changed to an entirely different tune. We synchronized with each other effortlessly—due to his skill, no doubt, not mine—as we hopped from song to song, laughing all the while.

Suddenly, an idea came to me. I had been searching for it for some time as I'd been thinking about ways in which torpedoes and submarines or ships could radio-communicate with each secretly. I lifted my fingers from the piano keys and turned to George. "I have a very strange request."

"Any request from Hedy Lamarr would be an honor."

My eyes pleading, I asked, "Would you work on a project with me? One that might help shorten the war?"

CHAPTER THIRTY-SEVEN

September 30, 1940
Los Angeles, California

So THIS IS WHAT A MOVIE STAR'S DRAWING ROOM LOOKS like?" George mused, wandering around the white space, pristine except for the jumble of work materials. "I confess that I thought the place would be scattered with pots of makeup, jewelry, and gowns, not drawing boards full of sketches and"—he lifted my volume of *Radiodynamics: The Wireless Control of Torpedoes and Other Mechanisms*, by B. F. Miessner, off the table—"incomprehensible books."

I laughed, gesturing around. "A scientific mess is what *this* movie star's drawing room looks like."

"I understand now why you are little seen outside the movie set these days."

"You've been checking up on me?" I didn't know whether to be flattered or irritated.

"I do my homework." He paused for effect. "Particularly if I'm about to embark on important war work with said movie star."

I decided to be flattered. "I'm pleased to hear that you're no stranger to homework, as you'll have loads more from now on."

"Is it finally time for me to hear what we'll be working on?"

"Yes, I suppose it is." I gestured for him to take the seat across from me.

I took a deep breath and began explaining to him about my life as Mrs. Mandl. Not the sordid details, of course, but the countless conversations I'd overheard about munitions and armaments and, most importantly for our purposes, torpedoes. In basic terms, I explained to him the flaws with wired torpedoes and my desire to craft a radio-guided torpedo system for the Allies that would be precise in its aim and that would use unjammable frequencies.

George looked stunned. Emitting a low whistle, he said, "I'm amazed at your deep understanding of this technology and your knowledge of what I'm guessing is guarded Third Reich military information. This is not at all what I thought we'd be discussing today, and I hardly know where to begin with my questions, Hedy."

"Ask me anything you'd like," I said and meant it. Speaking honestly with George about my past and my ambitions— instead of talking through the persona of Hedy Lamarr, movie star, that I played most of the day—felt liberating. In his tone, I heard not judgment or disappointment at meeting this Hedy but that was I recognized for the first time since I had arrived in Hollywood. And accepted.

"Why torpedoes? You obviously had access to all sorts of information about military plans and weaponry, but you're focused on torpedoes."

"I didn't initially zero in on torpedo systems. I actually wrote down everything I could remember overhearing about military strategy and weapons and hunted around for the area where I could make the most difference, but then *Benares* happened. And I vowed to use my knowledge to help the Allies sink every German submarine and ship out there. I never want to read about another *Benares* tragedy." This, of course, was only part of the reason. The motivation actually had its origin in my multifaceted guilt. Although we'd communicated so effortlessly, I couldn't yet entrust him with private past and my suspicions about Hitler's plans.

"That makes sense. *Benares* was a terrible loss." He shook his head. "All those poor children."

"Yes, it was." I willed my eyes not to well with tears as I continued. "I also had the unique experience of spending an hour or so with Germany's torpedo genius, Hellmuth Walter. We started out talking about his resolution of the submarine propulsion problem with hydrogen peroxide and moved on to the research he and his team were doing with remote control of torpedoes. At that time, indeed even now, most militaries favored wire guidance of torpedoes, in which the torpedo is attached to the submarine or ship with a thin, insulated wire that connects the torpedo electrically to the submariner or sailor who controls the aim of the torpedo. Walter was exploring remote control of torpedoes. He was examining the radio-control system used by glide bombs, which are winged bombs dropped from planes, in which each bomber and its single bomb are assigned one of eighteen different radio frequencies to communicate. His efforts weren't particularly fruitful, because the enemy could jam that bomber-to-bomb communication once the enemy detected which of the radio frequencies the bomber and bomb were using. But I thought maybe we could apply that glide-bomb concept to torpedoes in a slightly different way."

I paused, waiting to see if George had any comments or inquiries. His brows were knitted in utter confusion.

"You obviously have more questions," I said.

"Thousands," he said with a laugh. "I guess what I'm really struggling with is, well, why me? What makes you think that a composer with no scientific training can help you solve a problem that the best military minds presumably have been unable to resolve? Not that I don't want to help, of course."

"Well, you have all the qualities I need for a scientific partner in this project. You have a highly developed sense of mechanical instruments, and you're brilliant. You approach problems—the world, even—from a broad perspective, unlike most inventors and thinkers who are narrow in their views, which makes you more suitable for the job than any scientist. And you're..." I trailed off.

"I'm what?" he asked.

"A source of inspiration. When you and I played piano together the other evening at the Adrians, I solved the puzzle of how to create an unjammable remote-controlled torpedo." I smiled at the memory of that moment of clarity when I had suddenly understood how I might answer the torpedo question. "The big-picture solution anyway. And I could see very clearly how you could help me with it."

"Our duet did all that?" He looked incredulous.

"It did indeed." I took a moment to light myself a cigarette, offering one to George, who declined.

"How?"

"As I mentioned, the main problem of using remote-controlled torpedoes—which would allow for greater accuracy as there's no need for the limiting wire—is that an enemy can easily jam the radio frequency that the submariner or sailor launching the torpedo and the torpedo itself share. Even the great torpedo expert Walter hadn't been able to solve that problem."

"That part, I understand. But what on earth does that have to do with our playing piano together?"

"When you and I played our duet, we followed each other, hopping from tune to tune seamlessly. You started the tune, and I followed your lead. In some ways, you were operating like the transmitter of a signal—like a submariner or sailor—and I was operating like the receiver—like the torpedo. And I began thinking, what if the submariner or sailor and the torpedo constantly hopped from radio frequency to radio frequency just like you and I hopped from tune to tune? That would make the communication from submariner or sailor to the torpedo nearly unjammable by the enemy, wouldn't it? You could help me build an instrument that would do that."

George sunk back into his chair, silent as he processed my theory. "That's genius, Hedy," he said quietly.

A knock sounded on the drawing room door. "Come in, Mrs. Burton," I said, knowing that she was the only one of my household staff still on the premises.

The uniformed nanny opened the door, presenting Jamesie to me in his blue, footed pajamas. "The little gentleman is off to bed," she announced.

I sprung up to take him from her. "Give Mommy a kiss

before bedtime," I pleaded with him as I tickled his chunky, little feet.

Jamesie and I kissed, and I lingered with my nose in the curve of his neck, inhaling the baby scent of soap and powder. "Good night, sweet one," I whispered and reluctantly handed him back to Mrs. Burton.

I closed the door behind them and settled back into my chair across from George. "Okay, where were we?"

"You have a son?" He looked shocked.

"Yes, Gene Markey and I adopted him when we were married. He was eight months old when he joined us in October of 1939."

"And now that you're divorced?"

"He's all mine." I paused for a moment, deciding whether to trust George with my secret and Jamesie's secret as well. I decided to allow him in but only halfway. I gave him part of Jamesie's story. "He has no one else, you see. He's a European refugee."

"Ah." His brow smoothed in what he thought was understanding. "It's all making sense now: a refugee child, the *Benares*, torpedoes."

I nodded, allowing George to believe that my rescue of Jamesie coupled with *Benares* constituted the entire impetus for my inventing. But I knew that Jamesie was only one of the many victims of the Third Reich that I was compelled to save. I knew that when I escaped Austria without sharing my suspicions—or bringing anyone with me—that I became obliged to save many, many more.

CHAPTER THIRTY-EIGHT

October 19, 1940
Los Angeles, California

T HE WORK ENACTED CHANGES UPON MY BODY AND SPIRIT.
I no longer felt riven.

"Hedy, are you ever going to clean this place up?" George called to me from the entryway of my drawing room, where the detritus of our last few meetings remained scattered around the floor. We'd become very familiar and bantered casually with one another, like siblings, I thought. It was a refreshing change from the other sort of treatment I usually received from men— either the overeager, almost always unwelcome ministrations of men desperate to be suitors, or the standoffish orders of movie-makers who saw me as nothing more than an inanimate object appearing in their films.

George knew it was safe to yell out, because on Saturday afternoons, Mrs. Burton generally took Jamesie to the park, so the baby wouldn't be napping. The demands on my time from my new movie, *Ziegfeld Girl*, had been tremendous, necessitating weekend time with George. Previously, we'd met after work on weekdays, because I preferred to spend time with Jamesie on weekend days if not required to be on the movie set. George said he didn't mind, as his wife and son were on an extended stay on the East Coast visiting family, but I still felt like I was impinging on his privacy.

"Let's move out to the patio today. The weather's glorious," I yelled back from the kitchen, where I was organizing the coffee tray. We fueled our heated discussions, where we pushed each other along as we hunted for the mechanism by which our submarine and torpedo could synchronize their switching of radio frequencies, with copious amounts of coffee. I always tended to the coffee making myself, as I could never trust the staff to make good, strong Austrian-style coffee instead of the weak, watery American stuff they preferred.

Living as we did in California, the October afternoon was, of course, warm, but I sensed a slight brisk breeze underlying the heat emanating from the relentless sun. The hint of chill reminded me of the crisp, colorful Viennese autumns, and I suddenly felt homesick for Döbling and for Papa. The thought of Papa brought an unwanted tear to my eye, and I wondered if he'd be proud of the work I was doing now. After all, it was those Sunday afternoons where he had patiently explained the technical workings of the world that gave me the foundations and confidence for the project I attempted with George. Those hours had shaped me in ways I was only just now understanding. One thing I did know for certain: Papa would be proud of the efforts I'd undertaken to get Mama safely to Canada from bomb-riddled London.

Wiping away the tear, I picked up the heavy tray and walked out onto the patio. George had already set up the drawing board with a flip chart, where we'd written out the underlying structure of our invention. It had taken several meetings a week for several weeks, but we'd derived our three, interlocking goals and begun to solve for those goals. We listed them as: (1) create radio control of torpedoes to increase accuracy, (2) make system for radio signals between plane, submarine or ship, and torpedo, and (3) create mechanism that will synchronize hopping between radio frequencies in between communications to avoid jamming of signals by enemy forces.

I poured us each a steaming cup of coffee. Sipping slowly and staring at the board, we sat under the shade of an umbrella, listening to the wind rustle the leaves of the nearby fig, oak, and sycamore trees. It was a soothing, silvery sound.

"*Ziegfeld Girl* looks like it's taking a toll," George observed.

Glancing down at my wrinkled linen pants and patting my messily braided hair, I almost remarked that my clothing choice was a reflection of how comfortable I felt with George and should be perceived as a compliment, which was true enough. But I knew the long days of filming the musical about three hopeful performers alongside Judy Garland, Lana Turner, Tony Martin, and Jimmy Stewart had probably exacted the additional price of bloodshot eyes and dark circles. Jimmy was a dear man, so kind, but the tension between me, Lana, and Judy had been thick, as the women constantly angled for more screen time and meatier lines. Still, I couldn't regret the tariff as the light, airy musical brought levity into my acting résumé. And my dear friend Adrian and I got to spend hours together as he made my costumes, wonderful confections including a fantastical peacock headdress. I couldn't predict how the movie would be received, but I certainly welcomed its lighthearted tone.

"Maybe this is how I really look, underneath all the frills. Maybe this is the self I show to very few," I said as if in jest, although it was true. I'd lost myself for so long in other people's visions of me that I felt relief with George, as he demanded none of that artifice. Here, on my patio and in my drawing room with George, I felt safe enough to shed my other skins, even though the question of my deservedness continued to plague me. Having been granted the gift of transformation once before, I wondered if I really warranted another change.

"I feel honored," George said, and I knew he meant it. "But no one would believe it. *If* I told them, which I won't."

I laughed, knowing he was right. Reluctantly pushing myself out of the comfortable patio chair, I stood before the board. We'd made significant progress on our first two goals but knew we needed to tackle the third before we could get much further. "Are we ready for the next stage?" I asked.

"I hope so," he said, briskly rubbing together his hands as if he was warming up for the task.

I flipped to the next page of the chart, where we'd brain-stormed a list of ideas for the mechanism necessary to have the radio transmitter and receiver hopping together from frequency to frequency simultaneously. George and I sometimes called this device the *Frequenzsprungverfahren* when we reverted to German, as we occasionally did given that George's immigrant German parents had inculcated him in the language in his youth.

Currently, our plan, as it had evolved, worked as follows:

after the ship or submarine launched the torpedo, a plane over-head would signal course corrections, and the ship or subma-rine would signal them to the torpedo, and between each brief signal, the frequency would change manually at intervals of a minute. While this notion of switching frequencies to avoid detection and jamming was novel unto itself—a stroke of inspi-ration that came to me while George and I played that first duet—we wanted a more advanced system, one that didn't rely exclusively on the manual changing of frequencies by military men. Human hands often made mistakes, and the timing, so easy to get wrong, was critical.

But what form should that system take? What mechanism could undertake this task? We'd gone around and around on this question, and the chart reflected this. We needed to start fresh, so I flipped to a new page and wrote down our goal: "a synchronized alternating radio frequency device."

Coffee in hand, I began pacing around the patio, pondering the sort of device that could convey information about radio-frequency sequences and actually make the frequency change as well. When I finished with my coffee, I lit a cigarette and con-tinued my pacing. Inspiration wasn't coming from the bottom of my coffee cup or wisps of my cigarette smoke, and glanc-ing at George, I saw that he wasn't finding flashes of creativity there either. Maybe I'd set us to an impossible task. After all, if the brightest, formally educated scientific minds hadn't solved this conundrum, why did I think that an untrained actress and musician could successfully decipher it? I felt the fool.

I thought back to our duet. At the time, I'd been so cer-tain that George and I were the right partners for this project, even though our preparation for it was unorthodox, at best. Not only because that duet gave rise to my idea of synchronicity, but because I'd believed that George's unusual intellect and experience building machines—albeit of a musical nature—would serve the project well.

I slowed my pace. An idea was forming in my mind, teasing at the edges of my consciousness but not yet fully formed. What about George's sort of machines? The ribbons of the player pianos he'd used to create synchronicity in *Le Ballet mécanique*, for example? They contained perforations that operated as signals to the piano to change piano keys. Viewed from a slightly different perspective, couldn't the ribbons—or a device quite like them—serve as means to share synchronized instructions about changes in radio frequencies with the ship or submarine and the corresponding torpedo?

I picked up a red pen from the table and walked over to the flip chart. In bold capital letters on the nearly blank piece of paper on the front of our chart, I wrote *RIBBON*.

George looked over at me. "What do you mean by ribbon? Please don't tell me you're talking about a hair bow."

I was so excited about the possibilities for this idea that I didn't even get irritated at his insulting remark. I laughed. "No, silly. I'm thinking about the ribbon of a player piano. Couldn't we make an actual ribbonlike device for the ship or submarine and the torpedo that has holes—like the roll of a player piano—with instructions about the frequency-hopping radio sequence? One would operate as the transmitter and the other as the receiver."

George jumped up. "Oh my god, yes. Why didn't *I* think of it sooner? We could use matching rolls of paper for each, like the player piano ribbons, with slots to encode the changes in frequency."

"But how would it actually make the changes in the radio signal?"

He grabbed the red pen from my hand and began sketching out a design on the chart. "Look, Hedy." He directed me to his rough picture. "As the perforated ribbons roll around a control head, they could trigger a mechanism that could move specific switches connecting to an oscillator, which produces a radio signal."

"Eliminating the reliance on humans to switch the signal."

"Yes."

"It would allow for radio hopping all over the spectrum, not just a limited range. Jamming would be almost impossible."

"Exactly as you'd hoped."

"An unbreakable code." I almost whispered the words, like a mantra. Or a prayer.

We'd done it. We'd created a device that, minutes before, I'd questioned our ability to construct. I felt delight and pride of a sort I had never experienced with my acting career, and without thinking, I hugged George.

His arms reached around me, and he squeezed me back. Glancing down at him, as he was a few inches shorter than me, I smiled at him. Instead of smiling back, he craned his neck upward and kissed me on the lips.

I pushed him away, furious. Not at the liberty he'd tried to take but at the breach of our friendship. "How could you?"

His face burned bright red, and his hand flew to his mouth. "What have I done? Oh, Hedy, I'm so sorry."

"George, I'm used to men treating me like you just did—like I'm some object fashioned for their desires—but I expected more of you. A friendship and collaboration like ours has never happened to me before, and it means more to me than any affair. Do you understand?"

The crimson flush of his cheeks faded to pink, and he nodded at me. "I do. Can you ever forgive me?"

I'd pardoned far worse injuries to my body, but few people had exacted such harm on my mind and spirit. But peering into his face, I saw true penitence. I recognized it, because I saw the same contrition reflected back in my mirror every day. How could I deny him the sort of exoneration that I sought for myself? Wasn't forgiveness the impetus for this entire endeavor?

"Of course, George," I said solemnly. Then I gave him a playful shove to lighten the mood. "But don't you dare let it happen again."

CHAPTER THIRTY-NINE

October 26, 1940
Los Angeles, California

"WHAT ON EARTH DOES THAT OTHER SCRIBBLE SAY?" George asked, squinting and pointing to the phrase next to the word *ribbon*. "I swear you didn't learn to write or spell properly at your fancy Swiss finishing school."

I laughed. The inadequacy of my elite education was a frequent joke between me and George, particularly in comparison to the reams of technical, scientific information I'd taught myself. Somehow, with him, these topics didn't cause my defensive hackles to rise as they would have with another man. Or with Mama.

After a few days of awkwardness and stilted, formal exchanges, I once again felt as comfortable with George as the brother I'd often imagined but never had. I understood that his overture had been knee-jerk, as Susie liked to say, a behavior ingrained by society in most men. And I'd forgiven him.

"You know perfectly well it says 'Philco Remote Control,'" I ribbed him back.

Underneath *Philco Remote Control principle*, I'd spelled out the phrase *novel torpedo steering device*. This idea, inspired by the newly released Philco radio system that allowed for the remote changing of radio channels by consumers, referred to our basic design of the mechanism responsible for addressing the radio signals and converting them into steering directions for the torpedo, although we'd come up with our own idea. This had begun as the fragment of a notion we'd had to coax into the final, full-blown concept. We smiled at each other, as we confirmed the workability of this part of the idea as well. The rough design was becoming a viable reality. Soon, we thought, we'd be able to begin submitting it to the National Inventors' Council, the first step in the process toward military approval of any new technology. Ultimately, we hoped the navy would adopt it.

The front door, which I'd propped open to allow for a cross breeze, slammed shut. "Mrs. Burton," I called out. "Can you please bring Jamesie to see me before his nap?" I craved a tickle of my son's soft belly. Physical contact with his sweet skin helped appease the guilt I often felt over spending so much time apart from him.

Footsteps clattered across the marble entryway floor, but Mrs. Burton and Jamesie did not materialize. Perhaps the nanny hadn't heard me. "Mrs. Burton?" I called out again.

The footsteps grew louder, but it wasn't Mrs. Burton and Jamesie that opened my patio door. A small, quietly pretty woman, with dark hair and high, Slavic cheekbones, stepped through the doorframe onto the stones of the patio. Who on earth was she, and what was she doing in my house?

I began to yell out that we had an intruder when George spoke. "Boski, what are you doing here?"

Boski was George's wife. I'd thought that his wife and son were on an extended stay with George's family on the East Coast. That's what George had told me on our first meeting, and he hadn't mentioned their return, although he occasionally shared a funny anecdote about his son that Boski had told him about by letter.

Only then did I realize that her placid exterior hid a fury that raged beneath the surface. She yelled at George. "What am *I* doing here? What are *you* doing spending your Saturday with a movie star when your wife and son are finally home after two months on the East Coast helping your parents deal with the death of *your* brother? I had to see about this infidelity myself."

George started to stutter out an angry response, but I put up my hand to silence him. I understood this woman. I'd *been* this woman. A hurried explanation from her husband was not what she needed at the moment.

I walked toward Mrs. Antheil and reached out to take her hands in mine. She squirmed but finally acquiesced. "Mrs. Antheil, I assure you that nothing untoward has happened between your husband and myself." I didn't want to explain that I thought of George as a brother, never mind the pass he'd made only a week earlier. Or that in the time George and I had been collaborating, I'd divorced Gene Markey and dated the actor John Howard, playboy Jock Whitney, and the business tycoon Howard Hughes, who'd lent me a pair of his chemists and a lab to assist in my nonmilitary invention ideas, like the bouillon-type cubes that could turn water into a soda pop similar to Coca-Cola. I'd never once thought of George in the same romantic manner as any of these men, although, in many ways, he was far more important to me than any man I'd dated. I'd learned—from Fritz, from Gene, and from all those who followed—that losing myself in a man wouldn't shield me from my original self and all my guilt. I had to save myself, and George was my partner in that redemption.

I continued. "Your husband and I have been working on a project, one that we both hope might help in the war effort. As unlikely as it might sound, we are designing a new type of torpedo system."

Mrs. Antheil stared at me, her mouth slightly agape, and then she burst into hysterical laughter. In English even more heavily accented than my own, she said, "You expect me to believe this nonsense, Miss Lamarr? Please, I am not a stupid woman. My husband is a musician, not a scientist, and you are"—she stammered and then set free the righteous fury she'd been clamping down—"you are nothing but a pretty face."

Her label angered me as it touched upon a latent fear of mine—that the National Inventors' Council and the navy might reject our invention because *I* helped create it. Instead of lashing back, though, I kept my voice soothing and my words calm. I couldn't allow anything or anyone to jeopardize my partnership with George. What if she prohibited George from working with me? I couldn't bear the possibility that, having come so close to success, George and I might not be permitted to finish.

"It is *because* your husband is a musician that I sought him out. His symphony *Le Ballet mécanique* is all about machines talking to one another in synchronicity. This is the precise knowledge called for by the torpedo system I envisioned. May I show you our work?"

Guiding her across the patio and into the drawing room, I walked her past our flip charts, notes, models, mathematical calculations, and volumes on physics, torpedo systems, and radio frequencies. Her arms were folded and her brow furrowed. She hadn't so much as glanced at her husband as we went about this evidentiary process, but her hard, intelligent eyes took note of every detail of our labors.

Her face finally softened when I said, "My apologies for taking your husband away from you on a weekend. I promise that time will remain sacrosanct from now on. As will any project that will earn money for your family. And you and your son are welcome to join him anytime George comes to my house. Your son and mine could swim in the pool."

"You have a son?" she asked with surprise.

"Yes, he is eighteen months old."

Reluctantly, she said, "Thank you, Miss Lamarr."

"Please, call me Hedy. You are from Europe as well. Hungary, I believe?"

She nodded.

"Me too. I'm from Austria. The war has turned so many former friends into enemies. Let's not let a war effort keep us from becoming friends."

"All right," she answered hesitantly.

I took her by the hand, leading her to a section of the drawing room floor where we'd made a rough model of our system out of matchsticks. "Come, let me show you how your husband and I will help win the war."

CHAPTER FORTY

September 4, 1941
Los Angeles, California

I WAS STARING INTO THE MIRROR, WATCHING SUSIE TRANS-form my face, when my dressing room door crashed open without a single knock. George rushed in, clutching a single piece of paper in his hand.

"Hedy," George called out. "Hedy, you won't believe it."

Susie jumped at the brash interruption. She'd just finishing zipping up the back of the stylish yet no-nonsense dress I would be wearing for the upcoming scene of my new film *H. M. Pulham, Esq.*, one that showed the initial encounter between my character and her potential love interest, played by Robert Young. The filming had just begun, and I was more excited about this film than any I'd done excepting *Algiers*.

Staring at the red-faced, panting George, who'd never before come to the set of one of my films, Susie made the reasonable assumption that he was an interloper, albeit a non-threatening one given his stature and weakened state. "Shall I summon security, Miss Lamarr?"

"No, no, Susie, but I appreciate the offer. Mr. George

Antheil"—I paused to arch my eyebrow at him—"is a good friend, who sometimes, in his exuberance, forgets about the necessary proprieties."

"If you're certain, ma'am," Susie said with hesitation.

"I am," I answered. "Would you mind checking in to see what time they'll need me on set while I deal with Mr. Antheil here? I don't want to keep Mr. Vidor waiting."

I owed a tremendous debt to King Vidor, my director in this film and in *Comrade X*. After an unwelcome hiatus from moviemaking—due to a bout of pneumonia on my part and a bout of stinginess in loaning me out to another studio on Mr. Mayer's part—Vidor had asked me to perform the role of advertising executive Marvin Myles in his latest film, *H. M. Pulham, Esq.* Mr. Mayer resisted at first, but I'd fought for the unusual role, which Vidor pursued at my request. Instead of being cast as an exotic or a beautiful, icy statue, Vidor offered me the chance to play a character defined not by her looks but by her intellect and ambition. Somehow, Vidor saw beneath my exterior and understood, on some level, that this was the woman I secretly became off-screen, and he urged me to fully inhabit the role.

Susie shot a suspicious glance at George but acquiesced. "Yes, ma'am, I'll inquire," she said, closing the door behind her quietly.

"George, couldn't this have waited until this evening?" I asked, irritated. "This movie means a great deal to me."

George and I had plans to meet after dinner at my home that evening, much to the disappointment of John Howard, with whom I'd reunited after dating others. While John understood that my relationship with George was professional and platonic, he somehow sensed that I came alive with George in a way I didn't with him, and he loathed being marginalized, even when I explained that we were working on another military invention. This time, it was an antiaircraft shell that would explode automatically not when it hit the plane but when it neared the aircraft instead. I think on some level John didn't believe me, but in the end, I convinced him that his bitterness was unfounded and petty. If he hadn't changed his mind, it wouldn't have affected my meeting, and I would have jettisoned him for someone else; I would allow nothing to stand in the way of this work.

George and I had temporarily shifted our focus away from the torpedo system because we were awaiting word on our proposal. In the past December, we'd submitted a broad description of our torpedo and communications systems to the National Inventors' Council as we'd planned. From the start, we had every expectation that the council would react favorably not only because we believed in our invention, but also because our work and the council's shared a similar catalyst. While our system was ostensibly inspired by the horrible tragedy of the *Benares*, the council itself had been formed during the Great War when a passenger ship called the RMS *Lusitania* was torpedoed as it made its way across the Atlantic from New York to Liverpool. But it had been months since we'd turned in our proposal. While we tried to maintain a positive outlook by filing our patent in June at the suggestion of council member Lawrence Langner, who'd met with us to express his support of our proposal and even put us in touch with Caltech professor

Samuel McKeown and patent lawyers Lyon & Lyon to help in the patent process, we'd begun to lose hope.

The escalation of the war on all fronts had only made us more despondent. Daily, we read horrific news reports. Hitler expanded farther east into Europe and downward into Greece; fighting increased throughout Africa, including areas for which Fritz had provided Mussolini with weapons; the air raids continued over England, Scotland, Ireland, and Wales; the Nazis set up the Vichy government in France; and the German U-boat offensives increased in the Atlantic. Nothing appeared in the newspapers, however, about the escalating brutality against Jews and efforts to round them up into ghettos and concentration camps; those stories we learned from our European network. Even though America hadn't yet entered the fray, it felt as though we were under siege already, and I wanted our torpedo system in place when we made our inevitable war declaration.

The only bright light amid all this terrifying news was the development about Mama's immigration from Canada to America. For months, I'd had no luck lowering the high American barricade against the admission of wartime refugees. The fact that Mama was temporarily residing in the relative safety of Canada made it hard to argue for the necessity of her move, even though she posed no "economic burden" to America, a hurdle many immigrants couldn't clear. But finally, after working with lawyers and pressuring Mr. Mayer to assist me, I'd received unofficial word that her admission might be imminent.

"No, it cannot wait, Hedy. We've been waiting for months for word back, and now we finally have it."

I leaped up from my chair. "Is it the council's decision?"

"What else?" He held the paper close to his chest, a cryptic smile appearing on his lips.

I lunged for it, but he stood and swung it away from me. "Allow me to read the important excerpts to you," he taunted.

"Quickly, please. I'll have to go on set soon, and I don't think I can stand more delay."

"The letter is addressed to the United States Navy, but we were copied on the document, and the National Inventors' Council sent us a mimeographed copy. We can parse through every word later, but let me skip to the most important sentence." He paused and glanced over at me, unable to keep the boyish grin off his perpetually youthful face. "Oh yes, here it is. 'After clearing two layers of Council review, and after studying the proposal in great detail myself, it is the recommendation of the National Inventors' Council that the United States Navy place the submission of Mrs. Hedwig Kiesler Markey and Mr. George Antheil under consideration for military use.'"

I'd purposely chosen to use a name other than Hedy Lamarr. I worried that my celebrity might affect the council's decision negatively.

I squealed in delight, but before I could ask a barrage of questions, George added, "Best of all, Hedy, the person giving this recommendation is none other than Charles Kettering."

"*The* Charles Kettering?" The name sent me reeling. He was a famous inventor and head of the National Inventors' Council. He'd even been on the cover of *Time* a few years ago.

"The very same. And *he* thinks our invention is promising enough to recommend to the navy."

Did I dare say the thought running through my mind? Was it greedy to be so hopeful? "If Kettering thinks it shows that much potential, how can the navy do anything but concur?"

His wide blue eyes, so childish in appearance, sparkled. "That's what I've been thinking too."

"Now we just have to await word from the navy."

"Yup, the waiting game continues."

"Surely it's just a formality," I speculated.

"We can only hope, Hedy."

We grinned madly at each other, and a sense of euphoria coursed through me at this first public acknowledgment of my worth beyond that of my appearance. I felt like celebrating but knew the set of *H. M. Pulham, Esq.* would call soon. Still, the occasion was too momentous too ignore. I poured a glass of brandy for each of us, and we toasted to our invention.

Would it really be possible that in creating an invention to fight against the Third Reich, I could atone for my sins? That in saving the lives of those impacted by naval warfare, I could balance out the scales of justice for those I'd left behind in Austria? And was it possible that in the process, I might become known as more than Hedy, the "pretty face"?

No, I chastised myself silently, slamming down my brandy glass with a force that startled George. I was angry with myself. How dare I wish for a reward for doing my necessary penance? The war-shortening legacy of the invention alone would be enough.

CHAPTER FORTY-ONE

December 7, 1941
Los Angeles, California

E VEN THOUGH IT WAS SUNDAY, THE ENTIRE CAST AND crew was on the set of *Tortilla Flat*. We'd all grown accustomed to working every day of the week for this film adaptation of John Steinbeck's novel. Our director, Victor Fleming, demanded more of himself than his cast, so we never complained, no matter how many weekend evening plans I'd had to cancel with my new beau, the tall, Montana-born actor George Montgomery. Still, how I hated to miss a night with my other George, my romantic George, whose capacity for laughter drew me to him in otherwise dark times.

After arranging for Mrs. Burton to care for Jamesie on the day she usually had free, I returned to the set as the sun burned high above the Hollywood Hills. Susie and I worked silently as she helped me suit up into my simple costume. *Tortilla Flat* focused on the lives of a family of Hispanic Californians, and my character, Dolores Ramirez, worked in a cannery. The scene today called for a factory uniform and, unlike most of my film roles, only minimal makeup. I enjoyed the freedom of movement that the plain outfit and hair allowed.

I finished the last sip of the strong Austrian-style coffee I had prepared in my dressing room and walked down the long hallway toward the vast soundstage where a three-acre rural landscape, complete with an array of farm animals, had been re-created. My heels echoed throughout the largely empty building, and while I had expected to hear the usual sounds of the crew and equipment as I approached, I hadn't thought I'd hear a bloodcurdling wail.

I ran the remaining distance to the set, assuming someone had been injured, a not uncommon occurrence in filmmaking. On another film also directed by Fleming, *The Wizard of Oz*, an actress had been badly burned when a trapdoor delayed in opening and she was exposed to the fire and smoke. But when I arrived, I found another kind of catastrophe. Aside from a woman sobbing, the entire cast and crew stood frozen. They were listening to the blare of an earth-shattering radio report.

I ran over to my costars, Spencer Tracy and John Garfield, who were as immobile as everyone else. "What's going on?" I asked John, who I found more approachable than Spencer, with whom I'd worked on *I Take This Woman*. Even the experience of filming two movies together had not warmed him to me. Or me to him, it seemed.

Before John could answer, Spencer glared at me, placing his finger in his lips. "Shh," he hissed.

John, who played my character Dolores's love interest, drew closer to me and whispered in my ear, "Pearl Harbor's been bombed."

His words confused me. What or where was Pearl Harbor? I started to ask him more questions when the deep voice of a journalist returned to the radio, booming throughout the set.

"This is KGU in Honolulu, Hawaii. I am speaking from the roof of the Advertiser Publishing Company building. We have witnessed this morning a distant view of a brief full battle of Pearl Harbor and a severe bombing of Pearl Harbor by enemy planes, undoubtedly Japanese. The city of Honolulu has also been attacked and considerable damage done. This battle has been going on for nearly three hours. One of the bombs dropped within fifty feet of KGU tower. It is no joke. It is a real war. The public of Honolulu has been advised to keep in their homes and await results from the army and navy. There has been fierce fighting going on in the air and on the sea. The heavy shooting seems to be—one, two, three, four. Just a moment. We'll interrupt here. We cannot estimate yet how much damage has been done, but it has been a very severe attack. And the navy and army appear now to have the air and the sea under control."

No matter the reporter's protestations to the contrary, I couldn't stop thinking this was a joke. Threats from Europe, yes, those had been the topic of discussion for some time. Everyone had been following reports of the London Blitz and mapping out the response should our shores be similarly bombarded. But Japan? The newspapers and the politicians had mentioned nothing of attack from Asia, and neither had my European friends, who knew much more about the war than the newspapers and radio reports disclosed.

I glanced around. My fellow actors, the crew, and our director looked as stunned and disbelieving as I felt. We stood stock-still as horrific facts began pouring in, and I uncon-sciously reached for John's hand to steady me. Over three hun-dred Japanese bombers and planes had attacked the naval base in Oahu, Hawaii. Countless ships in the Pacific fleet had been hit, particularly the battleship USS *Arizona*. The number of the dead could not begin to be ascertained. We knew that it was only a matter of hours before America declared war.

When the radio report continued to repeat the same news and the cast and crew began talking, I quietly withdrew into a dark corner of the set, behind the rough building front that masqueraded as a farmhouse, and wept. For I comprehended better than anyone here the dark nature of the enemies America would be confronting. To the people surrounding me, those forces were faceless and speechless. But I had stared the leaders of our enemies in the eyes and turned my ear to their voices, and I knew the terror they meant to wreak upon our world.

CHAPTER FORTY-TWO

January 30, 1942
Los Angeles, California

I PACED ACROSS THE MARBLE ENTRYWAY FLOORS OF Hedgerow Farm, waiting for George Antheil, not Montgomery, who remained in the picture for the moment anyway. He'd sent me an urgent note earlier that day on the MGM set, where I was practicing scenes with my costar William Powell for my new movie *Crossroads*, a film noir, and we'd arranged to meet at my home in the late afternoon. While I traipsed, I held the script in my hand, ostensibly memorizing lines, but really, my mind could think of little else but the prospect of George's news.

In the seven weeks since America's war machine began grinding its gears against not only Japan but Europe, my restlessness had grown daily. The country prepared to send soldiers east and west, onto the very European ground from which I'd fled and across the ocean that I'd sailed. Official reports about downed planes and sunken ships had begun to pour in, alongside quieter stories passed among my European friends that American torpedoes targeted against Japanese ships often failed, either because they aimed too deeply or detonated too soon. Surely, I thought, the navy would adopt our system to address this failing. Surely the military wouldn't allow the enemy to proceed when George and I offered them a more effective option.

This anxiety reached a fever pitch as the whispers about a plan the Nazis called *Endlösung*—which, with its goal of annihilating European Jews, was the Third Reich strategy I'd been fearing—began winding its way down the corridors of Hollywood stage sets into the ears of my European friends. We gathered in dark bars and coffee shops to share the rumors we'd heard, finding the bright surreality of Hollywood too hard to bear as we shared unimaginable tales of Jewish ghettos, cattle cars, and concentration camps. We seemed to be the only ones in possession of these nightmares. Or perhaps, of all those who heard these murmurs, we were the only ones who believed that these nightmares could be real.

Images of the poor Austrian Jews inhabited my consciousness. So many of them were like myself. But they'd found it impossible to remove the stain of their heritage in the face of the Nazi invasion, no matter how hard they scrubbed with Teutonic vigor. Where were these people now? If they hadn't fled Vienna like Mama, were they in ghettos or camps? Or worse? Could I have done something?

I hoped that George's visit brought with it an invitation to action. We'd been waiting for months for word from the navy on our torpedo system. And sitting idly by on movie sets—costumed, bejeweled, and laden with guilt—was no longer an option.

The doorbells chimed, and even though I'd been marking time until they rang, I jumped. My housekeeper, Blanche, strode into the front hall to answer the door, but I shooed her away. I didn't need to stand on ceremony with George, and anyway, I didn't think I could withstand even a few minutes of pleasantries to discover his news.

I launched on him before he'd had the chance to remove his hat and topcoat. "What's the news?"

"Give me a moment, please. I'll tell you everything in time." He removed his hat, shaking the rain from it.

I honored his request in theory but couldn't hold back from a related inquiry. "Have you heard the reports about the navy's torpedo failures?"

"I have," he said, slipping his arm out from his coat sleeve.

"This will spur the navy on to adopt our system, don't you think? I mean, their own torpedoes are faring so poorly."

"Has your mother arrived?" he asked, hanging his trench coat on the coat stand. Why was he changing the topic?

Admittedly, George had been listening to my worries about Mama's well-being for months now. He'd lived through my hell of getting her out of London and into Canada. And he was all too familiar with how hard I'd lobbied the movie studio to help bring her the final distance to America. Of all people, he deserved an update. "She's on the train to California now. It'll take her three days to arrive here from Canada, so I'm expecting her on February 2."

"That must be a relief," George said as he trailed behind me into my drawing room where I'd set up a fresh flip chart on my board in anticipation of a new project.

"Yes," I said, but in truth, I had mixed feelings. I'd labored for so long to bring her to California, but now that she'd be standing in my home within a matter of days, I felt hesitant. What would it be like to have the famously difficult Mama as a fixture in my new world? Would the emotional insights she'd shared with me in her letter—that her reserve and negativity stemmed from a desire to balance Papa's indulgence—shape our relationship for the better? Could I believe in the love she professed to have for me? I decided to focus only upon the positive. I would have my mother here with me, safe and alive, when so many of our Viennese friends, neighbors, and family were in the Nazis' hands.

"Where will she live? Here with you and Jamesie?"

Without answering, I scrutinized my friend and colleague. My brother in arms. Why wasn't he sharing his urgent news? Why was he so curious about Mama, about whom he'd only tolerated discussions in the past? I'd never known him to be evasive before; if anything, I'd had to contain his brashness.

The answer arrived suddenly, but I couldn't bear to hear it from George's lips. Instead, I began to tread back and forth across the whitewashed planks of my drawing room floor, staring out at the sky periodically, while I responded to his ongoing queries about Mama. While the rain had stopped pouring and the skies had brightened, cloud shadows cast a periodic darkness upon the vivid green of my yard, and a sense of gloom descended upon me.

"The navy rejected us," I finally mustered the courage to say, because I knew he was struggling to muster up the courage to tell me the terrible news.

George sighed, finally admitting the truth. "Yes."

Without another word—I couldn't bear to speak about the refusal just yet—I trudged over to the sideboard and poured us each a tall Scotch. Gesturing for him to take the chair next to me, we sat side by side in my chocolate-brown leather armchairs. This time, however, we weren't excitedly brainstorming over our inventions. We were drinking in silence.

"On what grounds?" I finally asked. I almost didn't want to know.

"Well, you were right about the navy's torpedoes. I've heard rumors that over 60 percent of the torpedoes they've launched haven't hit their targets. It's awful." He deflected for a moment, then took a swig of the amber liquid and continued. "But these malfunctions didn't have the effect that you guessed at earlier. Like you, I'd thought that naval disappointment would lead to acceptance of our submission. Instead, the navy has decided to focus on getting their old-fashioned torpedoes to work, not in developing a completely new system with a complicated guidance system."

"Even though our system is superior?" I was incredulous.

"Even though." He paused, as if it pained him to explain further. "Of course, the navy is not openly admitting to their torpedo problems, so my sources tell me that they're blaming their decision to reject our proposal on the grounds that our system is too heavy."

"What? That makes no sense, George."

"I know. They said that our invention was too large to be used with the average torpedo."

"What?" I couldn't believe what George had just said. "Of

all the bases for rejection, that's the most ludicrous. Our mechanisms can fit inside a watch. We made that entirely clear in the papers we submitted to the National Inventors' Council and the navy."

"I know, and the council approved our designs. Honestly, Hedy, I wonder if they even fully read the submission. I think they saw the analogy between aspects of our system and the player piano and made a nonsensical extrapolation that they then latched upon as an excuse instead of admitting the truth: that they'd not given adequate funding to torpedo research for decades and, as result, the navy is saddled with an archaic, ineffective system that's too expensive to overhaul entirely."

George sounded defeated, but my rage had just begun to flare. I turned to him, screaming, "How could they reject an invention that could not only accurately steer an entire fleet of torpedoes to its destination, but would also be unjammable by the enemy, in favor of an old-fashioned system that never worked in the first place?"

"I don't know," George said dejectedly, but he had no fight in his voice, no anger. Who was this George?

I pushed against this acquiescence, testing its limits. "We should write to the navy and the National Inventors' Council, explain to them how they misinterpreted our submission. Tell them precisely how small our mechanisms can be built."

"I don't think it's worth it, Hedy. I doubt it'll change their minds." Why was he so oddly complacent? Maybe the long wait had finally worn down the ever-optimistic composer—no, inventor.

I rose from my leather armchair, my voice even stronger.

"We are going to Washington, DC, to explain our invention in person." I conjured all my power, as if standing onstage, and said, "George, if there's anything I've learned, right or wrong, it's this: Hedy Lamarr the actress, not the inventor standing before you, can change men's minds."

CHAPTER FORTY-THREE

April 20, 1942
Washington, DC

THE WAR SEEMED MORE REAL IN WASHINGTON, DC. FROM the window of our hired car, I saw troops amassing for training exercises, flags flying from every building, and heightened security forces on the exterior of critical government buildings. A palpable energy and pride pulsated throughout the citizens and heartened me for this war against the Third Reich.

The car let George and me off in front of the New War Building, as it was known, at the corner of Twenty-First Street and Virginia Avenue Northwest. We marched up the imposing stairs of the sandstone building that held the official offices of sections of the War Department, including the navy. A military officer let us pass into the revolving brass doors, and we walked up to two stunned guards helping police the citizens approved to enter and exit the building amid the throngs of army and navy men and women. Recognizing me, they guided us to the front of the security line, leading us past a fifty-foot mural that they told us was entitled "Defense of America's Freedoms."

"We have a one o'clock appointment," I said to the

receptionist, who sat behind a series of doors through which we'd been escorted. This appointment with naval higher-ups had been secured for us with George's "source," his government friend who'd kept us abreast of our submission's status throughout the process.

The young woman in a military uniform, who appeared to be sporting a blond version of the "Lamarr" look, stared at me. She stammered, "You're—you're Hedy—Hedy—" Mouth agape, she ceased speaking.

"Lamarr," I finished for her with a gentle smile. "Yes, I'm Hedy Lamarr, and this is Mr. George Antheil. And we have an appointment."

She sprung up. "Yes, Miss Lamarr, I'm so sorry. Please allow me to show you back to Colonel Smith's office."

As she led us through a warren of hallways, the receptionist periodically glanced back at us as if she couldn't quite believe a movie star was in their midst. She led us deeper into the labyrinth of naval operations until we finally reached a vast office that presided over an entire corner of the building. Before the young woman could knock, another man rounded the corner and greeted us.

"Bullitt," George called out, his hand already outstretched.

The men shook hands and clapped each other on their backs. I realized that this must be George's "source." William C. Bullitt was currently a senior member of the State Department but had been a journalist and diplomat when George and his wife first met him in Paris in 1925. Even though Bullitt was on the outs with President Roosevelt over his public dislike of Undersecretary of State Sumner Welles, a favorite of

Roosevelt's, he was still close enough to the corridors of power to provide George and me with solid inside information. He'd arranged the meeting and volunteered to accompany us to it.

The men finished their reunion and turned toward me. George introduced his friend, who stuck out his hand. "Call me Bullitt. So you are the famous Hedy Lamarr," he said with a certain amount of astonishment, even though he'd expected me. "When George told me he was working on an invention with you, I thought he was pulling a practical joke."

I didn't like this man's tone, even if he was a good friend of George's. "Because you couldn't imagine a woman working on a military invention?"

Bullitt's eyes widened. "Of course not. Because I couldn't imagine a beautiful movie star wanting to work with this guy," he said with a mock punch on George's arm. The men laughed. Perhaps I'd misread Bullitt. Anticipation over this meeting had stretched my nerves thin.

Turning toward the door, Bullitt called to us over his shoulder, "You folks ready?"

"As ready as we will ever be," George called back.

I reached over and squeezed his hand. I felt more nervous than stepping onto any stage or movie set, because today, I wasn't acting.

Bullitt held the door open for us, and we walked into a spacious office, where two uniformed men and a civilian gentleman awaited us. Bullitt introduced them as Colonel L. B. Lent, chief engineer of the National Inventors' Council; Colonel Smith, assistant to the chief procurement officer of the navy; and Mr. Robson, whose title remained curiously unspoken.

After we exchanged pleasantries, I stood before the men, glad I'd worn my most conservative navy suit. In my most authoritative voice, I began, "Good afternoon, gentlemen. Thank you for taking the time to see us, particularly in light of the demands the war effort must put upon you. Mr. Antheil and I understand that you initially declined to adopt our proposed torpedo system as part of your overall naval plan because of your concerns over the size of our system. Today, we would like to take a few minutes to explain exactly how small our system is. We would like to begin with the description we laid out in our patent application, which the United States Patent Office is currently considering."

The men exchanged surprised glances with one another. Had no one told them in advance that we had filed a patent, regardless of their denial? Or were the looks of astonishment a ruse? I continued with the prepared speech I'd labored over, holding up diagrams of the torpedo system and models demonstrating its small size. George took the helm at the designated moment, and we finished our presentation by emphasizing the accuracy of our system and inviting questions from the gentlemen.

Mr. Robson cleared his throat. "This has been a most illuminating talk, Mr. Antheil and Miss Lamarr. I think I speak for all of us when I say that we have a much greater appreciation for your torpedo system, in particular its size. It certainly isn't the behemoth we originally thought, and you've created an intriguing, novel invention."

George and I shot each other hopeful glances.

He continued, "However, we must stand by our earlier

decision to decline the adoption of your system. We have decided to continue with our existing torpedo system, with updates and modifications, of course."

I didn't understand. George glanced over at me quizzically.

"May I ask why?" I asked, trying to keep my voice even. "We have addressed your stated concerns over the size of our invention."

"Yes, you and Mr. Antheil have done that." The men gave one another furtive glances, and Mr. Robson hesitated before continuing, "Miss Lamarr, may I speak frankly?"

I nodded.

"I'm a big fan of your work, and I speak for all of us here in saying we appreciate the incredible efforts you and Mr. Antheil have undertaken here. But my advice to you is this—stick to your films. They help lift people's spirits. But if you're bound and determined to help with the war effort, we think you'd be better able to assist by selling war bonds than building torpedoes. Instead of focusing on all this weapons stuff, why don't you help us raise money to win the war against the Japs and the Krauts?"

No matter the misogyny that I knew well permeated the very fiber of my world, I couldn't believe his words. These men were rejecting a system that would enable a plane or ship to steer a whole fleet of torpedoes against enemy vessels with perfect accuracy, without any capacity on the enemy's part to jam the necessary radio signals. How could the military allow their soldiers and sailors to lose on the seas—to be killed in vast numbers—because they wouldn't use a weapon system designed by a woman?

My voice sounded calm, an emotion I certainly did not feel. What I felt was furious. "Let me understand. You are turning down our invention—which would have made your fleet unsurpassed in ocean warfare—because I'm a woman? A famous one that you'd rather have shilling war bonds than helping build effective systems? I can do both, you know—sell bonds and assist with your torpedoes, if that's what it takes."

Mr. Robson answered, "That isn't the sole reason we've decided to turn down your proposal, Miss Lamarr. But since you've raised it, I must admit it would be hard for us to sell our soldiers and sailors on a weapons system created by a woman. And we're not going to try."

I couldn't move. I couldn't speak. His words had stunned me into silent immobility. George and I had come so close, only to be stymied by naked prejudice. Seeing the expression on my face, George jumped in, desperately trying to stanch the wound by defending the merits of my "rather unfeminine occupation of inventor" and extolling my skills and intellect in building this unassailable torpedo system. But the wound was fatal.

As he continued to battle onward, arguing for the superiority of our system and the irrelevance of the gender of its creator, I sank back into the enveloping arms of my chair. It seemed the only solace available to me at the moment.

All the rage storming within me evaporated, leaving a hollow, if beautiful, shell. Perhaps the shell was all this world wanted from me. And perhaps the world would never allow me my penance.

CHAPTER FORTY-FOUR

September 4, 1942
Philadelphia, Pennsylvania

I HEARD THE ROAR OF THE CROWD FROM BEHIND THE SCAR-
let velvet curtain. The color and texture were so reminiscent
of the Theater an der Wien curtain that, for a moment, I was
transported back to Vienna, to my triumphant debut on the
stage as the iconic Bavarian empress Elizabeth. How long ago
that moment seemed, and how innocent that girl. Incredible
to think that I was once free of the guilt now stitched into the
fabric of my being.

I wondered how my guilt would be measured. Would an
accounting be done, tallying the lives I might have saved?
Would the scales tip more favorably in my direction because of
the efforts I made with my invention, even though its use was
thwarted by the military? The navy hadn't changed its mind
even when the United States Patent Office granted our application, giving the invention U.S. Patent Number 2,292,387,
a decision it would have made only if our design was viable.
Would I be granted any leniency in my sentence for the contributions I now made to halt the Nazis' evil in the sole way left

to me? "By selling war bonds instead of building torpedoes," as Mr. Robson had not-so-kindly suggested? I'd taken him at his word, which I doubted he intended me to take seriously.

The strains of violins and horns wafted over the din of the audience, and they slowly settled into respectful quiet after the prior act finished. The baritone host announced the next performance in the event to the Philadelphia Academy of Music patrons, and I readied myself for my act. For an act it was indeed.

The curtain rose, revealing an architectural confection of gold, crystal, and crimson evocative of the Vienna decor of my youth. How wounded, I wondered, was the Viennese landscape now and its people? Did even one of my childhood neighbors remain in the quaint cottages that lined the Döbling streets, including my family's street, Peter-Jordan-Strasse? Or had they already been shipped east to Poland and the camps? A tear threatened to escape from my eye and drip down my cheek, but I blinked it away.

Bringing myself back to the present, I listened as the audience gasped at the glittering offering I made. Dressed in a vermillion sequined gown designed to capture every facet of light on the stage, I didn't move, allowing the theatergoers to drink in my appearance. Then, I sauntered toward the audience members with hands outstretched, preparing them for the donation I'd be seeking. For I was both an offering *and* an invitation.

"Welcome to the United States Victory Show!" I announced in my best impression of an American accent, knowing that my natural Germanic accent wouldn't be received well tonight. I held my hand up in the now-famous "V for victory" symbol, and the audience did the same.

The audience lowered their hands to clap, and the theater thundered with the crowd's applause. "My name is Hedy Lamarr, and I am just a plain gold digger for Uncle Sam. I'm here to help win the war. I think you're here to see what that Lamarr dame looks like," I said with a comedic inflection, placing a jaunty hand on my hip. It was my best impersonation of the cheery Susie.

Laughter escaped from the theatergoers, as planned. Then I dropped my voice into a deeper octave to bring home my deadly serious point. "We should be here for the same purpose. What you think Hedy Lamarr looks like doesn't worry me as much as what Hirohito and Hitler are doing. Every time you dig into your pocketbooks, you tell those two rotten men the Yanks are coming. Let's make the end of the war come soon. Don't think about what the other fellow is doing. You buy bonds!"

The returning applause threatened to deafen, and while I waited for it to subside, I thought about the days to come, brimming with other events like this where I'd give some version of this speech. There would be parades and presentations and even luncheons for businessmen and leaders with five-thousand-dollar war bond minimums. How many millions could I raise for the Allies cause?

Putting my hand over my brows to provide shade while I looked out at the audience, I asked, "I say, do we have any of our military men in the audience tonight?"

The tour organizers had given tickets to a group of army and navy officers for this very purpose, and they'd planted in their ranks a very special sailor. He'd applied for this role, and we had practiced his routine beforehand. The military men, seated in the front section to the left, yelled out and raised their hands.

"Are we going to win this war, boys?"

This time, the entire audience cheered, although the military fellows yelled the loudest. Then, as we'd rehearsed, one particular sailor called out to me, "How about a kiss before we head out to war?"

Pretending to be shocked at his question, I let my jaw gape as I glanced in his direction. "Did you ask for a kiss, sailor?"

"Yes, ma'am," he yelled back.

I turned toward the audience. "Do you think I should give this brave young sailor a kiss?"

The crowd let out a resounding cry of "Yes!"

"These fine Americans think I should grant your request, Sailor. So come on up here."

The boy, in perfectly pressed navy whites, complete with the hat and tie, ran onto the stage. He'd appeared eager and bold until he stepped foot onto the wide dais, when a shy expression suddenly surfaced on his face. He'd never faced a crowd of thousands before. This was his first time onstage and the first time in this role, although he wasn't pretending to be a sailor about to be shipped out. His boat awaited him, as did the vast Pacific Ocean and fleets of enemy warships.

To calm his nerves, I greeted him with a warm handshake and invited him to introduce himself to the audience by his given name, Eddie Rhodes. I then focused my attention back on the crowd. "I'll make a deal with you, folks. I'll give our courageous serviceman Eddie Rhodes here a great big kiss if you pledge—right now—at least five hundred thousand dollars total. We've got girls with pledge sheets at the end of each aisle, ready to write your names and your donations down."

The girls, dressed in military uniform costumes themselves, passed the sign-up lists up and down the long aisles of the Academy of Music while Eddie and I waited onstage. Eddie's case of the stage jitters seemed to have passed, so he and I chatted easily for several minutes about his family back home while the orchestra played patriotic music. But then he shared his excitement about his assignment aboard a ship to the Pacific, and my stomach lurched. How I wished the navy had accepted our torpedo system. If it had, this poor young man would stand a much better chance at survival. I turned away so he wouldn't see the tears welling in my eyes.

A line of girls who had finished with their task began to form alongside the stage. "Have we reached our number?" I called over to our tour manager, who was busy adding the number of pledges. I watched as he conversed animatedly with the host, but no one responded to my question. Had we not reached our five-hundred-thousand-dollar goal? Maybe we'd asked for too much? We'd debated long and hard over the exact number to request from the patrons tonight, and I put incredible pressure on myself over this amount. I tabulated every dollar as if each one brought me closer to the Sisyphean state of redemption.

Eddie and I glanced at one another over the delay, the anxiety mounting in each of us. Finally, the host climbed the stairs leading to the stage. When he reached our side, I asked into the microphone, "Does our sailor deserve that kiss?"

"Well, Miss Lamarr, I have some news. We asked for a

tremendous amount from our audience tonight. Five hundred thousand dollars, as you know, is a veritable fortune."

"It sure is," I responded lightly, as if I wasn't bracing myself for the inevitable bad news.

"And tonight, we did not raise five hundred thousand dollars," he added, to the disappointment of the jeering audience.

"I'm so sorry," I said to Eddie. He looked crestfallen.

"Oh, don't be sorry, Miss Lamarr. And, Eddie, don't you be sorry either. Because tonight, we raised two million two hundred and fifty thousand dollars!" the host practically screamed, a necessity given the cacophony of sound coming from the crowd.

I was stunned. No war bond campaign event had ever raised five hundred thousand dollars, let alone over two million dollars. Only the high-roller luncheons with sky-high minimum donation fees targeting the big donors anticipated these figures. Not the typical war bond affair.

"Kiss him, kiss him," the audience began to chant, bringing me back to this moment. "Kiss him, kiss him."

I spun toward Eddie. He had earned that kiss, and so had the audience. As I readied for it, the floodlights blinded me for a moment, bringing me back again to my momentous opening night at the Theater an der Wien. Time buckled and then folded back onto itself, back to the night that changed everything. That night sent me on the path I stood upon today, one fraught with overwhelming guilt, the pursuit of redemption, and, occasionally, unexpected joy.

How many masks have I worn on my path? I wondered, unable to stop the tears from streaming down my face. Tears that Eddie Rhodes, my tour manager, and probably the audience thought were tears of joy from the wildly successful fundraising. Had I ever lowered one of my facades fully and braved my bare skin to the world since Papa's death? The closest I'd come was during my work with George, work that I'd been told was unacceptably "unfeminine." Work to which I'd refused to return after the navy's rejection, even when George begged me; I simply couldn't make myself that vulnerable again. Otherwise, I'd midwifed myself through multiple rebirths, donning a fresh persona with every new iteration, only to return to my original veneer again and again. Even tonight. Especially tonight.

Had I, in the end, become who they already thought I was? To everyone else, I was Hedy Lamarr, only a beautiful face and lissome body. I was never Hedy Kiesler, aspiring inventor, curious thinker, and Jew. Never the self I really was underneath the many roles I'd played on- and off-screen.

Or had I used the world's perception of me as a disguise, a sort of smoke screen to distract them while I achieved my ends? Had I taken the persona to which I'd been relegated and made myself into a weapon against the Third Reich after all, just not the instrument of destruction I'd intended? I wondered if it even mattered what—or who—they thought I was, if I'd gotten my revenge against the European suppressors by funding the Allies tonight and perhaps, along with it, the redemption I'd sought.

I had always been alone under my mask, the only woman in the room.

AUTHOR'S NOTE

We hold a piece of women's history in our hands every day. I do not mean this in a metaphorical sense but quite literally. Every day, nearly every one of us holds a piece of history created—in a roundabout fashion—by Hedy Lamarr.

What is this literal piece of history? It's one that the time period and scope of my novel would not allow me to address. It is your cell phone. But how on earth did an invention patented by a dazzling movie star in 1942 eventually become part of the foundation for the modern cell phone, a device that has transformed our world?

As you probably know by now, *The Only Woman in the Room* explores the singular and oftentimes unbelievable life of the woman better known as the movie star Hedy Lamarr. If I've done my job correctly, the book also reveals aspects of her life far less understood: her early life as a young Jewish woman in a very Catholic Austria; her astonishing, sometimes disturbing marriage to armaments manufacturer and arms dealer Friedrich "Fritz" Mandl from which she fled; and, perhaps most importantly, the time she spent creating inventions she hoped would help the Allies defeat the Nazis in World War II. It was during this later time period, almost entirely forgotten until recently, that the woman first known as the Austrian girl Hedwig Kiesler (alongside composer George Antheil) fashioned her frequency-hopping invention, in which radio signals transmitting from a ship or airplane to its torpedo would constantly change frequencies, making those signals impenetrable and improving the torpedoes' accuracy. This was Hedy's take on spread-spectrum technology.

After Hedy presented her invention to the navy and suffered through the disappointment of its refusal to use her design, despite the deficiencies in its own torpedo systems, Hedy assumed that the death knell had rung for her Secret Communication System. Interestingly, however, the military classified Patent 2,292,387 as top secret and, in the 1950s, gave it to a contractor for the construction of a sonobuoy that could detect submarines in the water and then transmit that information to an airplane above using Hedy's unjammable frequency-hopping idea. Later, the military and other private entities began to make their own inventions using this interpretation of spread-spectrum technology—without any recompense to Hedy, as the patent had expired—and today, aspects of her frequency-hopping idea can be found in the wireless devices we use every day. Hedy's role in these advancements was unknown until the 1990s, when she received a few awards for her invention, recognition she considered more important than the success of her movies.

So when we look at our cell phones—as almost everyone does countless times every day—we stare directly into the face of a scientific invention made, in part, upon Hedy Lamarr's invention. It is a tangible reminder of her life, beyond the films for which she is more famous. And who knows whether the cell phone as we know it today would have been constructed without her work?

But it seems to me that Hedy, her history, and her creation may have even greater symbolic importance. The manner in which her contribution to this world-changing device was largely lost—or ignored—for decades reflects the pervasive marginalization of women's contributions, a problem that is both historical and modern. Whether Hedy's work in spread-spectrum technology was purposefully disregarded or unconsciously forgotten, it appears that imbedded in that oversight were misconceptions about her abilities—about all women, really. Faulty assumptions about women's capabilities, stemming in part from the conscripted roles into which they'd been slotted, has caused many to think more narrowly about the manner in which the past has been shaped. But unless we begin to view historical women through a broader, more inclusive lens—and rewrite them back into the narrative—we will continue to view the past more restrictively than it likely was, and we risk carrying those perspectives over into the present.

Perhaps if Hedy's society had viewed her not simply as a blindingly beautiful creature, but as a human being with a sharp mind capable of significant contributions, they might have learned that her interior life was more interesting and fruitful than her exterior. Her invention might have been accepted by the navy when she offered it, and who knows what impact that might have had on the war? If only people had been willing to look behind "the only woman in the room" to examine the person she was beneath, they might have seen a woman capable of greatness, and not only on the screen.

*Read on for an excerpt from Marie Benedict's
next book from Sourcebooks Landmark*

LADY
CLEMENTINE

CHAPTER ONE

September 12, 1908
London, England

I ALWAYS FEEL DIFFERENT. NO MATTER THE SPHERE I
inhabit, I always feel set apart. Even today. Especially
today.

The weak, early September sun strains to break through the
darkness of the cold morning. The pallid rays illuminate the
cavernous bedroom assigned to me by my benefactress, Lady
St. Helier. They hit the white satin dress hanging on the mannequin, reminding me that the gown waits for me.

As I finger the delicately embroidered, square-cut bodice,
its sleek Venetian fabric finer than any I've ever worn, I am
seized by a sensation fiercer than the usual isolation that often
besets me. I crave connection.

I hunt for the clothes the maids unpacked from my trunk
and placed into the dresser drawers and mirrored armoire when
I arrived at 52 Portland Place a fortnight ago. But I find nothing other than the corset and undergarments meant to be worn
under the white gown today. Only then do I realize that the
maids must have packed my belongings back into my trunk for

my journey afterward. The mere thought of afterward sends a shiver through me.

Tying my gray silk dressing gown tightly around my waist, I tiptoe down the grand staircase of Lady St. Helier's mansion. At first, I don't know precisely what I am seeking, but I have an epiphany when I spot a housemaid working in the parlor. She's kneeling before the fireplace grate.

The sound of my footfalls startles the poor girl, and she jumps. "Morning, Miss Hozier. May I help you with anythin'?" she says, wiping her blackened fingers on the cloth dangling from her apron.

I hesitate. Will I endanger the girl if I enlist her help? Surely Lady St. Helier will forgive any protocol breach I cause today.

"As a matter of fact, I could use your assistance. If it is not too much trouble, that is." The apology is heavy in my voice.

After I explain my predicament to the girl, whose age must match my own, she races away down the back hallway toward the kitchen. At first, I think she may have misunderstood my request or thought me mad. But I follow her, and when she scurries across the rough wooden kitchen floor toward the servants' staircase, I understand.

Wincing at the loud clatter of her work boots stomping up the stairway and down the hallway of the attic where the servants' bedrooms are, I wait. I silently pray that her racket does not rouse the rest of the staff. I fear that if they appear for their morning chores and find me in the kitchen, one of them will alert Lady St. Helier. When the girl returns with a bundle in hand—without any additional servants in tow—I sigh in relief.

"What is your name?" I ask, reaching for the bundle.

"Mary, miss," she answers with a minuscule curtsy.

"I shall be forever in your debt, Mary."

"It's my pleasure, Miss Hozier." She gives me a conspiratorial smile, and I realize that she is enjoying her part in this unorthodox plan. It may be the only deviation in the sameness of her days.

As I pivot and walk back toward the grand staircase, Mary whispers, "Why don't you change in the pantry, miss? Less chance of being found out than if you head back up them stairs. I'll make sure your clothes are returned to your bedroom before anyone notices them."

The girl is right. Every step I take up that creaky grand staircase is one step closer to waking the lady of the house and her servants. Taking her advice, I enter the jar-lined pantry and close the door only partially to ensure some light will reach the enclosed space. I let my dressing gown and robe slide down and puddle on the floor, and I unwrap the bundle. Pulling out a surprisingly sweet floral dress, I shimmy into its floor-grazing cotton and then lace up the black boots Mary thoughtfully included.

"Fits you right well, Miss Hozier," the girl says when I step back into the kitchen. As she hands me her coat off the peg on the wall, she says, "Godspeed to you."

I hurry out the servants' door at the rear of the house and make my way down an alleyway that runs behind the row of luxurious Georgian homes lining Portland Place. I pass by kitchen windows beginning to glow with lamps lit by servants readying the house for their masters. A bustling world lies behind the mansions of Lady St. Helier and her friends, but because I always enter through the front doors, I've never witnessed the province at the back.

The alley lets out onto Weymouth Street, where a motorbus stops. It's heading west to Kensington, and I know the route fairly well as I've taken it the other direction toward Lady St. Helier's on several occasions. Mary's wool coat is too thin for the brisk morning, and as I wait for the bus, I wrap it tightly around me in the vain hope of extracting a bit more warmth from its meager fibers.

The unadorned hat that Mary leant me bears only a small brim, and consequently, the working girl disguise does nothing to mask my face. When I step onto the bus, the driver recognizes me from the photographs that have run in the newspapers in recent days. He stares at me but says nothing at first. Finally, he sputters, "Surely you're in the wrong place, Miss"—he drops his voice to a whisper, realizing that he shouldn't reveal my identity—"Hozier."

"I am precisely where I mean to be, sir," I answer in a tone that I hope is kind yet firm. His eyes never leave my face as he takes the fare Mary had given me from her savings—which I plan to replace multifold—but he doesn't say another word.

I keep my gaze lowered to shield my face from the curious onlookers who have been alerted to the oddness of my presence by the driver's reaction. I hop off the bus the moment it nears Abingdon Villas, and I feel lighter the closer I come to the cream-colored stucco house bearing the number 51. By the time I reach up to lift the heavy brass knocker, the tightness in my chest begins to loosen, and I breathe with ease. No one answers the door immediately, but I am not surprised. Here, no bevy of servants lies in wait in the kitchen, ever ready to answer the knock of a front door or the ring of a master's bell. Here, one servant does the work of many, and the household inhabitants do the rest.

I wait, and after several long minutes, my patience is rewarded with an open door. The face of my beloved sister Nellie, still creased with sleep, appears. She rushes in for an embrace before the shock of seeing me registers and she freezes.

"What on earth are you doing here, Clementine? And in *those* clothes?" she asks. Her expression is quizzical. "Today is your wedding day."

CHAPTER TWO

September 12, 1908
London, England

T HE COMFORTING SMELL OF STEEPING TEA RISES TO MY
nostrils, and I allow the steam to warm my face and hands.
Nellie has not pressed me to answer her question, not yet. I
know she will soon insist on an explanation for my unexpected
visit, but for now, I indulge in the temporary quiet of the parlor.
These silent moments alone with my sister, here at home, may
be enough to carry me through the day.

"You are not thinking of calling off the wedding, Clemmie?"
Nellie interrupts the silence with a tremulous whisper. Neither
of us wishes to waken a single member of the sleeping
household—least of all Mother.

"No, no, Nellie," I whisper back, reaching for her hand. My
knuckles brush across the table where my sister and I used to spend
hours doing needlework for our cousin Lena Whyte's dressmak-
ing business, a necessity to help with household expenses.

Relief softens her features. I hadn't realized how fearful the
very idea that I might cancel *this* wedding made her. It had been
cruel of me not to justify my appearance from the beginning.

"Nothing like that, dearest. I simply needed the familiarity of home for a moment. To calm my nerves, as it were."

"Nerves over what? The wedding ceremony itself? Or the man you are marrying?" Nellie, my little sister and the twin to my only brother, surprises me with her astuteness. For too long, I'd considered her youthful and inexperienced, not at all the confidante that my indomitable elder sister Kitty would have been had she lived beyond sixteen, had my beautiful, fearless sister not succumbed to typhoid. I should not have underestimated Nellie.

Her question awakens a memory of the first time I met my intended. It was an evening at Lady St. Helier's mansion, the very place from which I'd just fled. I had initially resisted my benefactress's invitation to dinner on that cool March night. My suitable gowns were in need of mending, and I had no clean white gloves, I'd lamented to Mother. In truth, my long afternoon tutoring French had exhausted me, but I didn't dare speak plainly, as Mother loathed any reminder that we girls needed to contribute to the household upkeep. She preferred to believe her title and aristocratic heritage would magically provide funds for housing, food, and servants, a strange contradiction with her decidedly bohemian views on the malleability of the marital vow and her clear focus on her extramarital relationships and little else, certainly not us children. She would brook no excuse to turn down an invitation by my generous, wealthy patroness, who was Mother's aunt and adored helping the young make their way into proper society. So Mother loaned me her own gloves and Nellie's simple white satin princess dress, and off I dutifully went, if a bit past schedule.

But late as I was, the dinner guest to my right still had not materialized by the time the staff served the second of five courses. I'd begun to despair of any conversation other than the boring weather reports recounted by the elderly gentleman to my left when the dining room door swung open with a slam. Before the butler could announce the tardy guest, a round-faced man with a sheepish half grin marched in, offering his apologies to Lady St. Helier before settling into the ornately carved chair next to me. As the chair's feet scraped loudly against the wooden floor, drowning out the butler's announcement of his name, my attention was drawn to the man. His cheeks had the softness of boyhood, but on his forehead, I saw the deep grooves of adult worries.

Who was this gentleman? He looked familiar, although I could not place his face. Had I met him at another social occasion? There had been so many.

"Miss, I regret any inconvenience my delinquency caused you. An empty seat at a formal dinner is no easy matter. Please excuse me," he said, meeting my gaze with unsettling directness.

Unaccustomed as I was to such candor, my surprise precipitated a blunt response. "It is no inconvenience at all, sir. I arrived only moments before you, my work having delayed my own arrival." I immediately regretted my words, as girls of my class were not meant to have employment.

He looked startled. "You have a position?"

"Yes," I answered, a bit on the defensive. "I am an instructor of French." I didn't dare mention the income-generating needlework that Nellie and I also undertook.

His eyes shimmered with enthusiasm. "That...that is

wondrous, miss. To know something of work and the world is invaluable."

Did he mean it? Or was this a bit of mockery? I didn't know how to respond, so I decided to thread the needle with an innocuous response.

"If you say so, sir."

"I do indeed. It is refreshing. And your regular immersion in French and its culture, ah…of that, I am jealous. I have always held a healthy appreciation for the cultural and political contributions France has made to Europe, particularly the fostering of personal liberty and the rights of man."

He seemed in earnest, and his views matched my own. I took a chance and responded in kind. "I agree wholeheartedly, sir. I even considered studying French, its culture, and its politics at university. In fact, my headmistress encouraged me to do so."

"Indeed?" Again, he seemed surprised, and I wondered if I'd been too honest about my youthful ambitions. I did not know this man or his views.

I softened my aspirations with gentle humor. "Yes. Although, in the end, I had to settle for a winter in Paris, where I attended lectures at the Sorbonne, visited art galleries, and dined with the artist Camille Pissarro."

"No small solace," he offered with a smile, his eyes lingering on mine. Did I imagine a glimmer of respect in his light-blue eyes? In the low candlelight, their color shifted from pale aquamarine to the color of the dawn sky.

We grew quiet for a moment, and it seemed as though the rest of the guests—an illustrious mix of political figures, journalists, and the odd American heiress—had reached a lull in their conversations as well. Or perhaps they had been listening quietly to us all along. I realized that I'd been so engrossed in discussion with my tablemate that I'd quite forgotten the other diners.

The gentleman stammered for a moment, and to avoid embarrassment, I returned to the chicken on my plate, now grown quite cold. I felt his eyes on me but didn't turn. Our exchange had been unusually personal for a first meeting, and I didn't know what to say next.

"Please forgive me, miss." His words were unexpected.

"For what, sir?"

"For my unforgivable lapse in manners."

"I do not know what you mean."

"A woman like yourself deserves every courtesy. I realize now that I have not offered even the bare minimum—an introduction beyond the butler's announcement. This is particularly inexcusable given that I arrived too late for the usual formalities. Will you allow me to introduce myself?"

I gave him a small nod, wondering what he meant by "a woman like yourself." What sort of woman did he think I was?

"My name is Winston Churchill."

Ah, I thought with a start. The familiarity of his appearance was explained. While I believed I'd met him in passing several years earlier, I knew his face not from that earlier social occasion but from the newspapers. The gentleman sitting next to me was a prominent member of Parliament and rumored to soon become the next president of the Board of Trade, which would make him one of the most important members of the government. His rise through the leadership ranks had been riddled with controversy, as he'd changed parties from Conservative to Liberal a few years before, favoring free trade and a more active government with legislation protecting the welfare of its citizens. This led to constant coverage in the dailies, including a lengthy interview in the *Daily Chronicle* by the *Dracula* author, Bram Stoker, a few months ago.

If I recalled correctly, some years before, this Mr. Churchill had actually voted in favor of the female suffrage bill, an issue quite dear to me. During my school years at Berkhamsted School for Girls, my headmistress, Beatrice Harris, had instilled in me a taste for female independence. Her lectures on suffragism had fallen upon keen ears, because, having grown up with a mother who professed nonconformist beliefs but actually relied upon her aristocratic status and many liaisons for sustenance, I wanted to pursued a path of purpose and, if possible, independence. And now, sitting before me was one of the few politicians who had publicly backed an early effort for the women's vote. I suddenly felt quite nervous but exhilarated at the same time.

The rest of the table had grown quiet, but my dinner partner didn't seem to notice, because he cleared his throat loudly and continued. "I hope the mere name Winston Churchill doesn't scare you off. I'm quite the pariah these days in most households."

A fierce heat spread across my usually pale cheeks, not from his words but from my worry that my ignorance of his identity might have led me into some kind of gaffe. *Had I said anything inappropriate?* I wondered as I quickly reviewed our exchange. I did not think so. If Kitty had been in my place, she would have

managed this interaction with aplomb and humor instead of
with my awkward pauses and nerves.

I settled upon a response. "No, sir, not at all. I find your
views quite in line with my own, and I am delighted to make
your acquaintance."

"Not delighted enough to share your name, it seems."

My cheeks flamed even hotter. "I am Miss Clementine
Hozier."

"It is *my* pleasure, Miss Hozier."

~

I smile at the memory now. Before I can answer Nellie, her
twin, Bill, bounds into the room. Bill is my younger brother
and still schoolboy gangly despite his position as an officer in
the Royal Navy. He is midbite into an enormous apple that
promptly clambers to the floor when he sees me. "What in the
devil are you doing here? Not skipping out on another commitment, I hope?"

Leaping to my feet, I jab his arm for the reference to my not
one but two jilted fiancés—Sidney Cornwallis Peel, grandson
of the former prime minister Sir Robert Peel, and Lionel Earle,
men with lofty titles or positions and the promise of financial
security but with whom I foresaw a life of staid decorum and
scant hope of purpose. While I eschew the unconventional life
led by my mother, I found that I could not commit to either
of these fine gentlemen solely for the sake of propriety when I
longed for a life of meaning and, dare I think it, emotion, even
though decorousness was a powerful lure.

Nellie, Bill, and I burst into laughter, and I feel impossibly light. The heavy sense of isolation I felt in the long hours before dawn fades away, and in the presence of my siblings, the aisle-long march to my new life no longer seems an insurmountable journey. Until Mother walks into the room.

For the first time in memory, Mother is speechless. No judgmental lectures on her pet topics, no public redressing for perceived slights, no under-the-breath yet audible remarks about bourgeois acquaintances. And most incredibly, it is me—the least favored and often ignored of her children—who has rendered mute the outspoken Lady Blanche Hozier.

Nellie, the favorite, leaps in to defend me. "Clemmie is here only for tea and a quick visit, Mama."

Mother rises up to her full height and finds her voice. In a shrill, mocking tone, she says, "A visit? At dawn? On the morning of her wedding?"

No one answers. Such questions are not meant to be answered.

With her blond hair in disheveled strands around her still-beautiful face, she stares at each of us in turn, making yet another criticism dressed up as a rhetorical question. "Can any of you think of anything *less* appropriate?"

I almost snort with laughter at our bohemian mother, never one to follow the strictures of society, church, or family, doubting the *appropriateness* of her children's behavior. She, whose own behavior has long flouted the traditions of marriage and child-rearing through multiple simultaneous affairs and long absences. And we, who cling to convention as a life raft in the sea of our mother's tempestuousness.

Glancing at Nellie and Bill, I recognize the cowed

expressions beginning to form on their faces, and I remind myself what today means. For me, for our family. Instead of submitting to Mother's irritation and hoping a remorseful look will dissipate her foul humor, I assemble my own features into an air of amusement. Today, I will assume a powerful mantle, and this is my first effort at making plain that the balance has shifted.

"Surely you don't begrudge your daughter a brief trip across town to see her family on the morning of her wedding, Mama?" I ask with a smile. I'm trying to sound like Grandmother, also called Lady Blanche, who, as a Stanley of Alderley inhabiting Airlie Castle, embodies all the strong and assertive qualities the Stanley matriarchs are known for, including female education. Not that Mother follows suit in her own beliefs; she is unorthodox in every view except on the subject of female education. I cannot understand it, but I suppose it's that Mother's focus lies on her relationships with men, most of whom find female education distasteful.

Mother doesn't answer at first, unused to being challenged. Finally, she speaks, in a forced and deliberate manner. "Of course not, Clementine. But I will arrange for a brougham to pick you up and take you back to prepare at Lady St. Helier's within the hour. After all, there will be over a thousand people watching you walk down the aisle."

READING GROUP GUIDE

1. As *The Only Woman in the Room* opens, Hedy's father expresses concern for his daughter's welfare—for all Jewish people, really—in the wake of Hitler's desire to annex their home country, Austria, to the overtly anti-Semitic Germany. Hedy views this as a problem faced by the *Ostjuden*, the nonconforming Eastern Jewish people, but not the fully assimilated Viennese Jews like her and her family. Did her initial reaction surprise you, and if so, do you think modern-day readers would find her response disconcerting thanks to the benefit of hindsight? How do you think you might have acted in this time period?

2. As a very young woman, Hedy marries one of the richest men in Austria, the munitions manufacturer Fritz Mandl. How did you feel about her encounters with high-ranking Austrian, Italian, and even Nazi political figures as Mrs. Mandl? How did her beauty make her both noticed by these men and invisible to them? What impact do these experiences have on her later life?

3. When Hedy finally escapes from her troubling marriage to weapons manufacturer Fritz Mandl, she flees to London,

where she secures an introduction to Louis B. Mayer of MGM Studios, who is in Europe, in part, to scout European Jewish actors, writers, and directors who can no longer work due to the anti-Semitic Nuremberg Laws. Although her circumstances are somewhat different, Hedy gets swept up in the wave of Louis B. Mayer's recruits, and she sails for Hollywood. Were you surprised at the large number of European refugees, many of them Jewish, who became prominent Hollywood figures (although they were never permitted to admit their heritage)? What did you think about the process by which they assimilated into American society?

4. Despite their conflicted relationship, Hedy struggles to bring her mother from war-torn Austria to America and only finds success because of the connections garnered by her fame. What was your reaction to Hedy's mother's initial resistance to leaving? How knowledgeable were you about America's immigration policies during World War II, and what are your views on them?

5. The book explores the inspiration behind Hedy's invention, as well as the moment when the ideas converged to fashion the "secret communication system." Please discuss the various events that may have served as catalysts for her invention. Has Hedy's story caused you to wonder about the process of creation and the stories behind other innovations, particularly the roles that women may have played?

6. Would you be surprised to learn that Hedy's groundbreaking invention became the basis, in part, for the creation of Wi-Fi technology? Please discuss the fact that her contribution to this world-changing innovation was largely lost—or ignored—for decades.

7. The title of the novel is subject to several interpretations. What meanings can you glean from the title, and how did your understanding of the meaning of *The Only Woman in the Room* change from the beginning of the novel to the end, if at all?

8. How might Hedy have symbolic importance in our time? Do you think it is important to uncover the voices and stories of historical women, and if so, why?

ACKNOWLEDGMENTS

The opportunity to share the incredible legacy of Hedy Lamarr, both historic and modern, is possible only because of the support, encouragement, and hard work of many, many people. I must start, as always, by thanking my extraordinary agent, Laura Dail, whose wise counsel serves as a constant source of inspiration and guidance. The marvelous Sourcebooks team deserves my endless appreciation. Without the championing by my brilliant editor, Shana Drehs, the phenomenal Dominique Raccah, along with the fantastic Valerie Pierce, Heidi Weiland, Heather Moore, Liz Kelsch, Kaitlyn Kennedy, Heather Hall, Stephanie Graham, Margaret Coffee, Beth Oleniczak, Tiffany Schultz, Adrienne Krogh, Will Riley, Danielle McNaughton, Katherine McGovern, Lizzie Lewandowski, Sean Murray, Todd Stocke, Bill Preston, Chris Bauerle, and Travis Hasenour, this story could never have come to light. And I am so grateful to the tremendous booksellers, librarians, and readers who have been supportive of me and my work.

While family and friends were integral to the creation of this book, particularly my Sewickley crew, Illana Raia, Kelly Close, and Ponny Conomos Jahn, without the love of my boys, Jim, Jack, and Ben, none of this would be possible. I am indebted to them for *everything*.

ABOUT THE AUTHOR

Marie Benedict is a lawyer with more than ten years' experience as a litigator at two of the country's premier law firms and Fortune 500 companies. She is a magna cum laude graduate of Boston College with a focus on history and a cum laude graduate of the Boston University School of Law. She is also the author of *The Other Einstein,* as well as *Carnegie's Maid.* She lives in Pittsburgh with her family.

THE OTHER EINSTEIN

In the tradition of *The Paris Wife* and *Mrs. Poe*, the story
of a relationship as fascinating as it is troubling

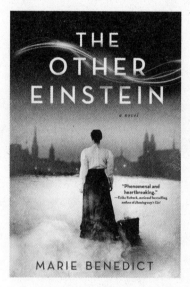

What secrets may have lurked in
the shadows of Albert Einstein's
fame? In 1896, the extraordinarily
gifted Mileva "Mitza" Marić is
the only woman studying physics
at an elite school in Zurich. For
her, science seems like an easier
path than marriage, until she falls
in love with fellow student Albert
Einstein. Charismatic and brilliant,
Albert promises to treat her as an
equal in both love and science. But
as Albert's fame grows, is there
room for more than one genius in
a marriage?

The Other Einstein reveals the forgotten woman whose light was lost
in Einstein's enormous shadow.

*"Superb…the haunting story of Einstein's first
wife who was lost in his shadow."*
**—Sue Monk Kidd, *New York Times* bestselling
author of *The Invention of Wings***

For more Marie Benedict, visit:
sourcebooks.com

CARNEGIE'S MAID

The mesmerizing tale of the woman who could
have inspired an American dynasty

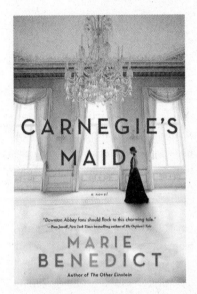

Clara Kelley is not who they think she is. She's not the experienced Irish maid who was hired to work in one of Pittsburgh's grandest houses. She's a poor farmer's daughter with nowhere to go. But the other Clara has vanished, and pretending to be her might be her best option. If she can keep up the ruse, that is. Serving as a lady's maid in the household of Andrew Carnegie requires skills she doesn't have, answering to an icy mistress who rules her sons and her domain with an iron fist. What Clara does have is a resolve as strong as the steel Pittsburgh is becoming famous for, coupled with an uncanny understanding of business, and Andrew begins to rely on her. But Clara can't let her guard down, even when Andrew becomes something more than an employer. Revealing her past might her ruin her future—and her family's.

Carnegie's Maid tells the story of the brilliant woman who may have spurred Andrew Carnegie's transformation from ruthless industrialist to the world's first true philanthropist.

"Downton Abbey *fans should flock to this charming tale."*
**—Pam Jenoff, New York Times bestselling
author of The Orphan's Tale**

LADY CLEMENTINE

An incredible novel of the brilliant woman whose unsung influence helped shape two World Wars: Clementine Churchill

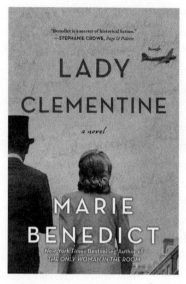

In 1909, Clementine steps off a train with her new husband, Winston. An angry woman emerges from the crowd to attack, shoving him in the direction of an oncoming train. Just before he stumbles, Clementine grabs him by his suit jacket. This will not be the last time Clementine Churchill will save her husband.

Lady Clementine is the ferocious story of the ambitious woman beside Winston Churchill, the story of a partner who did not flinch through the sweeping darkness of war, and who would not surrender either to expectations or to enemies.

For more Marie Benedict, visit:
sourcebooks.com